A Convict Story

I0534924

Dyshum Jones

Black Authors INK LLC

A Convict Story

Copyright © 2016 Dyshum Jones

This book is a work of fiction. Names, characters, places, and incidents are products of the authors imagination or are used fictitiously. Any resemblance to actual events or locales or persons, living or dead, is entirely coincidental.

All rights reserved. No part of this book may be reproduced in any form or by any means including electronic, mechanical, or photocopying, or stored in retrieval systems without the written permission from the publisher, except by a reviewer who may quote brief passages to be included in the review.

The publisher makes no representation or warranties with respect to the accuracy or completeness of the contents of this book and specifically disclaim any implied warranties of merchantability or fitness for a particular purpose. Neither author nor publisher accepts any liability or responsibility to any person or entity with respect to any loss or damage alleged to have been caused, directly or indirectly, by the information, ideas, opinions or other content in this book. The statements, opinions and data contained in this publication are solely those of the individual authors and contributors and not of the publisher and the editor.

For information regarding special discounts for wholesale purchases, please contact Sales at blackauthorsink@gmail.com or mail inquiry to Black Authors INK, P.O. Box 271, Mauldin, SC 29662

Interior Format: BlackAuthorsINK
Editor: Shelby R.Lazenby MBA
Cover Design: HotBookCovers

ISBN-10: 0-9971572-2-4
ISBN-13: 978-0-9971572-2-2

First Black Authors INK trade paperback edition 2016
Printed in the United States of America

Black Authors INK
P.O. Box 271
Mauldin, SC 29662

Black Authors INK

A Convict Story

Dyshum Jones

ACKNOWLEDGMENTS

I want to thank and give all worship and praise to Allah first and foremost, because with Allah, there is nothing possible. He provides all things, from the water we drink to the air we breathe, so thank you my creator.

To all the true real convicts I came across during my thirty (30) year prison sentence, thank you, especially those convicts who provided me jewels and rules to live by, and showed me how to walk like a man, and look at the world through another set of eyes.

To Ms. Kimmiko Anita Davis Holloway, I thank you for being there for me. All though we are no longer together, and the love was destroyed, know that I understand, and that without you ever touching the space in my life, then I wouldn't be who I am today. Look what came out of the fire. (Smiles)

To my father Walter Michael Convict Jones and Uncle Irving Daniel Jones, may you rest in peace. Hopefully Allah's will is for me to see you again in Janna. I love you man.

To all my sisters and brother, I have so many. I thank you for showing me the difference between family and kin folks.

To my partners, Herbert Waco Wakefield, Joey Adair, Willie Brown, Lee Wardlaw, Mike Smith, Lazenzo Sullivan, Preston John Auston III, Brian Huggins, Ant McGee, and the entire Nichol Town Squad and Cannaberry Young Thugs, I thank you for keeping it real in this new world, where this generation does not know the real definition of keeping it real.

To any and everybody who has their hands in seeing this first born published and placed on the shelves in any and all cities and town.

Last, I like to thank any and all of the haters, fuck niggas, bitch niggas, and snitch niggas, because without you, my game would not be super tight. Also, if you stop spending all your time on hating others, and put that time on your grind, then you can be where real niggas stand.

Oh I forgot, wrong I remembered, and will always remember, thanks to all my friends you are now resting in the ground, and special thanks to the ones resting in the ground for my life to continue.

Prologue

Imprisonment by whatever name it is called is a harsh thing and the discipline that must be exercised over human beings in close confinement can never be wholly agreeable to those subjected to it. When an attempt is made to hide the harsh realities of criminal justice behind euphemistic descriptions, a corrupting irony may be introduced into ordinary speed that is fully as frightening as Orwell's Newpeak.

Prison is a complex of physical arrangement and of measures, all wholly governmental, and all wholly performed by agents of government which determines the total existence of certain human beings from sunup to sundown, sleeping, walking, speaking, working, playing, viewing, eating, voiding, vending, alone, with others, it is not so with members of the general adult populations to rise at a certain hour, retire at a certain hour, eat at a certain hour, live for a period of time with no companionship whatsoever, wear certain clothing, or submit to oral and anal searches after or before visiting hours, nor have the state governments undertake steps to prohibit members of the general adult population from speaking to one another, wearing beards, embracing their spouse, or corresponding with their lovers.

However, prisoners are people whom most of us would rather not talk about. Banished from everyday sight, they exist in a shadow world that only dimly enters our awareness. They are members of a "Total Institution" that controls their daily existence in a way that few of us can imagine.

CHAPTER 1

I It was a hot, muggy night on March 9th, 2004 at approximately 3:45 A.M. at Perry Correctional Institution when Convict Jones was suddenly awakened out of his sleep due to loud pounding and kicking on the prison cell doors, consolidated with other inmates yelling.

Fire in the hole is a term prisoner's use when prison officials or guards come to shakedown for contraband or to take someone to lock up.

Convict Jones rubbed the cold sleep out of his eyes. When he brought his hand down, he noticed two prison officials standing at his cell door. Once the cell door opened, the two prison guards entered the cell. One of the prison guards was a short, fat, round white man in his mid-40's, who wore a white dress shirt with electric plated gold symbols on his right and left collar, identifying him as a sergeant, coupled with coffee stains spread here and there on the white shirt. This prison guard's name was Sergeant John Wilson.

"Inmate Jones," Sergeant Wilson called.

"Yeah, what up?" Convict Jones asked.

"What's your prison number?" Sergeant Wilson asked.

"Two-one-four-seven-four-seven."

"Mr. Jones, we were informed to come pack you and your belongings because you are being transferred out of here."

"Where am I being shipped to?" Convict Jones asked Sergeant Wilson, looking around the small cell.

"You will find out when you get there, inmate," the other prison guard replied, whose name was Officer Reggie Green rudely stated, cutting Sergeant Wilson off from replying.

Officer Reggie Green was a tall, skinny, black man with a bad right leg and a dead left eye. He was better known to all the prisoners as Toothpick. Prisoners would call him everything from house nigga, black cracker, to Uncle Tom when he came to work because he would treat his own black brother like a dog for no justifiable reason. Officer Green could not comprehend that he was only a pawn used to carry out the order of the Willie Lynch Doctrine. Every time Officer Green came to work, he brought with him his problems from home. He figured that since he could not control his household, he would try to control the prisoners who were already under restraints. When Officer Green came to work, one of two things would happen, either certain prisoners were going to lock up or the unit or dorm would be locked down.

Using his better judgment, Convict Jones decided to keep his mouth shut. There was no need in beating a dead bush. Making any type of remark would have led to a confrontation with Officer Green and Convict Jones did not want that for good reasons. Convict Jones was going before a parole board in eight months, and had a post-conviction relief application pending in the *Greenville County Courthouse*. Officer Green threw a big, green duffle bag in the middle of the cell floor and informed Convict Jones to unlock his wall locker. Convict Jones did as was ordered. Officer Green immediately began throwing Convict Jones' belongings into the bag, onto the floor, and anywhere else he felt was appropriate. Sergeant Wilson stood looking, shaking his head, knowing Officer Green was wrong, but he refused to go against his officer for a prisoner.

"I don't have all night for this shit," Officer Green growled as he continued tossing items out of the locker.

After packing Convict Jones' belongings without completing a proper inventory sheet, Officer Green informed Convict Jones to turn around to be handcuffed. Sergeant Wilson then intervened.

"No, handcuff him in the front because he has to carry his own property."

"What about the rest of my property on the floor?" Convict Jones asked.

"What don't fit in the green duffle bag stays behind," Green replied.

Convict Jones was then escorted to the head of operations. The head of operations is in the control center for the entire institution. Without the head, the body would fall. Once at the head of operations, Convict Jones was roughly pushed into a small cell by Officer Green. The cell was only big enough for a body and a chair. Convict Jones resided in this cell for the next four hours, without having the chance to use the bathroom or eat breakfast. After four hours passed, two big black prison officials came to the small holding cell and informed Convict Jones to take all his clothing off. After Convict Jones was stripped, he was ordered to turn around, bend over, and cough as the officers watched his rectum like it was a movie while holding a conversation between each other about his ass cheeks. Once Convict Jones put his clothing back on, he was informed to turn around and put his hands and nose on the wall. Convict Jones complied with the order. The guards then unlocked the holding cell door, entered, and placed prison shackles on Convict Jones's wrist, waist, and ankles. Convict Jones was then escorted through several corridors within the prison, and out a back door to a gray prison van with tinted windows and bars covering the windows. Once in the van, Convict Jones noticed another prisoner. This prisoner was locked into the van in a small cage in the back, smaller than the holding cell he had just exited. The prisoner looked like a caged animal. He had a full beard with a head full of hair. The prisoner in the cage had on a bright red jumpsuit. The red jumpsuit represented that the prisoner was on lock-up for violation of a major rule of the prison system. Later during the ride, Convict Jones found out that the brother was on his way to supermax in Columbia, South Carolina.

CHAPTER 2

Supermax is short for maximum security. Only the most dangerous and violent prisoners are placed in supermax, as well as prisoners who either committed murder or assault on prison guards or prisoners or a prisoner who was a threat to the security of the prison system itself, mostly legal litigating prisoners. It is said that anything goes in supermax. It is said that some prisoners that go to supermax never make it back out alive. They either get killed by prison guards or they kill themselves, but most of the time it's the prison guards who are responsible for their deaths, even the suicidal ones. This is the place where the prisoners get lost in the system.

The prisoner in the back of the van on his way to supermax was Bernard Clark, but everybody began calling him *Gangsta* after the incident which got him sent to supermax. Gangsta was a prisoner who had entered into a sexual relationship with a prison official named Lieutenant Debbie Clinkscale. Lieutenant Clinkscale was a light-skinned black woman with no booty and very large breasts. She was fair game for convicts who had been serving a lot of time, and had not had sex in years. In fact, she was the prisoner's favorite prison guard, but only for the right price. Rumor has it that Gangsta murdered Lieutenant Clinkscale in cold-blood in front of the majority of the prison population for giving him AIDS.

True or not, Gangsta who was serving a twenty-five year prison sentence under the eighty-five percent law for possession of crack cocaine and possession of a firearm during the commission of a violent crime had been in a sexual relationship with Lieutenant Clinkscale for eight months. Gangsta, who had already served six years on his prison sentence, had a good chance of having his case overturned in the next six months through a writ of Habeas Corpus. Out of the six years served, he had only had sex with his wife Tina Thomas, who everybody knew as *Tot Tot*. Those sexual encounters with Tot Tot took place during conjugal visits. The last one was at least a year ago. Gangsta and Lieutenant Clinkscale had been having sex every chance they got. In fact, feelings had started developing between the two of them, but neither one would admit to it. Tot Tot had been holding her husband Gangsta down for the last six years like a champ. She vowed with her life not to abandon him during his trials and tribulations in prison. She knew firsthand how hard it was for her husband because she also had a little brother who was serving a ten year sentence under the eighty-five percent law, who would call home every other day complaining about her not sending him any money.

One morning Gangsta woke up feeling ill, and decided to go to the prison medical facility. It was not like they were going to do anything, and if they did all they were going to do was tell him to take two Tylenols and lay down. Once he got to the medical facility, the nurses checked his blood pressure, weighed him, took some blood, and then sent Gangsta back to his unit. Three days later, the medical facility summoned Gangsta. Once Gangsta got to medical, a nurse immediately took him into a tall, slim, white doctor's office, who sat looking at a computer. Gangsta took a seat.

"Inmate Clark, I hate to be the one to inform you, but you have contracted a very serious virus. We would like to run some more test and draw some more blood from you," the doctor said, looking down at some paperwork.

"What serious virus are you talking about?" Gangsta asked, squinting his eyes at the doctor as the nurse immediately exited the office to get security.

"Please calm down, sir. We need to also ask you a few questions."

"Questions like what?" Gangsta asked as the nurse and three prison guards entered the office.

"Sir, have you had any sexual contact with homosexuals since your incarceration?" Doctor Epps asked, looking Gangsta straight in the eyes.

"Hell no!"

"Well sir, you have contracted a sexual transmitted virus from someone and we need to know who so that we can contact and help them too," the doctor replied, looking up at the nurse who immediately left the office again.

Gangsta's thoughts began running and immediately Lieutenant Clinkscale came to mind. He already knew that due to the code he lived by he would not snitch her or anybody out.

"I know this bitch," he said referring to Lieutenant Clinkscale, "ain't given me no yeast infection," Gangsta said to himself.

Gangsta's thoughts were then interrupted by the nurse.

"Excuse me Inmate Clark. The doctor is still talking to you."

She noticed that Gangsta's mind had drifted off somewhere.

"Oh, okay," he replied.

"Inmate Clark, I don't think that there is any other way to tell you this so I am going to spit it right out. Know this isn't the end of the world. There are medications to help you with your illness," the doctor babbled on.

"Doc, would you spit it out," Gangsta said, looking him in the eyes.

"Alright, you have contracted the HIV AIDS virus."

Gangsta's heart immediately seemed to drop to his stomach. He felt as if his bowels were giving way, and he was about to shit on himself. His entire life began flashing before his eyes, while sweat formed on his forehead and dropped into his eyes.

"Would you please follow Nurse Aulston? She will provide you with a pen and paper to write down the names of the people you have been sexually intimate with in the last five years," Doctor Epps stated, closing the file on the table in front of him.

"Would you please follow me?" Nurse Aulston asked.

Gangsta stood to his feet. The bad news had him a little dizzy. Gangsta followed Nurse Aulston to another location within the medical facility. Once there, Nurse Aulston instructed Gangsta to have a seat outside the office door while she continued on down the hall to another office. Gangsta stood back up and exited the medical facility. He was still dazed and in shock from the revelation of having AIDS then he walked back to the yard

Pursuant to the South Carolina Department of Corrections prison policy concerning medical procedures, Nurse Aulston was required to contact Gangsta's next of kin to inform them of his medical condition. Nurse Aulston retrieved Gangsta's medical files from Doctor Epps, and proceeded to another office within the medical facility to make the phone call. Nurse Aulston dialed the phone number in his files. The phone rang three times before a soft, lovely voice answered.

"Hello."

"May I speak with Mrs. Tina Thomas Clark?" Nurse Aulston asked.

"Yes, this is she," Tot Tot replied.

"My name is Tammy Aulston, and I am a nurse at Perry Correctional Institution, and we have an inmate Bernard Clark here in our medical facility. Do you know him?"

"Yes, he is my husband," Tot Tot replied, her heart pounding, thinking that something had happened to Gangsta.

"Well, Mrs. Clark, I truly hate to be the one to tell you," Nurse Aulston stated as Tot Tot began screaming.

"Ain't nothing happened to my husband has it?"

"Mrs. Clark, please calm down and let me explain first. Your husband has contracted the HIV AIDS virus through sexual intercourse. We are still running test to make sure that we have not made a mistake. There is a lot of sexual intercourse going on between the inmates at this prison. We, the medical staff, are bound by prison policy to contact the inmates family and inform them of such medical conditions when they occur."

"Thank you for calling," Tot Tot replied dryly, hanging the phone up on the nurse.

Nurse Aulston hung the phone up and wiped the perspiration dripping down her forehead. She hated this part of her job that involved calling family members to inform them that something had happened to one of their own. While Nurse Aulston beat herself up about the part of her job she did not like, Tot Tot sat on her bed crying and screamed at the top of her lungs. She was sitting in a trance, not believing what she had just learned.

CHAPTER 3

Gangsta walked back to the compound, went to his unit, and went directly to his cell. Once in his cell, he sat down on his bunk and dropped his head in his hands. There was no doubt in his mind that Lieutenant Clinkscale was the person who gave him the deadly virus. As Lieutenant Clinkscale filled his thoughts, rage seemed to emerge out of him. He then thought about his wife Tot Tot, and how he was going to explain first, that he had been having sex with another female, and second, that same female gave him the HIV AIDS virus.

Gangsta got up from his bed, walked out of his prison cell, and headed to the telephones on the wall to make a collect phone call to his wife. After dialing his home number and waiting for the operator to explain the procedures for his wife to accept the collect phone call, the once lovely, soft voice he grew to love came on the line but with rage and venom.

"Motherfucker, what's this I hear about you having sex with other men?"

Her accusation threw Gangsta for a loop.

"Hold up, baby," Gangsta tried to defuse the hostility to no avail.

"Don't hold up baby me with your faggot ass," Tot Tot shot back.

Gangsta had never heard Tot Tot speak in this manner, and especially towards him. He knew then that the situation was volatile.

"Listen baby," he stated, trying to calm her down. "I don't know what's going on, but those tests have to be wrong."

He listened to her breathe hard on the other end of the phone.

Out of hurl and rage, Tot Tot informed her husband that she was done with holding him down. She hung up, leaving Gangsta staring at the phone with a tear running down his cheek.

Gangsta left the phone hanging from the wall and went back to his cell with tears in his eyes. Anyone could see that he was not in his right state of mind. Once inside his cell he began throwing everything around the room, trashing his cell while screaming Lieutenant Clinkscale's name with profane words. Other prisoners walked by the cell, but did not stop to consider the brothers cries and pains. He then immediately came to a conclusion if he was going to die, he was not going out alone. He reached under his bed and pulled his chopper which was lawnmower blade sharpened down to look like a machete. He then opened his locker, reached in, and pulled out a nine-inch icepick. He placed the icepick in his waistline. Gangsta put on his coat and tucked the chopper under his arm, concealing it from other prisoners and officers. He exited his cell with one thing on his mind, heading to the mess hall where he knew Lieutenant Clinkscale was stationed to work. Gangsta spotted Lieutenant Clinkscale instructing prisoners that they had five minutes to finish their lunch. It was clear that Lieutenant Clinkscale made a real good slave driver the way she was shouting at the prisoners and ordering them around.

Gangsta walked towards Lieutenant Clinkscale slowly, while she was facing the opposite direction. This was going to be hard for him because he truly loved Lieutenant Clinkscale, but they were from two different worlds. She was the police, and he was a criminal. Opposites attracted in the wrong place at the wrong time. Had it not been that, they could have made it work. Once he got within five feet of Lieutenant Clinkscale, he leaped in the air like a bobcat with the nine-inch ice pick in his hand. He drove the icepick into Lieutenant Clinkscale's neck, sending her falling to the floor. While Gangsta stabbed Lieutenant Clinkscale over-and-over, she was able to turn over, making eye contact. Lieutenant Clinkscale's mouth moved, forming the question why as she stared into the eyes of Gangsta which were void of life. Gangsta hit her twelve more times with the icepick before finally leaving it stuck in her chest.

While Lieutenant Clinkscale lay in the middle of the floor with blood escaping her body, she took long, deep, heavy breaths, trying to fill her lungs with air to no avail compliments of the icepick. Gangsta's mind was now totally gone. He stood to his feet, pulled out the chopper, and began chopping Lieutenant Clinkscale into pieces. Other prisoners and prison guards just stood around and looked in amazement. Not one prison official went to the aid of their fallen comrade. Other prisoners cheered Gangsta on due to the way Lieutenant Clinkscale treated them. Some prisoners wanted to help her, but did not think going up against Gangsta would be wise. Gangsta was out of breath, dripping in sweat, and tired from swinging the chopper. He was tackled to the floor by prison officials who had entered the mess hall in riot gear. Meanwhile, Lieutenant Clinkscale's body parts were laying everywhere by the time other prison officials with enough heart to help her came to her aid. She was already dead.

One year and four months later, Gangsta plead guilty by reason of temporary insanity. He informed the judge that although he murdered Lieutenant Clinkscale, he had good reason.

"Mr. Clark, what gave you the right to take her life?" Judge Floyd asked.

"Because she took my life, sir," Gangsta replied.

"And how did she do that, sir?" Judge Floyd wanted to know because the claim that Gangsta placed before the courts did not add up with the evidence before the court.

"She gave me the AIDS virus," Gangsta replied, ratting out the dead to save his life.

"Mr. Clark, Lieutenant Debbie Clinkscale's test result for HIV or AIDS came back negative. In fact, your test taken two weeks prior to this trial also came back negative," The judge informed Gangsta.

"But they—" Gangsta was trying to state when the prosecutor for the state interrupted him.

"Your Honor, Mr. Clark has already been found guilty on both counts of murder. We, the state, ask for the toughest penalties to be imposed due to the fact that she was a state official, and he failed to prove that he had AIDS or that she gave him AIDS."

"I object your Honor," Gangsta's attorney said, shifting through some paperwork. "We are waiting on the DNA test of the child involved in this case."

"Well," the judge replied, "if the DNA test comes back with something different he'll get relief on appeal, but as of today I sentence Bernard Clark to two life sentences."

He slammed his gravel down.

Gangsta looked at the crowded courtroom and saw his wife Tot Tot who had tears running down her face, forgiving him, now knowing the truth. Doctor Epps and Nurse Aulston sat in the back of the courtroom hiding their face, ashamed because they also knew the truth. They intentionally took the stand and provided false testimony, stating they had no records indicating that Gangsta had AIDS or that they informed him of such. Gangsta was then escorted out the courthouse with two life sentences that he would never be able to complete. One for Lieutenant Debbie Clinkscale and one for his unborn seed.

Two hours later, coming down 4444 Broad River Road in Columbia, South Carolina, the gray prison van pulled into *Kirkland Correctional Institution.* Entering the prison, Convict Jones counted ten-prison officials all in white shirts with electric gold plated bars holding shotguns. Once the van stopped, Gangsta was removed from the small cage in the back of the van and escorted away by two prison guards to supermax. The two prison officials that drove the van handed over some paperwork to the other prison officials and returned back to the van where Convict Jones sat watching from the window. As Convict Jones watched, he thanked Allah that he had turned down Lieutenant Clinkscale's offer some months back when she came to him with a proposition. It is possible that had Convict Jones took the offer, it would have been him in Gangsta's position. Convict Jones thoughts were interrupted by the prison van engine starting up again. Coming out of Kirkland Correctional Institution, the prison van went further south. It seemed as if the two black prison guards driving the van took each and every back road in the state of South Carolina. Two and a half hours later the van stopped at another prison where the guards parked the van.

The prison guard getting out of the passenger's side of the can stated, "Inmate Jones, welcome to your new home," laughing as he walked off around the van.

CHAPTER 4

Convict Jones exited the prison van and was escorted to the back door of a building that was separate from the prison. Once inside the building, the guards escorted Convict Jones down a long corridor, approximately twenty-five feet long and seven feet wide. At the end of the corridor, they entered a series of steel doors, some double before stopping in front of another door made of steel and fiberglass with bars on the window which was a holding cell. After being handed a set of keys by the holding cell official, the guard opened the holding cell and ordered Convict Jones in. Convict Jones entered the holding cell and stopped dead in his tracks at the door of the holding cell due to a very loud and foul odor inside.

"Hey man, I'm not going in there!" Convict Jones stated.

"Inmate Jones, we don't have time for this. You won't be in there long," the guard replied.

Convict Jones then entered the holding cell under the assumption that he would not be in there too long. Inside the holding cell was unbelievable. It was straight up nasty. In the far left corner of the holding cell sat a puddle of urine mixed with vomit. There were flies and cockroaches everywhere. The holding cell was the true meaning of an eighth amendment rights violation. The benches in the holding cell had defecation smeared all over them, as well as parts of the floor. Convict Jones found a spot to stand in until he was released from the cell. After thirty minutes of standing, Convict Jones coped a squat where he stood which was not that nasty, and made a short prayer to Allah.

"So Inmate Convict Jones has arrived?" a very large man asked another prison guard under his order, who name was Major Walter Riley.

"Yes sir. He arrived thirty minutes ago. He's been placed in the shit hold," Sergeant Bobby Jackson replied.

"Good then. I believe you have all the proper paperwork so that the head office in Columbia won't be breathing down our neck," Major Riley stated, assuring that his prior orders had been carried out to the tee.

"Yes sir. We followed your orders."

"Well Sergeant, I do believe the welcome committee is ready and prepared to welcome Inmate Convict Jones to Evans. Am I right?" Major Riley asked, standing up from behind his desk and closing a folder.

"Yes sir, I notified them right before I came to your office," Sergeant Jackson replied.

"Good boy Sergeant. Let's go welcome Inmate Convict Jones to Evans Correctional Institution."

Major Riley stood to his feet and walked out of his office with Sergeant Jackson following him like a trained dog.

Sergeant Bobby Jackson had been employed by the South Carolina Department of Corrections for the last six years. A trained military corporal in the United States Army, he had come from the Gulf War with the after effects of the Asian Orange Chemical. Those after effects only allowed him to do but so much. Sergeant Jackson was also known as Major Riley's ass cleaner or do boy by the other prison officials at Evans Correctional Institution. Sergeant Jackson spent most of his time at the prison, even on his off days. He had to be forced to take his sick day leave, and even then he continued to work for free. Evans Correctional Institution was Sergeant Jackson's life after the Gulf War. In other words he was a loser who had given up on life. He had no children, wife, or even a girlfriend. He made the staff and administration of Evans Correctional Institution his family.

After thirty-five minutes passed by, Major Riley and Sergeant Jackson entered the nasty holding cell where they had placed Convict Jones. Sergeant Jackson had in his possession a brown paper bag, which was Convict Jones' dinner. The food in the bag consisted of a piece of mystery meat, two old hard biscuits baked four days earlier, and half of a rotten carrot. By order of Major Riley, Sergeant Jackson handed him the brown paper bag.

Major Riley then said, "Inmate Convict Jones catch."

He tossed the bag in a corner where it landed in a puddle of urine, vomit, and God knows what else.

"Enjoy your meal, Inmate Jones," Major Riley stated, laughing as Sergeant Jackson followed suit.

Convict Jones attempted to find out where he had been transferred to when he was rudely cut off by Major Riley.

"Did anybody tell you to talk boy?" Major Riley stated, staring Convict Jones in the eyes. "You talk when told to talk boy! Do you understand?" Major Riley shouted.

"I understand that you can suck my dick," Convict Jones immediately replied.

With a sinister grin on his face, Major Riley replied, "That's just what I wanted to hear."

Sergeant Jackson immediately exited the holding cell, leaving Major Riley staring at Convict Jones with hate in his eyes.

Sergeant Jackson returned to the holding cell within five seconds with three other black prison officials. To this very day, had Convict Jones known where he had been transferred and the type of individuals he was dealing with, he would have not spoken one word. If he did talk, he would have agreed with any and everything Major Riley said in an attempt to soften the blows he received. The three officials that followed Sergeant Jackson into the holding cell were all big, muscular black me with not one ounce of fat on their bodies. The three prison guards began cracking their knuckles after placing on black leather gloves. Convict Jones already knew what was coming, and there was nothing he could do or say to prevent the ass cutting he was about to receive.

"Inmate Jones, pull out that little dick of yours so I can suck it. You do want me to suck your dick, right? That's what you said a few seconds ago," Major Riley stated as the prison guards surrounded Convict Jones.

Major Riley then walked up to Convict Jones and cowboy punched him in the gut. Convict Jones immediately dropped like a sack of potatoes. After that blow, it was all she wrote. Until this day, Convict Jones could not tell you how many times he was lifted in the air and dropped on his head. He was repeatedly kicked in his ass and ribs, and stomped in his face and chest. As Convict Jones received his beating, he swore that one day that he would repay each and every prison official that assaulted him in that cell with death of their loved ones or themselves.

After the prison guards beat Convict Jones until they became exhausted, they grabbed him by his feet and dragged him through his own blood mixed with the urine to another cell then tossed him in it. Once Convict Jones landed hard on the cement floor, the guards entered into the cell, took all of Convict Jones' clothing, and exited the cell. Convict Jones lay in the floor in the same spot for the next two hours before he attempted to move. The pain he was in restricted him from moving too much. Convict Jones lay on the floor for another hour and a half, and then tried to move again using the remaining energy he had left in his body. He somehow managed to pull himself up by the bed in the cell. He then flopped down on the bed, which did not have a mattress, landing on the cold steel that sent shocks through his body. Convict Jones' face was swollen with deep cuts and lacerations. His body parts felt as if they belonged to the wrong body. Two of Convict Jones' fingers where either jammed or broken. His left thumb was also dislocated as well as his shoulder.

Convict Jones lay on the cold steel bunk in the nude, in pain, in the dark, and freezing. Convict

Jones' eyes were shut closed due to swelling, and he could only moan due to his jawbone being crushed. Ten minutes later, the pain in and of itself knocked Convict Jones out cold.

CHAPTER 5

"Sergeant Jackson, how is Inmate Convict Jones doing?" Major Riley asked, checking on Convict Jones.

"Well sir, I contacted medical, and they have informed me that Inmate Convict Jones is busted up pretty badly. It ain't nothing that three weeks of healing wouldn't take care of," Sergeant Jackson replied.

"Very good. What I want you to do now is to contact the shift supervisor in the mess hall, and inform them to place Inmate Convict Jones on a Nutra Loaf Diet. I also want you to make sure that he gets no showers unless they are cold showers. Do not let any mail of his leave the institution. Do not allow him any phone call privileges until he returns to population, and do anything else that you feel would make his stay here at Evans uncomfortable. Do you understand me?" Major Riley barked.

"Yes sir."

"Then what the hell are you waiting on then?" Major Riley shouted.

"Done yesterday," Sergeant Jackson assured, feeding Major Riley's ego.

"One more thing," Major Riley stated. "I do not want Inmate Convict Jones off of lock-up until all of his injuries heal up. Do you understand?"

"Yes sir," Sergeant Jackson replied and hurried out of Major Riley's office.

Convict Jones had been on lock up for three weeks. His injuries healed fast, although medical and staff were ordered not to assist in his healing. Had it not been for certain convicts providing Convict Jones with help, it could have been possible that he would still be in bad shape. Day-by-day Convict Jones became stronger mentally, physically, and spiritually. Convict Jones had also written over six letters, which were returned to him only after Major Riley read each and every one. Convict Jones even tried sending letters out in other inmate's name, and those letters were returned to him, allowing him to know that he was under investigation. Convict Jones was only placed on lock-up so that his injuries could heal before anybody could see him or he could contact anybody for help.

Although the physical injuries healed, the mental injuries needed redress. Convict Jones spent his time in lock-up doing a daily exercise program, which consisted of two hundred pushups, five hundred back arms, five hundred squats, two hundred pull-ups off the cell bars, and two hundred crunches. Convict Jones lost seven pounds, but his body began ripping up. After twenty-one days in lock-up, having to consume cold Nutra Loaf in the morning, noon, and night, Convict Jones was still confused as to what was going on. After completing his daily exercises, Convict Jones was standing over the sink connected to the toilet washing his face with a cool rag. Convict Jones then heard someone calling his name.

"Yo Dyson! Yo Dyse! Yo Dyson!"

"Yo who that be?" Convict Jones asked.

"Your boy Raw Raw," a familiar voice replied.

Convict Jones then began thinking, trying to match a name with the voice then put a face to the name and voice.

"They told me you was up here!" Raw Raw shouted.

Convict Jones listened closely to the voice and knew exactly who Raw Raw was. Convict Jones continued the conversation to make sure that he had the right Raw Raw because he knew a lot of cats that went by the same name.

"Yeah, what's happening partner?" Convict Jones asked.

"What brings you down in these neck of the woods?" Raw Raw asked.

"That's a good question that's worthy of a answer I don't have," Convict Jones stated placing the rag on the side of the sink.

Convict Jones and Raw Raw conversed for the next twenty minutes until Convict Jones informed Raw Raw that he was about to fall back and take a nap.

"Alright, big homie. One love and keep your thoughts clear brother," Raw Raw replied, ending the conversation.

Convict Jones walked back over to the cell bed and laid down with his hands folded behind his head. He began searching his memory, placing Raw Raw's face with his name. As he lay back, he watched a brown recluse spider persistently climb a moist wall and slide back down the slick molded brick wall. Convict Jones realized that his position was no different from the spiders. So many attempts by the spider to climb the wall to freedom but to no avail. This was the same as Convict Jones' so many attempts to get the courts to agree with him on his legal matters, but the state showed no reciprocity or concerns. As Convict Jones watched the spider, his thoughts drifted back to the name Raw Raw and his face appeared in his mind's eye.

CHAPTER 6

The first time Convict Jones met Raw Raw was not good at all. However, in the end, it turned out to be one of the best friendships you could have, considering it was prison. Raw Raw was a young kid at the age of nineteen who entered into a grown man's world without the understanding of the things you could do and the things you should not do. Nor did Raw Raw have the concept of when to speak and when not to speak.

Raw Raw was sentenced to life without parole for the murder of an elderly woman, while trying to feed his crack habit. When Convict Jones and Raw Raw first met they bumped heads. Convict Jones being the wiser, older, and stronger lion of course prevailed. It was Raw Raw and two other young cats that were serving football numbers under the eighty-five percent law, who would do 15 to 25 years or more before they would see the streets again. They robbed one of Convict Jones' mules. A mule is a prisoner who puts contraband in their rectum to conceal from prison guards when coming off visit through shake down strip searches. Convict Jones' mule was a tall, slim white boy named Bill McBee.

McBee was considered a convict. He would always put his convict word on something to get what he wanted. Later down the line, many found that McBee's convict word wasn't shit! McBee had been serving time since the year 1982 for a string of bank robberies and house break-ins. When they finally caught up with McBee, the courts broke him off with one hundred and twenty-five years because one of the break-ins was one of the Judge's friend's house.

McBee was also known as a fighting ass white boy. Most of the time he got his ass kicked, but no matter what he would still fight. Rumors had it that McBee was also a girl behind the wall in the early eighties, but Convict Jones' only concern in dealing with McBee was simply business. No more, no less.

It was one Saturday after visitation was called over and McBee made it through shakedown with Convict Jones' package of four ounces of marijuana that Raw Raw and his two partners stuck homemade knifes to McBee's throat and demanded Convict Jones' package. When McBee refused to give up the marijuana, the three young boys punched him in the gut and made him shit out the four ounces of compressed marijuana. Other prisoner said that it did not happen that way, and that McBee was lying about the whole ordeal. Word was that Raw Raw and his two partners caught McBee in his cell dipping in Convict Jones' package, which later Convict Jones found out to be true. Either way, Raw Raw and his crew had to be handled, as well as McBee for biting the hand that fed them.

Convict Jones and two other convicts from Convict Jones' neighborhood, Valentino and Waco, approached Raw Raw in the mess hall as he sat at the table eating lunch. The area was not five feet away from where Lieutenant Debbie Clinkscale was butchered by Gangsta. Raw Raw was not paying any attention to his surroundings because he allowed Valentino to creep up behind him without being noticed, while Convict Jones approached his table in full view and took a seat.

Once Convict Jones sat down at the table he said, "Listen little punk." As Waco stood blocking the view of any prison official that could see what was going on, Convict Jones continued, "I want my shit back by five o'clock today!"

Raw Raw gave Convict Jones a hard look, which immediately changed into a wide eye look due to Waco placing him in a chokehold. Valentino then came over and assisted Waco by grabbing Raw Raw by the feet, whereby they picked him up and carried him to the back of the mess hall without the prison guards noticing what was going on. Once in the back of the kitchen, both men slung Raw Raw over by a big deep fryer and large cooler. Convict Jones followed behind with authority in his step as other prisoners watched in plain sight.

By this time, Raw Raw had fear in his eyes and voice then asked, "What's up, man?"

He was wiggling and trying to get free from Waco and Valentino's tight grip.

"Shut the fuck up and listen nigga. I want my shit back by five o'clock today." Waco and Valentino slung Raw Raw to the hard wet floor.

For good measure, Waco then kicked Raw Raw twice in the ribs stating. "By five o'clock, nigga!"

Convict Jones and his partners then exited the back of the mess hall, leaving Raw Raw stretched out on the floor.

Five o'clock came around fast. Raw Raw made his way out of the place to Convict Jones' dorm, risking picking up a disciplinary infraction to hand deliver Convict Jones his product. Raw Raw actually returned two ounces of the four ounces of marijuana, coupled with three hundred and fifty dollars cash money.

As Convict Jones took the money from Raw Raw, Raw Raw stated, "I will give you another three hundred and fifty dollars next week when I come off visit."

"What happened to the other ounce?" Convict Jones asked.

"One of the cats that was with me checked in protective custody with it after hearing about our altercation in the kitchen earlier."

"Don't worry about it little man. I'll take the loss this time," Convict Jones replied, opening one of the ounces of marijuana.

Raw Raw began walking towards the door of Convict Jones' cell, when Convict Jones said.

"Hold up little man. Where are you going?" Convict Jones was looking at Raw Raw eye-to-eye and he seemed to be shook. Convict Jones then said, "Have a seat for a minute."

Convict Jones then informed Raw Raw that he liked his style, and that it was real smart move on his behalf to return what did not belong to him. Convict Jones knew that any other prisoner would have officials to get Convict Jones pinched to avoid any beef behind their wrong deeds. Convict Jones stood up, walked past Raw Raw to his cell door, and opened it. He then called Valentino over and informed him to go get a gallon of swamp fire homemade buck. Valentino immediately set out to go get the homemade wine, while Convict Jones walked back over to his bunk and sat down. Convict Jones then took one of the two ounces that Raw Raw returned and broke it down the middle and handed a half of the ounce to Raw Raw.

Convict Jones said, "Get on your feet."

Both men locked eyes with one another.

Big lion to young lion, Convict Jones began dropping the jewels and old school rules to the game on the young cat that needed the guidance in the worst way. Convict Jones then twisted up a hog leg street blunt from the other half of ounce he had, which was filed with nothing but buds and set fire to it.

As the fire touched the tip of the blunt, Valentino walked in the cell, and said, "I'm right on time."

CHAPTER 7

A prison guard was yelling Convict Jones' name, snatching him out of his daydream.

"Inmate Jones!" the prison guard yelled as he was looking at a sheet of paper.

"Yes sir," Convict Jones replied respectfully, having now wised up from the ass cutting.

"Pack all your belongings. You're going to the yard."

Convict Jones immediately began packing his belongings into a dingy pillowcase he received with a set of sheets one week after being placed in lock-up. The prison guard opened the cell door and Convict Jones exited the cell. He then followed the prison guard down a long hallway with cells spaced out on each side. As Convict Jones followed the prison guard down the hallway, they passed Raw Raw's cell. Without being noticed by the prison guard, Convict Jones slid a book under the cell door to Raw Raw, which contained two and a half packs of cigarettes Convict Jones had received from the prisoners that worked in lock-up.

"I'll see you when you hit the yard young blood," Convict Jones replied.

"True, true," Raw Raw replied, all smiles as he ducked.

Convict Jones continued following the prison guard.

The prison guard said, "Inmate Jones, before we proceed to the yard the Major wants to have a chat with you."

They made a right and went through a small steel door.

"Cool," Convict Jones replied, not really caring because he was just happy to be out of lock-up.

Coming into the Major's office door, he noticed a sign in big bold red print that read: *Enter at your own risk*.

The prison guard knocked on the hard oak wood door three times, then a voice from the other side of the door said, "Enter."

Once inside the Major's office, Major Riley sat behind a large desk made of mahogany wood. The same three prison guards who put it on Convict Jones' ass stood at attention with all their fingers in their pants pocket except for their pinky. Upon seeing this set up, a dreadful cold chill ran through Convict Jones' spine and bones. Convict Jones understood that each and every prison official that was in Major Riley's office felt and believed in inflicting violence and harming all prisoners.

"Inmate Jones, please take a seat in that chair in the corner." Major Riley instructed, pointing in the direction of the chair with a snarl on his face as he continued, "I am the Major of this institution. You have already learned firsthand, witnessed, and felt how we run this institution and handle wise guys like yourself. The same type of treatment will continue on a regular basis if you choose to refuse to do what you are told to do, inmate." Major Riley stopped to spit in the trash can beside his desk and continued. "I have a very low tolerance for disrespect such as you informing me to suck your nasty ass little dick. Do you understand?" Major Riley shouted.

Due to Convict Jones' pride and figuring Major Riley was trying to play with him, Convict Jones tightened his face and remained silent. This was coupled by the fact, he couldn't help but remember the ass cutting he received some three weeks back. Suddenly, a sharp pain exploded in Convict Jones' rib cage from a nightstick held by one of the prison guards standing in the office. This was a clear sign to Convict Jones that he had to answer Major Riley's questions whether he wanted to or not.

Convict Jones then mumbled, "Yes, I understand clearly."

He spoke while pure hate and rage ran through his mind and heart.

"Good then, and address me by sir," Major Riley stated, looking Convict Jones in the eyes then dropping his head back down to look into a folder. "I have your warden's jacket right here in front of me, and from the looks of it you have been a very busy boy. Let's see, you entered the South Carolina Department of Corrections on July 24th, 1988, and your max out of date is now reading January 1st, 2009." He looked up from the folder into Convict Jones' eyes, allowing Convict Jones to know that he did not like him. Major Riley continued, "Since your incarceration, you have had fifteen assaultive disciplinary infractions on or against SCDC prison officials, thirteen inciting a riot and or creating a disturbance infractions, sixteen fighting with or without a weapon disciplinary infractions, thirty disrespect disciplinary infractions, which is not hard to believe, two drug disciplinary infraction charges, and more than enough institutional rule violations." Major Riley paused, and then continued, "Inmate Convict Jones what I don't understand, and you need to answer this question if you know what's good for you. How is it that out of all these disciplinary infractions you have picked up listed in your files, you have only been convicted of twice disobeying a direct order?" Major Riley awaited a reply.

"Despite the law, money, power, and respect," Convict Jones spoke with a cockiness and pride that Major Riley could not stand.

"You listen you little piece of shit." Major Riley was becoming angry as he shouted, "Your money is no good here nigga! We have our own money and power." Major Riley started laughing, and continued,"I am all the power there is around here, and you shall soon know this nigga. As for respect, I expect that out of you at all time nigga, or I'll beat it out of you nigga." Major Riley made his point, clearly allowing Convict Jones to know what he thought of him as being ignorant. Major Riley continued, "Inmate Jones, we summoned you. I mean, you have been sent to us for rehabilitation and corrections. There will be no breaking of any of my rules, regulations, or policies. There will be no drugs sold or used on my compound, and if you do other that what I expect of you to do you will be punished for such violations of policy, rules, or regulations as I see fit. I am the law around here, and what I say goes. My officers standing here in this office, which you have already met upon your arrival here will make sure you follow the policies, rules, and regulations. You can make your stay here hard or easy. It really doesn't make any difference to me. I'd rather you choose to make it hard so that I can get a full erection from beating your stupid ass every chance I get. Plus, my new girlfriend loves when one of you son of a bitches violate my rules because she knows that my dick will be hard and stiff when I get home to beat her back out," Major Riley stated laughing, looking at his guards who joined in on the laughter. "Now, boy do you understand?" Major Riley asked, wanting Convict Jones not to answer.

"Yes, I believe I do understand you clearly. I agree that your rules, your policies, and your regulations were made to correct inmates, and they should never be broken." Smiling while he continued to answer Major Riley. "However, why all the hostility?" Convict Jones asked.

"Another stupid smart aleck. Get that piece of shit out of my office," Major Riley stated with a frown surfacing on his face and ordered the prison guard who brought Convict Jones down from lock up. "Officer, also tell Sergeant Jackson to get a rag with some soap, bleach, and water then clean my chair where his nasty ass sat."

He was holding his breath and clenching his teeth.

The prison guard along with Convict Jones exited Major Riley's office and delivered the message to Sergeant Jackson. After receiving Major Riley's orders, Sergeant Jackson came into his office five minutes later. Major Riley was on the phone yelling demands into some poor officer's ear when Sergeant Jackson was directed to take a seat.

After another five minutes on the phone, Major Riley slammed the phone down on the receiver and shouted, "Stupid asshole!"

"Sir, did you call for me?" Sergeant Jackson asked ready to serve Major Riley.

"Yes Sergeant. I need you to contact my peeps on the compound and inform them that we have a meeting at 7:30 tonight," he said, standing up from his desk and walking over towards a file cabinet.

"Yes sir. I am right on it."

Sergeant Jackson hopped out of his chair like fire ants were in his pants and headed towards the office door, whereby he was stopped in his tracks when Major Riley gave him further instructions.

"Also Sergeant, please tell them not to be late or drunk, and to slow down on making that damn buck."

He grabbed his jacket off the back of his chair.

"Yes sir," Sergeant Jackson replied and walked out of Major Riley's office door, heading to the yard to carry out his orders.

CHAPTER 8

Across the prison compound, two young prisoners sat in a cell in dorm three drinking homemade wine. One of the prisoners name was Terry Johnson, who went by the alias *O-Dog*. The other prisoner's name was David Smith, who went by the name of *Dirty Dee*. O-Dog was a young, short, thick, black male with nappy hair, and always wore his pants hanging off his ass. O-Dog was also known for playing with shanks and icepicks. Wherever he went confusion followed. He also made it his business to put it down on the weaker, new inmates who were scared to death upon entering prison. However, his partner, Dirty Dee was the total opposite.

Dirty Dee, although he ran with O-Dog doing dirt, every Sunday and Monday night he attended church service faithfully. If it was not for Dirty Dee and Major Riley, the twenty-five years under the eighty-five percent O-Dog was serving for murder, would have easily been turned into a natural life sentence or death sentence for the stupid things O-Dog was doing.

Sergeant Jackson walked into dorm three and looked around the rock. He noticed several inmates freeze in their tracks and yell fire in the hole. Other inmates just watched him as he watched them. Sergeant Jackson walked up several stairs, passed four cells on his right, and stopped in front of the fifth cell. Sergeant Jackson then knocked on the door and opened it. Once he entered inside, he saw O-Dog and Dirty Dee sitting on a bottom bunk drinking the homemade wine.

"Hey boys," Sergeant Jackson stated as he looked around the cell. "The Major wants to see you two tonight at 7 o'clock, and don't be late."

He then turned around and walked back out of the cell.

"Man, I wonder what Major Riley wants?" Dirty Dee asked, passing O-Dog the creamer of wine.

"Shit! Who knows? He always wants something or has some type of mission," O-Dog replied in a sluggish tone.

"Well, we better get ready because it's about that time."

"When I finish this creamer," O-Dog replied, turning the creamer up to his lips.

"Hurry up," Dirty Dee informed O-Dog then got up off the bed and walked over to the toilet to take a leak.

As Dirty Dee used the john, O-Dog went to his locker and rumbled around for a few minutes. He pulled a kitchen knife out and concealed it in his waistline.

"Let's be out, homie," Dirty Dee stated, flushing the toilet.

Both prisoners exited O-Dog's cell and headed to Major Riley's office for their meeting.

After Convict Jones was escorted from Major Riley's office, he had been standing in the hallway of operations with another inmate named Michael Sullivan for an hour and a half. One of the prison guards, Sergeant Paul White was also a member of the welcoming committee. He was completing the paperwork for assigning Convict Jones and Sullivan to dorms and cells. Sergeant White was a high-ranking Mason that belonged to the Blue Lodge in Florence, South Carolina. He was also responsible for the majority of the drugs, cell phones, and DVD's that flooded the compound, which was before the federal government infiltrated Sergeant White's operation that he had been up and running for the last six years. It was said when the federal government infiltrated Sergeant White's operation over fifteen prison officials at Evans Correctional Institution were indicted, and some were ever fired on the spot for failing to cooperate in the investigation. However, Sergeant White escaped the wrath by his chinney chin chin.

Sergeant White exited the office then approached Convict Jones and Sullivan in the hallway, and said, "Inmate Convict Jones and Sullivan." Getting the prisoner's attention, "The computers are down right now, and it's more than likely they will remain that way for a while. In that case, you two inmates go ahead to the kitchen and report back here immediately after you finish eating."

Convict Jones and Sullivan exited the double doors to operation and headed in the direction of the mess hall. During the walk to the kitchen, Sullivan insisted on carrying on a conversation with Convict Jones. Sullivan talked about everything, even things he had no business talking about. Convict Jones just remained silent and answered Sullivan's questions with yeah or nah. The vibe Sullivan gave off to Convict Jones was strange. Convict Jones figured that he was a yes man or snitch. As Sullivan babbled on during the walk to the mess hall, Convict Jones thought about the ass cutting he received from Major Riley and his boys. He considered that Sullivan acted the way he acted because he may have received a similar ass cutting. If that was so it explained a lot to Convict Jones, but by no means whatsoever was he going to assume that to be true.

"How long have you been in lock up?" Sullivan asked.

"About three weeks," Convict Jones replied.

"Shit, I been up there for three months for making wine."

Sullivan was providing information Convict Jones did not ask for.

Convict Jones and Sullivan reached the mess hall and made a right at the corner of the building. The two prisoners then went in between two rails, and then into a side door of the cafeteria. Once inside the mess hall, Convict Jones couldn't help but to acknowledge the familiar looks on the faces of the prisoners. Their faces were filled with hate, misery, sadness, and madness. Their eyes told the story of the misery in which they lived. It was clear they accepted the pain that was forced into their lives. Few faces wore smiles and the ones that did were masks to hide traces of grief.

CHAPTER 9

As Convict Jones stood in the crowded line in back of Sullivan, waiting to pick up a dog tray filled with slop through a hole in a steel plated wall, which separated the prisoners from the prisoners who worked in the kitchen on the line, Convict Jones couldn't help but to study his surroundings with precaution. He watched two prisoners having a conversation and pointing in his direction. He saw the younger prisoner of the two, hot potato an eight-inch blade to the older prisoner. The older prisoner's name was Ray Williams, but he earned the name *Straps* due to the fact that he stayed strapped with some form of weapon and was not scared to use it. Convict Jones later found out that Straps was a convict from the old days. Straps was serving a life sentence. He had already served twenty-six years in the prison system day for day.

Straps' track record was not a pretty picture. Whether true or false, it was said that during Straps' tenth year in prison, while serving his time behind the wall Straps had beat and raped a white boy. He had already killed four prisoners while serving his time. Shockingly Straps, when he first came to prison, only had three years to serve. However, he managed to turn it into a life sentence. After Straps cuffed the blade close to his leg, concealing it from the other prisoners and guards in the mess hall, he began sliding through the crowd of prisoners towards Convict Jones' direction. Convict Jones realized due to experience that a hit was about to go down, and it was possible that he was the target.

Convict Jones bumped Sullivan's arm to place him on point and stated, "In coming at your right."

Sullivan brushed Convict Jones' statement off because he was too concerned about getting an extra piece of cake off the food line.

When Straps was within five feet of Convict Jones, Sullivan, and a few more prisoners, Convict Jones stepped back into defense mode with his hands balled in a fist.

"What's hood, nigga?" he yelled ready to fight for his life.

Convict Jones' outburst got Sullivan's attention. However, when Sullivan turned around to see who Convict Jones was talking to, Straps leaped in the air like a wild mountain lion on his prey and drove the blade straight through Sullivan's juggler, crushing his windpipe instantly. This attack immediately stopped any and all screams of pain or calls for help that may have escaped his mouth.

Prisoners began moving out of the way as Straps went to work on Sullivan. Straps drove the blade through Sullivan's neck and chest area. Convict Jones backed up and watched, wondering whether to help Sullivan. Convict rules dictated that Convict Jones would go against his better judgment to intervene in matters that did not involve him or his peeps. Convict Jones believed that you would live much longer if people would just mind their own damn business. Convict Jones' attention was brought back to the violence taking place before him when a thick gooey substance spewed across his face and mouth. Convict Jones immediately could taste and smell the unpleasantness of Sullivan's soul. Straps hit Sullivan five more times for good measure before getting up off of him. Convict Jones actually watched the blade go straight through Sullivan's body and chip the very crappy tile on the mess hall floor. Blood was everywhere now.

Every time Straps plunged the blade into Sullivan's body, he screamed, "Die snitch bitch."

As Sullivan laid there damn near floating in his own blood, Convict Jones and Straps locked eyes. In this area of the game, real has to recognize real.

Convict Jones grunted, and asked, "What is it nigga?"

His fist were still balled up.

Straps broke eye contact and looked down at Sullivan, who now seemed to be running out of breath and time. Convict Jones followed Straps' eyes down to where Sullivan laid slowly dying, watching Sullivan's mouth form the word help inaudibly.

Convict Jones said, "Fuck that snitch."

Then he spit on Sullivan.

Straps looked back at Convict Jones and smiled. He then tucked the blade and disappeared into the crowd of prisoners, whereby Convict Jones did the same.

CHAPTER 10

Convict Jones departed from the cafeteria unnoticed as several prison officials entered the cafeteria with riot gear. Medical staff soon followed the prison guards. Convict Jones then put some pep in his step, heading back towards operations and getting away from the area where the murder was committed. Convict Jones had no intention of being investigated about the matter. Coming up the sidewalk to operations, Convict Jones noticed several specs of splattered blood on his uniform and sneakers. Convict Jones licked his fingers and removed some of the specs of blood. Of the blood he could not remove, he made a duwa or prayer that no one noticed it.

Entering the double doors of operations, he was met by Sergeant White who immediately asked, "Where is Inmate Sullivan?"

He looked behind Convict Jones.

"I don't know. When we went into the cafeteria, we went our separate ways."

"What happened down there?" Sergeant White asked, fishing for information.

"Don't know, plus I don't do that," Convict Jones replied, talking about snitching.

White looked at Convict Jones hard, and then turned around and walked back into the office to go get his paperwork for dorm and cell assignment. Convict Jones knew something was wrong because he could feel it. He later found out the reason why Sergeant White asked so many questions about Sullivan was because Straps took the hit up for Sergeant White due to Sullivan's snitching on Sergeant White's operation which was infiltrated by the federal government.

Sergeant White exited the office with paperwork in his hand and handed Convict Jones a sheet of paper with his dorm and cell assignment. Convict Jones was then informed where dorm two was located and released into the prison population. He got to the dorm in five minutes, having to walk across a very large yard. Entering the dorm, he was faced with over three hundred inmates on the side of the dorm he would be housed in. Some prisoners were sitting around playing cards, while others were tuned into four televisions hanging from the ceiling. Other prisoners walked around in circles bored out of their mind, while others sat around sleep dreaming, thinking that they were awake.

Convict Jones noticed several prisoners going to and from a certain cell located in the corner of the dorm. He made a mental note that that was where the happenings were going down, and intended to check it out when he got stationary. The dormitory was somewhat spotless. The air condition unit pumped out more cold air than anyone wanted, except for the white boys who loved the created cold area due to their original habitat is in the Caucasus Mountains located in Southeastern Europe.

Little did many prisoners know was that the air condition blew out cold air for a reason and a purpose. The more prisoners come in from outside where they are forced to work until they are dripping with sweat then come into a cold building, without a doubt the prisoners would catch either a cold or pneumonia.

Prisoners would then have to go to medical to be treated. However, despite universal laws, once you lock a person in a cage you automatically assume the responsibility for feeding the prisoner, clothing the prisoner, and providing the prisoner with medical treatment providing he gets sick. However, once a prisoner gets sick from the tactics used to get the prisoner sick, they charge the prisoner five dollars every time he goes to medical for treatment. The only services that the prisoner receives from the medical facility is information to take two Tylenol and lay down.

Convict Jones rubbed his bare arms and looked back at the piece of paper with his cell number on it. He then proceeded to walk to cell 116. Entering cell 116 another prisoner whose name was Michael Smith, who also occupied the cell, stood to his feet and just looked at Convict Jones hard with a frown on his face like something smelled foul. Convict Jones paid him no attention and tossed the little property he brought from lock-up on the bottom bunk he was assigned to.

CHAPTER 11

Inmate Michael Smith was another mid aged black male weighing in at one hundred and eighty pounds, six pounds heavier than Convict Jones. Smith had a very fucked up attitude about everything. He felt that the world owed him something. Nobody owed him anything, at least Convict Jones didn't. Convict Jones sat down on the bottom bunk he was assigned to, not saying a word to Smith because he was in deep thought and contemplating his next move. After five minutes passed, Convict Jones got up off the bunk and proceeded out of the cell to check out his surroundings.

Convict Jones looked across the rock and saw the phones on the wall. He immediately headed in the direction of the wall phones. Once at the phones, he picked one up and dialed his home phone number then his pin number, only to find out that his pin number was deactivated.

"Shit!" Convict Jones shouted under his breath and headed back to the cell.

While Convict Jones was heading to his cell, he came across an old timer who was another convict to heart.

"Luther Moses!" Convict Jones shouted happy to see an old friend still kicking and alive. "What's happening, man?" Convict Jones asked.

Luther Moses, who everybody called *Mo*, looked at Convict Jones strange at first because it had been over eight years since he had last seen him.

When he did recognize Convict Jones, he replied, "Mr. Jones," he said, smiling ear-to-ear. "How in the hell have you been doing?" Mo asked with a country slang.

"I'm good," Convict Jones replied, and asked, "How long has it been, old friend?"

He was looking past Mo at some young boys who were picking on an older white gentleman.

"It's been a long time, friend. What brings you down here in this crazy house?"

"Mo, all I know is that one night I was awakened out of my sleep and transferred here."

Convict Jones gave him the simple version before he went into how they kicked his ass and locked him up.

"That's fucked up," Mo replied after listening to Convict Jones. "How is your canteen looking?"

"I don't have shit right now, but as soon as I get to the canteen things will get better."

He was laughing to keep from crying, thinking how fucked up they had him.

"Follow me," Mo informed Convict Jones and walked off.

Convict Jones followed Mo to his cell, which was located on the second floor of the dormitory. Mo was an old convict who had been serving time since the early eighties for a brutal double murder. Mo's murder made O.J. Simpson's murder look like a peaceful tea party for five year old girls.

Mo had killed his best friend and his very first and only love. Convict Jones remembered Mo telling him the story like it was yesterday. Many times before, Mo informed Convict Jones that if he could take it back he would but it was too late. If he had the chance to do it all over again, he would controlled his emotions better than he did. However, who can control their emotions in the face of betrayal at the highest lever known to man. Convict Jones' mind drifted back to the story Mo told him, which seemed to be so vivid in his mind.

It was a cold prom night in a small town on the backside of South Carolina. Mo had just dropped his first love and her girlfriend off at home. They had just finished having the time of their lives at the school prom. Actually, the tradition in this small town was for those who attended the prom to afterwards to get a motel room and allow nature to take its course. However, in Mo's case this did not happen because his girlfriend, Tina Floyd, refused to submit to Mo's sexual advances. Tina's claim to fame was that she was a good Christian girl and would only have sexual intercourse with the man she married.

After the prom was over, Mo and Tina hung out a little while with Tina fighting him off of her. When he realized that she was not going to give him sex, he called it a night and took her home. Mo loved him some Tina. He worshipped the ground she walked on. Nobody, not even Mo's mother and father, could tell him something was wrong with Tina. She was the apple of his eye and the blood that flowed through his heart. Pulling up to Tina's house at 3:15 A.M. in his brown rusty Ford pickup truck, she leaned over and kissed Mo on the cheek then jumped out of his truck.

"I love you," she stated as she walked away from the truck and disappeared into her house.

Mo smiled and pulled off feeling like the happiest man on Earth. Coming to the corner of her street, he stopped to make a right turn then realized he forgot to give her the gold diamond locket he bought for her. The locket was a deep expression of the love he had for her. It took Mo three weeks of shoveling shit at the horse stable to purchase the locket. Pulling his truck over and searching through his inside pocket for the locket, he noticed Tina's back door open. He watched as Tina came out the back door.

Mo said to himself, "This girl is so crazy."

He was smiling as he just sat and watched her.

Tina began walking away from her house, which caused Mo concern. She began walking down towards the small stream behind her house. This small stream ran all around the bottom part of the small town that they lived in. It was also a mile and a half upstream where Mo and his childhood best friend, Billy Jordan, had built their treehouse when they were young. Until that day, Mo and Billy spent a lot of time in that treehouse they grew up in. They smoked marijuana in that treehouse, amongst other things they both swore to never tell and take it to the grave with them.

Mo exited his truck and began following Tina without her noticing him. Tina went down through the overpass and between the underbrush. Mo then stood behind a large oak tree to conceal his presence when he noticed Tina had stopped and began looking around. Mo then watched another figure, he could tell was a male, appear out of the darkness. Tina immediately ran to the figure and jumped into his arms. Tina and the figure began kissing one another with passion. The kiss seemed to last forever to Mo. His heart was being ripped out of his chest with every taste the figure got from Tina's lips.

Once Tina and the figure stopped kissing, Mo was shocked when he saw that the figure was his best friend, Billy. Visions of violence shot through his entire being. Mo fell back against the oak tree and grabbed his chest as tears ran down his face. Mo's movement rattled the leaves where he was standing, getting the attention of Billy and Tina.

"What was that?" Tina asked, looking around in the direction of the large oak tree and grabbing on tightly to Billy.

"Probably a rodent going back into its hole," Billy replied, grabbing her by the hand. "Come on, let's go."

Mo turned around and headed back towards his truck hurting. He couldn't stop the tears from flowing down his face. Once at the truck, he opened the door, got in, and started the engine.

Mo then screamed, "Fuck no! Oh hell no!"

He jumped back out of the truck.

Mo slammed the truck door, and walked around to the bed of the truck. He reached into the bed of the truck and grabbed one of the largest axes he could find. The entire time he was talking to himself in a weird mumbling voice. Mo headed back down behind Tina's house and into the wooded area.

CHAPTER 12

Mo stopped beside another tree with the large ax in hand, clutched to the side of his leg. He heard Billy's voice.

"Yeah, right there baby." As Mo moved closer to hear clearer, he heard Billy state, "Oooh, I love you."

Mo moved closer-and-closer so he could see them. When Mo finally got a full view of Tina and Billy, the view was not a pretty picture. He watched as Tina's head bobbed up and down on Billy's rock hard white cock. Moans escaped from Tina's mouth as she licked the large vein that ran down the base of Billy's penis.

She then began sucking his balls slowly as Billy squealed, and said, "Sssstop."

Cold chills shot threw his body.

Tina followed Billy's instruction and came up for air, allowing him to regroup. Billy then lifted her prom dress that Mo had also bought with his hard earned money, and snatched her panties clean off her ass.

"Uhhh," Tina grunted and licked her lips.

Billy turned Tina around, grabbed her by the neck, and bent her over. He then took his hard white penis and entered her from behind.

"Ohhhh Billy." She was moaning his name and continued, "Fuck me Bill! Fuck me good!"

Her pink and black pussy lips gripped Billy's Johnson making a tight fit.

"Who black pussy is this?" Billy asked, pumping hard slow thrusts.

"Yours baby, always yours," She said, throwing her pussy back at Billy even harder until both of them came.

Mo was now in a daze as he appeared from behind another large tree. He watched a couple more minutes as they continued to have sex then made his presence known.

"Are y'all enjoying y'all self?" he asked as Billy jumped back from Tina, his dick hard and dripping Tina's juices.

"Mmmo man, it's not what it looks like," Billy replied. "Just take it easy big boy and calm down."

Billy tried to pull up his pants, while Tina backed behind him.

"How could y'all do me like this?" Mo asked, overcome with emotion down to his chest.

Mo brought his head back up and stared directly into Tina's eyes. Tina could see the fire burning in his eyes as Mo began transforming right before them.

"I loved you both," Mo said, speaking in the past tense.

Tina then noticed the tension in Mo's grip on the ax. As she took a step to run for safety, she was cut down from the waist by the swing of Mo's ax. Tina fell to the ground screaming.

"Please Mo, I'm sorry!" She yelled, meaning every word of it now.

Billy tried to compromise with his best friend, and that's all it was, a compromise, because the sharp end of the blade split Billy's forehead open, killing him instantly. Mo then turned his attention on Tina, who was trying to crawl away. Without a second thought, and ignoring her plea for mercy, Mo began chopping her up into pieces. It was stated later that all of Tina's body parts have not been found. Mo came back to reality and looked around at the mess he had created. He was dripping in blood and tired from swinging the ax. Startled at the revelation of what he had done, Mo dropped the ax and took off running back to his truck. The ax that Mo left behind was the only evidence, which lead to his involvement in the double murder.

Fourteen months later during Mo's trial, Mo plead guilty to twenty to life. He was only afforded this deal because it was proven that he was temporarily insane at the time of the double murder. However, until this day, there are people who say that the only reason Mo was convicted and received time for the murders was because Billy was the son of a Grand Red Dragon of the KKK.

Convict Jones' thoughts were interrupted by the sound of a loud fire alarm, but there was no fire. The fire alarm seemed to go off every fifteen minutes. True or false, it was stated that the prison guard set the alarm to go off every fifteen minutes, which was another tactic by prison officials to break the spirit of prisoners by driving them insane. Once at Mo's cell, Mo gave Convict Jones the run down about what was going on with the prison guards and the prisoners. While Mo was talking, he was also going into his locker and pulling out canteen items then handing them to Convict Jones.

"Good look out. I'll return your stuff with interest when I get to the canteen."

"Don't worry about that. I get my blessing back from the creator," Mo replied because he was a very religious man.

Convict Jones and Mo conversed for a little while longer until Convict Jones informed Mo that he had to go make a move and handle some business. Convict Jones informed Mo that he would get back up with him later and walked out of Mo's cell with the canteen. Convict Jones walked back into his cell and dropped the canteen off. He then exited back out of his cell, went back to the wall phones and tried to make a call, only to find that his phone pin number was still not in service.

CHAPTER 13

Convict Jones entered his cell and saw that Smith had several other prisoners in the cell. Convict Jones automatically figured that the other prisoners were either his homeboys from his hometown, or just guys that he was cool with. Convict Jones was not slow by a long shot. He knew that the other prisoners were there to see who he was. The other prisoners really wanted to know if Convict Jones was a pussy or a stand-up guy. Two of the other three prisoners were sitting back on Convict Jones' bed like it was their own. This was no more than a test to Convict Jones, which he accepted with open arms. Convict Jones, having already served fourteen years on his sentence, knew the ins and outs of a situation such as the one he was now facing. He knew exactly what the prisoners were up to, but they had the wrong prisoner. They had a convict on their hands.

Convict Jones walked past one of those prisoners that were standing up and intentionally bumped him, damn near knocking him down. Convict

Jones did not supply an excuse me or anything. He was ready for whatever they were willing to dish out. The prisoner he bumped looked at Convict Jones like he was hard and getting ready to do something.

"What nigga?" Convict Jones asked, testing the other prisoner's gangsta status.

The prisoner immediately dropped his head, showing a sign of cowardice. Convict Jones thought to himself upon the prisoner's reaction, *Pussy ass nigga.* He checked his surrounding, just in case the other prisoner tried to steal off on him.

Finding that none of the inmates were making any moves Convict Jones continued.

"Y'all get the fuck off my bed," he said as he stared the prisoners down.

The prisoners that were sitting on Convict Jones' bed immediately got off, submitting their my bads.

However, Smith not liking what he saw jumped off his top bunk, and yelled, "Nigga, you don't run nothing around here."

He was getting in Convict Jones' face.

"Alright," was all Convict Jones said, knowing that he would have to handle him later.

Convict Jones then backed his back up against the wall ready to fight, but none of the prisoners made a move, not even Smith. When Smith did not follow through with his tough talk, Jones knew that he was built for what he had coming. However, Convict Jones made another mental note to touch his ass up later. Whether he won or lost, one thing was for sure, Smith and Convict Jones were going to bump heads later on when the dorm would be locked down.

"Allah-who-ack-bar. Allah-who-ack-bar."
"Allah-who-ack-bar. Allah-who-ack-bar."
"Ash-sha-du-an-la-illaha-ilaha-la."
"Ash-sha-du-an-la-illaha-ilaha-la."
"Ash-sha-du-anna-muhummada-ra-sual-allah."
"Ash-sha-du-anna-muhummada-ra-sual-allah."
"High-yalel-salat."
"High-yalel-salat."
"High-yalel-fa-lat."
"High-yalel-fa-lat."
"Allah-who-ack-bar. Allah-who-ack-bar."
"La-ilaha-illaha-la."

This was the fourth time that day Convict Jones heard the singing sound of those words. He knew that it had something to do with the Muslims, but he had no idea what it meant. He made a mental note to find out what they were saying when he got the chance. All Convict Jones knew was that when that sound was made, Muslims from everywhere appeared and joined each other in prayer. Convict Jones walked out of his cell behind the other prisoners and thought, *Muslims are coming from out of everywhere to join in praying.*

"You two boys are so hard headed that I don't know what to do with y'all. Just look at you!" Major Riley yelled with a frown on his face as he bashed the two prisoners sitting before him. "Drunk! Drunk! Drunk!"

Major Riley was sucking his teeth and slamming his radio down on his desk. O-Dog giggled under his breath, unable to control his alcohol.

"Yo Dog man, chill out," Dirty Dee whispered to his partner. "You are going to get us in trouble."

Dirty Dee was staring at O-Dog hard, letting him know he meant business.

Major Riley sat down at his desk, looked at the two prisoners, and said, "Okay boys. Playtime is over. Get serious or I'm going to have to cut you out of my will."

That caused O-Dog to immediately sober up and stare Major Riley in the eyes with a confused look.

"Now y'all listen and listen good. Especially you, Terry. Our boy showed up three weeks ago, but I had him in lock-up until he healed from the ass cutting the welcome committee put on his narrow ass."

"Who?" O-Dog asked, not knowing who Major Riley was talking about.

"See, that's what I am talking about. Terry you never listen or pay attention to what's going on. That is one of the reasons you're serving this time because you don't listen. Now pay attention fool," Major Riley spat.

O-Dog sucked his teeth as usual because he didn't care to hear the lecture that Major Riley always beat him in the head with.

"He's talking about that Jones cat," Dirty Dee informed O-Dog, putting him up on game.

"Oh," O-Dog replied dumbfounded.

"I'm glad someone is listening and paying attention around here because shit is about to get serious around here." Major Riley said, standing up from his desk and walking over to a small cabinet in the corner of his office.

Major Riley opened the cabinet, reached in, grabbed a small brown paper bag out of the cabinet, and tossed it to Dirty Dee.

Then Major Riley said, "Make that last."

He said speaking of the dime bag of marijuana he gave them.

"I've been waiting to put some work in on that nigga," O-Dog stated, being the most violent out of him and Dirty Dee.

"Now you have your chance, but make sure you be clean about it," he said, letting O-Dog know he meant business. "And I don't want the incident to lead back to me, the institution, or for that matter, the South Carolina Department of Corrections. Do you understand?" Major Riley spoke while providing instruction to the two young black males.

While Major Riley was talking, like always O-Dog daydreamed, thinking about how he was going to murder Convict Jones. He was no longer paying attention to what Major Riley was saying, nor did he care. All O-Dog wanted to do was kill Convict Jones.

"Terry, Terry, Terry! What the hell is wrong with you?" Major Riley asked, breaking O-Dog's thoughts. "Did you hear what I said?" Major Riley shouted, getting upset with O-Dog.

"Huh," O-Dog replied because he was caught off guard.

Major Riley became furious. He grabbed his head and began shaking it not believing that he was going through with what he was going through with.

"Big guy," Dirty Dee got Major Riley's attention. "I heard you. I'll get dog straight and have a talk with him."

"Thank you, David," Major Riley replied, calming down.

The entire time Major Riley and Dirty Dee were having a conversation about O-Dog, O-Dog watched and listened to them. Anger immediately filled O-Dog's heart because he felt like they were trying to play him.

"Well boys, I believe this meeting is over. Please leave out the back way so no one will see you coming out of my office," Major Riley informed them, wanting to keep their association unknown.

O-Dog and Dirty Dee got up out of their chairs and left out of Major Riley's office. They then walked out the back entrance of operation where they could not be seen by other prisoners or guards. Stepping out of the back door of operations, an older prisoner stood beside the door picking up garbage. The older prisoner listened to O-Dog and Dirty Dee arguing and discussing the same matter they had spoken about in Major Riley's office. However, O-Dog and Dirty Dee did not pay attention, therefore they had no clue that the older prisoner was there, much less hearing everything they said.

CHAPTER 14

"Attention in the area. Lockdown roll call count will be conducted in fifteen minutes," the institutional p.a. intercom system announced throughout the institution.

Prisoners began scattering like little roaches all over the rock area. Some of the prisoners went to get a last minute warm-up at the microwave, while other prisoners made pit stops to say a last few words to other prisoners, just in case Allah didn't see fit for them to see another day. Convict Jones headed to his cell and entered. Once inside the cell, Convict Jones noticed Smith sitting on his top bunk with a pair of Koss headphones on his ears listening to the radio. Convict Jones had already intended to bust his ass, but Smith made it that much more known when he began singing out loud like a trick bitch.

"I'm a king," Smith sung in a low squeaky voice, pissing Convict Jones off that much more.

Convict Jones sat down on the toilet connected to the sink and strapped his boots up.

As soon as the prison officials made their roll call count and left the wing, Convict Jones got up, walked over to the bed, and asked, "What's up nigga?"

He was expecting anything.

Smith looked at Convict Jones all wide eyed with his nose turned up towards the ceiling, and stated, "What's up?"

It was like he didn't know what was good in the hood.

Smith then jumped off the top bunk and stood close to Convict Jones' face, breathing heavy like a big bull. Out of nowhere, Convict Jones slapped the cowboy dog shit out of him, instantly deflating the air in his chest. Expecting some type of retaliation, Convict Jones was still like a deer in headlights.

Smith dropped his pants, and said, "Here, you don't have to take it."

Smith had his bare ass pointing in Convict Jones' direction.

Out of dislike for homos, Convict Jones football kicked Smith directly in the crack of his ass, sending him crashing between the toilet and wall. For the rest of the night, Smith stayed in the corner in the same position whimpering like a child until breakfast was called the next morning.

The following morning, Unit Two headed out to breakfast at 5:45. All the prisoners were made to line up in a straight line and walk to and from the cafeteria in the same fashion. This also occurred for every destination in the institution that prisoners went to. This form of action was called controlled movement. This was one of the criteria of the prison system that prisoners had to follow. Inside the cafeteria, Convict Jones stood in a long crowded line of prisoners waiting to receive his meal on a dog tray.

Prisoner's food would come through a slot in the hole of a steel wall, which consisted of two boiled eggs, two cold hard biscuits, and a half of scoop of unclean yellow grits. Prisoners were also allowed to get as much juice as they wanted. That's because the juice was watered down. Whenever the prisoners were provided milk, which was far and few, they were served milk that was cut down to its lowest degree. Sometimes you could see maggots forming in the milk. The coffee they served prisoners made their shit smell something awful.

Prison guards stood around the cafeteria watching the prisoners eat screaming, "Five minutes!"

They were walking through the tables, standing over inmates while they ate.

Convict Jones proceeded towards the orange juice containers, which was an ice cooler, when he heard his name being called. Convict Jones refused to turn around and kept moving like it was not his name, but he did cut his eyes to see who was calling his name. Once Convict Jones saw the caller of his name, he made his way over while he watched another set of eyes follow his every move.

"What's up, boy?" L.C. Floyd shouted, happy to see an old friend.

"It's been about six years, ain't it?" Convict Jones asked, and answering a question with a question, all the while keeping his eyes on his surroundings.

"Where you coming from?" L.C. Floyd asked, sitting down at one of the mess hall tables.

"Where you left me at."

"Well, I can tell you now, you have come to the wrong place. These motherfuckers are crazy down here, and I'm not just talking about the prisoners. I'm speaking about the prison guards," L.C. Floyd explained with emotion.

Convict Jones and L.C. Floyd went way back before the eighty-five percent law, control movement, and close custody. These two prisoners were convicts who had been in the prison system prior to Director Michael Moore and Governor David Beasley taking office in South Carolina. There was no such thing as one, two, or three custody levels. Prisoners had their own clothing, televisions, radios, and just about anything the people on the streets had. It was back when prisoners could do their time without the bullshit from prison guards. Convict Jones considered L.C. Floyd to be a true blue convict to the heart. L.C. Floyd was serving a seventy-five year prison sentence for a double homicide. Actually it was self-defense, but because L.C. Floyd was a black man from Tampa Bay, Florida, and it was two white boys who were killed, the State of South Carolina stuck it to him. Convict Jones remembered how L.C. Floyd told him it went down, which only caused Convict Jones to grab his head and shake it.

It was the early 1980's when the railroad tracks were laid for L.C. Floyd at gunpoint in broad daylight in the middle of the street in downtown Columbia, South Carolina. The two white boys whose names were Dan Jordan and Jason Johnson had followed L.C. Floyd from a small bar where he had picked up a white woman named Mechelle Henderson. L.C. Floyd and Mechelle had already had several drinks and decided that they would leave the bar together, go get a motel room, and have a little fun. What L.C. Floyd did not know was that he was nothing more than a trick or lick for Mechelle, Jason, and Dan. Before leaving the bar, L.C. Floyd ordered another round of drinks for him and Mechelle.

"What else you want to drink?" He asked in a sluggish tone.

"Nothing baby," she replied, rubbing L.C. Floyd's leg. "Just get a bottle so we can take it to the room with us."

"You do girl?" L.C. Floyd asked while pulling out a large knot of money.

"Yeah baby, how much you got?" she asked, fishing for information while Dan and Jason watched from the other side of the bar.

"Enough sugar," L.C. Floyd replied, placing a hundred dollar bill on the counter to pay his tab.

"Hold up, baby. I have to use the ladies room," Mechelle informed L.C. Floyd.

When Mechelle got up and went to the bathroom so did Dan and Jason. Inside the bathroom, Mechelle informed them that L.C. Floyd had a lot of money and drugs, although she didn't see any drugs. Dan and Jason told Mechelle to ride with him and they would do the rest. Mechelle walked back out the bathroom, and told L.C. Floyd that she was ready to go. Coming down Main Street in Columbia, South Carolina, Dan and Jason pulled up in front of L.C. Floyd's gray Buick with their greenish blue I-Roc and blocked his car from moving. Dan and Jason jumped out of their vehicle with their guns in hand and drew down on L.C. Floyd. Mechelle immediately opened L.C. Floyd's car door, exited his vehicle, and took off running. Pedestrians stopped walking and stood in shock, looking at what was going on.

L.C. Floyd was only in Columbia, South Carolina to visit his sister. He was on leave from the military. L.C. Floyd being a military man, always stayed strapped with a military issued .45 handgun filled with full metal jackets. Dan and Jason without warning, and high on heroin and meth, immediately opened fire on L.C. Floyd's vehicle. One slug found its way into L.C. Floyd's left shoulder, while another slug found its way into his left arm.

"Ahhhhh!" L.C. Floyd screamed, not knowing what was going on.

L.C. Floyd's military instincts immediately kicked. He ducked down in his car at the same time reaching under his seat for his military.45 handgun with his right hand. Dan and Jason moved in quick. The only thing on the white boys mind was getting the drugs and money, whether they got the drugs off L.C. Floyd's body, dead or alive. L.C. Floyd struggled, but he got his car door open, rolled out of the vehicle, and let off two rounds. Dan and Jason ducked for cover as people began running and ducking behind cars and buildings. L.C. Floyd placed his back up against his vehicle, clutching his weapon.

The meth consolidated with heroin had Jason feeling as if he could not be stopped. Jason ran around L.C. Floyd's vehicle and caught a bullet in the mouth, followed by one to his forehead, killing him before he could ask Allah for forgiveness for all the wrong things he had done in his life. Dan watched wide-eyed as Jason fell to the ground dead. He yelled and ran at L.C. Floyd, letting off his entire clip. All that screaming, yelling, and shooting came to an immediate stop with one slug hitting him in the heart, while another slug struck him in the throat and knocked half of his face off.

Police rolled up to the area, and immediately drew down on L.C. Floyd. L.C. Floyd was arrested and taken to jail. A year later, after sitting in the county jail, L.C. Floyd went to trial and was convicted for a double murder, although he had several witnesses who testified that he was being attacked by Dan and Jason. Testimony also came in from Mechelle Henderson that she was part of the set up, and that she did not know that Dan and Jason would shoot L.C. Floyd first. The court still ruled out self-defense based upon L.C. Floyd's Commanding General, General Pratt, who was not only from South Carolina, but also gave testimony that L.C. Floyd was trained to kill.

"So you're saying that he was a one hundred percent at the shooting range?" the State Attorney asked General Pratt.

"Yes, that is correct."

The State Attorney then twisted the facts around in closing arguments before an all-white jury stating, "L.C. Floyd did not have to kill Dan Jordan and Jason Johnson. He could have easily wounded them." Looking the jury in the eyes he went on to say, "Mr. Floyd wanted to murder. It's in his blood to murder. No military training would cause you to do that, despite what General Pratt stated about him being a trained killer."

Picking up the military .45 off the table, which was used to kill Dan and Jason, the State's Attorney continued, "You heard the General, Mr. Floyd scored out on the shooting range a one hundred percent. A trained gunman by the United States of Amy. This was not self-defense because if it was he could have wounded them. He did not have to kill, I mean murder them."

Based on that argument consolidated with it being an all-white jury, L.C. Floyd was found guilty of a double homicide. The court then sentenced L.C. Floyd to seventy-five years in the South Carolina Department of Corrections. The strangest thing about his sentence was that the court ordered that his sentence be non-violent.

CHAPTER 15

While Convict Jones and L.C. Floyd held a conversation, catching up on old times, discussing other convicts who got out of prison or came back to prison, and the ones who have never been seen from or heard about again, Convict Jones could not help but feel the same set of eyes burning holes in his skull. Without turning around, Convict Jones cut his eyes around his surroundings and noticed a young prisoner evil eyeing him. Convict Jones placed his hand over his mouth as if he was coughing and began talking to L.C. Floyd.

"L.C., we are being monitored like a motherfucker by the young cat at the back table by the window to my right."

Now removing his hand from his mouth as L.C. Floyd placed a spoon full of eggs in his mouth, not to eat, but to conceal what he was about to say.

"Yeah, I noticed that young brother too five minutes ago."

"Do you know him?" Convict Jones asked, whipping his face and making it hard for anybody to read his lips.

"No, but I have seen him around. He keeps a whole lot of bullshit with him, and I mean a whole lot."

That caused Convict Jones' brain to start storming.

"What's his name?" he asked, seeking information with concern in his voice, "and where is he from, and what's his M.O.?" Convict Jones asked doing his homework, rather to be safe than sorry.

Old school rules of convicts is that if any threat or potential threat arises one must do his personal investigation so as to find out everything they can about the threat or person, so that you can always be prepared for the unexpected.

"They call him O-Dog. He stays in a lot of arguments with other prisoners. Most of the arguments, if not all of them, is about bullshit."

L.C. Floyd started thinking back to a time when he witnessed O-Dog starting a fight over a basketball game he was not playing in.

L.C. Floyd then continued, "These inmates don't do nothing about it because of the reputation that the young cat has for stabbing another old school convict some years back. Most of the new arrivals are scared to death of him, but frankly the young bitch knows his place and boundaries," L.C. Floyd explained.

"Well, I don't sleep on no nigga, and I don't like the way he watching me," Convict Jones replied, becoming irritated.

The two convict's conversation was interrupted by a prison guard yelling that breakfast was over and they had forty seconds to evacuate the cafeteria. Both convicts stood from their seats at the table.

As Convict Jones gave L.C. Floyd a pound, he stated in a low whisper, "Keep your ears to the concrete walls."

"Yeah, always," L.C. Floyd replied and walked off in a different direction, disappearing into the crowd of prisoners leaving the mess hall.

As Convict Jones watched L.C. Floyd disappear, he picked up his tray of food, grabbed the two boiled eggs, and stuffed them in his pocket. The other prisoners in the cafeteria were all departing. As Convict Jones proceeded to the area where you dropped the tray off to be washed, he noticed the young cat, O-Dog, still evil eyeing him. Convict Jones exited the cafeteria, making a mental note to find out what was on the young cat's mind for watching him so close. Many prisoners have gotten killed for that same type of act in watching a nigga, as well as being killed for lesser things than that in prison.

Once outside the mess hall, Convict Jones with Unit Two, walked back towards the unit. During the walk, O-Dog's face appeared in Convict Jones' mind's eye, and he realized that he had seen O-Dog's face somewhere before. He didn't know if it was on another prison yard or if it was on the street, but one thing was for certain and two things are for sure, Convict Jones had seen O-Dog's face somewhere before. Convict Jones also considered that O-Dog may be his cellmate's homeboy or partner, looking to get redress for his homeboy but immediately ruled that out. If Michael Smith was a bitch, then what hung around him was also bitchafide. However, Convict Jones didn't give a shit if O-Dog was his daddy, he would handle anything that came his way or get handled.

All the prisoners got back to the dorm at approximately 6:00 A.M. where Convict Jones drunk him a cup of coffee, smoked a cigarette, and then went back to his cell to get some rest. As Convict Jones lay in his bunk thinking for ten minutes, he remembered that Sergeant White had informed him that he had to pick-up his property from the property room at 10 o'clock on the dot. Ten minutes later, Convict Jones had dozed off into a peaceful sleep.

CHAPTER 16

Hundreds of miles away in the State of Oklahoma, Federal Agent Paul Johnson sat at his desk looking through stacks of folders and files full of pictures of the most wanted criminals in America. All the suspects and criminals were wanted for murder. One particular suspect was alleged to be wanted for murders in South Carolina, Georgia, New York, Florida, and several other states.

"Damn John!" Federal Agent Johnson screamed and continued, "We almost had him."

Federal Agent Johnson closed the file on the desk.

"We will get him," Federal Agent John Williams replied, straightening his tie. "We always get our man."

Agent John Williams and Agent Paul Johnson were partners. They had been working together for the last sixteen years. Both agents were married with kids, but of course their job caused problems in the household because their jobs came first. Agent Williams had three children, two of which were about to start high school, while the oldest was about to start college. Agent Johnson also had three children, except all his children were by different women.

In Agent Johnson's younger days, you couldn't tell him he wasn't a player, and that of course was when the children started showing up. He decided to revoke his player's card. Being a mixed child coming up in life had its perks, just as it had its problems. However, Agent Johnson overcame all of it, although it was rough. Agent Williams, on the other hand, was a black man from North Carolina, stationed to work in Washington D.C. on assignment with Agent Johnson. Both agents took their jobs too seriously, and sometimes sought injustice to bring forth justice.

Agent Williams and Agent Johnson had been on this particular case for over five years. Sometimes it felt to them, like they were chasing a ghost. The only evidence that the agents had on their suspect was a blurred photo of the suspect leaving a murder scene. However, the photo was taken of the side of his face, but with new technology, Agent Williams and Agent Johnson were able to come to a close composite of the suspect. Running data after data on the photo, nothing came up that could identify who the suspect was. There were no arrest records on the photo or anything that would explain something about the suspect. The agents didn't even have a name for the suspect so to humor themselves they called the suspect Casper. All the agents had was a bad photo that wouldn't hold up in a court of law. However, today was their lucky day. Casper had struck again, and this is why the agents were in Oklahoma.

"Excuse me, sir. My name is Agent Johnson and this is my partner, Agent Williams," Agent Johnson said, introducing them to an eyewitness at the crime scene.

"Yes, how are you doing?" the shaken eyewitness asked.

"I was informed that you witnessed the incident that took place across the street in the blue building," Agent Johnson stated while pulling out a pen and pad to take down notes.

"Yes sir. It was horrible," the eyewitness stated, feeling free to give any and all information to the federal government.

"Can you please tell me and my partner what you saw so that we can get to the bottom of the matter?" Agent Williams asked.

"Well, I was sitting over there on the bench," he started explaining as he directed the agent's attention with his finger, "next to the blue building where I sit every day to catch the bus downtown to Fifth Street. That's when I saw this black guy standing around the blue building. Two minutes later as I was waiting on the bus, I heard several gunshots. When I turned to look in the direction of the gunshots, which came out of the blue building, I saw the black guy come out with two big brown grocery bags. The black guy looked in my direction and noticed that I had seen him. He looked at me and raised his index finger to his mouth. I guess he was indicating for me to be quiet. Then he took the same fingers and pointed at me as if he had a gun, and pretended to pull the trigger then blow the barrel. I immediately got up off the bench, headed in the other direction, and went into *Tony's Beef and Grill* right there on the corner. As I looked back, once in Tony's, the guy got into a black van and drove off going east, just as he had pulled up."

"Thank you very much, sir. Is that all you can remember, sir?" Agent Williams asked.

"Well, that's what I saw."

"Okay. I want to show you a picture, and tell me if this is the guy you saw."

Agent Williams handed the eyewitness the photo of Casper.

The eyewitness took one good luck at the photo, and said, "This could be him, but I don't know. I don't see too good these days."

"Sir, please try to remember. It is very important that we stop this guy and get him off the street," Agent Johnson stated, breaking into the conversation.

"Well, let me see the picture again."

The eyewitness grabbed the photo and began studying the picture.

After reviewing the picture, the eyewitness said, "I believe that is the guy."

"Why do you say that?" Agent Williams asked as he began taking down notes again.

"Because the same ring on his hand in the picture is the same ring that was on the black guys hand when he acted like he was going to shoot me," the eyewitness stated.

Agent Johnson and Agent Williams took down the eyewitness' name, phone number, and address then they headed back to their unmarked vehicle after going into the blue building to further investigate the crime scene.

CHAPTER 17

The tapping on Convict Jones' cell door woke him out of his sleep. He turned over and looked at the door. Convict Jones motioned with his hand for Mo to enter his cell.

Once inside the cell, Mo sat down on the table and asked, "You going to the canteen?"

Mo looked around the cell.

"Yeah," Convict Jones replied in a deep voice.

"Well, you better get up and get ready because they will be calling for us to line-up in about five minutes."

"I'll be ready."

Convict Jones started raising up out of the bed and placing his feet on the cold brick floor.

Mo got up from the table and exited Convict Jones' cell so that he could get himself together. Convict Jones got up off his bunk, went to the toilet, and took an early morning piss. After using the toilet, he washed his face with a cold rag, and brushed his teeth with some state Bob Barker toothpaste. Convict Jones only used the state issued items because at that very moment he did not have his own. While Convict Jones was getting ready, his cellmate Michael Smith laid in the top bunk like a bitch watching Convict Jones' every movement, but at the same time pretending to be asleep. Smith would grunt and moan, while tossing, turning, and sucking his teeth like a true bitch.

"You got a problem, nigga!" Convict Jones shouted because he was tired of the bitch shit.

"You making too much noise. I can't sleep," Smith replied in a soft, passionate tone.

With a disgusting and aggressive tone, Convict Jones spat, "Shut the fuck up, bitch!"

Convict Jones exited the cell.

As soon as he exited the cell, Convict Jones saw Mo waiting and the rest of the prisoners lined up and leaving the unit.

Convict Jones caught up with Mo, and asked, "Canteen line?"

"Yeah, fall in with me," Mo replied, moving out of the way to make room for Convict Jones.

Once at the canteen, Convict Jones, Mo, and twenty-five more prisoners waited for their orders to be filled. Convict Jones watched the other prisoners that worked in the canteen penny pinch their fellow prisoners by robbing them blind. When all is said and done every penny the prisoners in the canteen stole would add up to a great amount. The fact was that a prisoner's family members worked hard and sent their loved ones in prison their hard-earned money. Upon the prisoner receiving the money, first and foremost the South Carolina Department of Corrections would take their five percent for DNA testing. Then they will get their five dollars for every visit you may have taken to the medical facility, consolidated with another five dollars for each time you received medication from them for your serious medical needs. Then you have the prisoners who work in the canteen robbing you.

This is insane because a prisoner would be lucky to have ten dollars left out of fifty dollars sent to him if that prisoner owed the canteen man in the dorm, other prisoners for drugs or cigarettes, or had to pay restitution to the state courts. Convict Jones returned back from the canteen with Mo carrying three big bags of canteen after spending one hundred and twenty five dollars. The other prisoners in the dorm stood around the rock area eye hustling Convict Jones' bags so that they could later come and beg for something they saw in the bags or break into Convict Jones' locker when he was gone. However, before robbing or stealing, they needed to get to know Convict Jones to even try him like that. If they did they surely wouldn't attempt any bullshit games with Convict Jones.

Convict Jones and Mo entered his cell where they put all Convict Jones' canteen bags on the bottom bunk. Convict Jones then threw his white blanket over the bags of to conceal them from roaming eyes. Convict Jones and Mo then walked back outside of his cell. Mo went in one direction, while Convict Jones went in another direction. Convict Jones headed back out the door, and walked back up towards the head of operation to pick up his property in the green army duffle bag that was packed by Officer Green at Perry Correctional Institution. Coming across the prison compound, which was pretty big, Convict Jones counted five units. Other prisoners were walking to and from on the compounds.

Convict Jones stopped one of the prisoners, and asked, "Where is the property room partner?"

"Right there by the double doors," the prisoner replied, pointing in the direction of operations.

Convict Jones followed the directions given to him by the other prisoner and ended up at the property room back door.

Going through the back door of the property room, a short, fat, ugly, white woman with red freckles all over her face, in a white shirt and dusty blue khaki pants asked Convict Jones, "Do you have an OTR?"

She was speaking of a piece of paper, which is called an order to report.

"No, I was instructed by Sergeant White to come and pick up my property today," Convict Jones replied, looking around the small property room of prisoner's property.

"Oh, you must be Jones," she stated then continued, "I've heard about you."

She was smiling from ear-to-ear.

"Was it bad or good?" Convict Jones asked, finding the white woman vulnerable because she was so unattractive.

"It's not important," she replied, allowing Convict Jones to know that she was with the order of the institution, and then continued. "What's your inmate number?"

"Two-one-four-seven-four-seven," Convict Jones replied, thinking to himself what did the white woman mean by, *I heard about you.*

The white woman left the area for about five minutes and returned with Convict Jones' property. Convict Jones snatched up the green duffle bag and placed it over his shoulder.

"Shaquan,"

Convict Jones said thank you in Arabic.

"Huh?" she asked, not understanding what he meant.

"Thank you, and have a nice day,"

Convict Jones started walking out the back door of the small property room.

Once outside the property room, Convict Jones watched a long line of prisoners walking towards the cafeteria. He knew that lunch had begun. To Convict Jones' right, an older man was planting flowers in the garden, which was next to the entrance to medical.

The older prisoner looked at Convict Jones long and hard before Convict Jones asked, "What's happening old time?"

He was wondering why he was looking at him like that.

"Be careful youngblood," the older prisoner replied and walked away into the medical double doors.

Alarms immediately went off in Convict Jones' head. *Why would the old timer inform me to be careful, when I do not even know him?* Convict Jones started walking back across the compound towards his assigned unit. Once back at the unit and going into his cell, Smith was just getting up out of bed. Convict Jones dropped his property on his bottom bunk with the concealed canteen, and headed back out of the cell so that Smith could get himself together by washing his face and brushing his teeth. Convict Jones knew that Smith would be coming out of the cell anytime because the institutional intercom had announced for Unit Two to line-up for lunch, which meant that Unit Two had five minutes before they left for the cafeteria.

Three minutes later Smith came out of the cell, and Convict Jones entered back into the cell. Once inside the cell, Convict Jones immediately covered his cell window by placing a towel in the window with a toothbrush holding it in place. As Unit Two prisoners left, Convict Jones began dumping his property out of the green duffle bag onto his bed. Convict Jones then saw what he was looking for, and grabbed the new day baby powder container. He then got some newspapers from the side of the toilet, and a white towel out of his property. First, he placed the towel down on the bed, and then placed the newspaper over the towel. Next, he dropped the lid of the container of baby powder and poured everything out of the container. Inside the container of the baby powder, wrapped up in plastic and electrical tape were three ounces of compressed marijuana. Convict Jones also had four hundred dollar bills wrapped in plastic and electrical tape. It was by luck that Convict Jones had put the marijuana and money in the baby powder container. The very same night, prior to Sergeant Wilson and Officer Green waking him up and packing his belongings, he had just placed the marijuana and money in the container.

The only reason why Convict Jones was holding his own stash was because his hold man was informed that he was going to court the following morning or possibly transferred to another prison. Just so happened, his hold man was being transferred because in the following weeks, Convict Jones saw him working in the cafeteria. Opening the plastic bag full of marijuana, the scent smacked him in the face. He pulled a large bud out of the marijuana, wrapped it back up, and put it back in the container. The four hundred dollar bills, he placed in the tongue of his Converse tennis shoes very neatly to where you couldn't tell it was there. He then bagged up ten sacks of marijuana from the big bud of marijuana he removed from the rest. The remainder of the marijuana left from the big bud, he placed inside of a blunt he bought from the canteen earlier that day. After rolling the blunt, Convict Jones set it in the window so that it could dry.

While the blunt dried, he placed all of his property and canteen in his locker neatly. After all his belongings and canteen items were placed in the locker, he grabbed a master lock he also bought from the canteen and locked his property in the locker. It wasn't that Convict Jones feared his belongings getting taken from him by others, it was just that you don't ever give others the opportunity to try you in that manner because it would be your own fault.

Convict Jones then reached up in the window and grabbed the blunt he rolled and set fire to it. He took five deep pulls off the blunt then he heard the prisoners returning from lunch. He quickly put out the blunt and lit homemade incense made out of Muslim Oil and tissue. Convict Jones then fired up a cigarette to further cover the smell of smoked marijuana. Two minutes later, Smith entered back into the cell looking around and sniffing the air like a bloodhound.

Then he stated, "It sure does smell good in here."

He was not talking about the Muslim Oil or cigarette.

After Smith's remark, Convict Jones walked out of the cell without responding, but thinking to himself, *Nosy bitch!*

Convict Jones realized that he was crazy high because his focus was enhanced several notches higher. He could smell better, see better, taste better, hell he could even jump higher. Convict Jones could damn near hear a roach piss on cotton. He had become more aware of his surroundings.

Convict Jones then noticed Mo heading to his cell. He   followed slowly behind Mo to his cell without Mo knowing that he was being followed. When Mo got to his cell and opened the door, Convict Jones stopped the door with his hand, startling Mo. Quick as a wink, Mo had already had the blade pulled up against Convict Jones' rib cage.

Convict Jones glanced down at the blade, and said, "Damn, chill out partner!"

He looked back up into Mo's eyes.

"Don't do that man, and stop playing all them damn games. That's the quickest way to get turned into a pin cushion," Mo stated really mad. "Plus you have done too much time to be running around here playing them games."

Mo was serious as a heart attack.

"Fuck that shit you talking. Let's go in the cell," Convict Jones replied, paying no attention to Mo's remarks, even though he knew Mo was telling the truth. Convict Jones then continued, "I got something for you."

Mo opened his cell.

Both of the convicts then entered the cell, closed the door behind them, and placed a towel and toothbrush in the cell window.

CHAPTER 18

Boom! Boom! Boom!

Gunshots rang throughout the streets of Atlanta, Georgia as people dove behind vehicles to duck stray bullets. Two middle aged black men lay dead in the middle of the street with bullets in their chest and neck area. A lone black man disappeared around a corner and leapt into the front seat of a black van.

"Damn that was close!" he screamed breathing hard, placing the van in gear while pulling off.

While he pulled away from the curb, he immediately began changing his jacket and placing on another pair of glasses while passing the two black males in the street. As the black man rode down the street, he began laughing to himself. He made a bunch of left and right turns, and fifteen minutes later he pulled behind an eight story abandoned building. After getting out of the van, he ran around to the back of the van, opened the doors, and took out three large black duffle bags. He then closed the van doors, picked up the three large heavy bags, and entered the eight story abandoned building.

After walking up six flights of stairs, he dipped into a hole in the wall and climbed a ladder with the bags into the ceiling of the building. He ended up in the attic of the building. Looking around the attic of the building, there was a big brown desk sitting in the corner facing the window, which gave an all-around view of his surroundings. Four TV monitors were displayed and built into the wall. These monitors were also connected to eight different recording cameras that were located outside the building. These cameras would pick up anything moving within a half-mile radius. The black man's name was Rico Cross. He was known to the federal agents as *Casper the Ghost*.

Rico dumped the three bags down next to the desk. The three bags held large amounts of money. There were hundred dollar bills wrapped tight with rubber bands. Rico then reached down and grabbed his .45 nickel plated Smith and Wesson, slammed it down on the desk, and then sat down. He then reached over and opened one of the bags. He began removing the money from the bag, placing it on the desk in stacks then he started counting the money.

"Yeah," he screamed to himself and continued, "it's on and poppin' now!"

After counting four hundred thousand dollars, he loaded the money back up in the bags and took it to another room in the building. Once inside the room, he opened up a safe that he had built into the wall. The safe was the size of a large walk in closet. Casper placed the money inside the safe with the rest of the money that was already in there. Casper then locked up the safe, walked back to the attic room, and sat down at his desk. After firing up a cigar and taking two pulls, he pulled out his cell phone and punched in a number.

The phone rang three times, a female voice picked up the phone, and said, "Evans Correctional Institution, may I help you?"

O-Dog and Dirty Dee were sitting in O-Dog's cell watching a football game and drinking a creamer of homemade wine.

"Yo Dirrrrty," O-Dog stated in a sluggish tone. "I saw our boy just this morning."

He downed the rest of his creamer and smacked his lips.

"Who?" Dirty Dee asked.

"That cat Jones," a snarl spread across O-Dog's face as he spoke the name. "He was talking to that old ass convict L.C. at breakfast."

"Well, that's good but we have to wait to make a move on him," Dirty Dee stated, remembering what Major Riley had told them.

"We don't have to wait on shit!" O-Dog shouted, allowing the alcohol to think and talk for him. "We can move on that motherfucker right now."

He pulled out his rusty icepick and waved it around.

"Hold up, dog. If we are going to hit this nigga, we going to hit him right. I'm not trying to get caught up in no fuck shit, and I am definitely not trying to catch no more time. I got babies at home that miss daddy," Dirty Dee replied with a serious look on his face.

O-Dog grabbed Dirty Dee's creamer, took the last swig of wine, and said, "I'll be right back."

O-Dog started to walk out the cell door, while Dirty Dee followed asking, "Where you going?"

"I'll be right back," O-Dog answered.

O-Dog exited the cell and turned a corner at the end of the hallway.

CHAPTER 19

"I don't know why you got me putting up this flap," Mo stated, placing the toothbrush in the window to hold the towel in place. "Ain't nobody out there."

Mo peeped back out the window through the crack of the towel.

"Man just put the flap up. I got something for you," Convict Jones informed Mo.

After Mo got finished with putting the towel in the window, he walked back over to his bed, sat down, and asked, "Okay, what's good little brother?"

Convict Jones went down in the front of his pants and pulled out a sock. He then emptied the contents of the socks on the bed. The ten bags of marijuana he bagged up landed on the bed.

"Oh shit!" Mo shouted excitedly. "Where you get some weed from?"

Mo's eyes locked on the marijuana on his bed.

"Don't worry about all that. Just take these two bags for that canteen you gave me yesterday. That should cover me, right?" Convict Jones asked because he was a true believer in being a good paymaster.

"Man, it's been dry as leaves around this bitch for months. Ever since the SLED and Feds came up in this prison, it's been hard to score on visit. The prison guards are scared to death to take a chance bringing something in."

Mo informed Convict Jones of everything that had been going on around the institution.

"It can't be that damn dry because my homeboy just hit me off with this little bit here. He told me he will holla at me later on some other shit," Convict Jones informed Mo, lying through his two front teeth for good reasons.

Convict Jones then pulled out the remainder of the blunt he had lit up and put out in his cell. As Convict Jones sparked the blunt back up, he thought that it was crazy that out of five dormitory's on the compound and the prison population consisted of over thirty five hundred inmates, that there no weed on the yard for four months. Convict Jones began to really question himself, asking where in the hell had they transferred him to.

"Damn!" Mo said. "That's that bomb shit, ain't it?" he asked.

Convict Jones replied, "And you know it."

He inhaled the smoke and blew it out in Mo's direction.

Convict Jones then passed the blunt to Mo then he walked back over to the window and peeped out the side of the towel.

"Mo, I holla back at you later. I have to go handle something. Oh yeah, don't tell nobody I got nothing, and if they ask just tell them that I don't get down like that. If they want to buy some I'll holla at my homeboy and get some more, but you will be conducting the transactions. Under no circumstances, allow nobody to know whether by sight or mouth that I have anything, or where you getting the weed from because the streets are always watching with their ears to these prison walls," Convict Jones lectured Mo like a child.

Mo just looked at him like he was crazy, and replied, "Why you trying to play me like that, boy?" Mo hit the roach of the blunt. "You know damn well I'm not going to bring your name into nothing, nigga."

He tossed the roach in the toilet and flushed it.

"Alright," Convict Jones replied then opened the cell door and walked out.

As Convict Jones headed back to his cell, he was stopped by another prisoner who everybody called *Pill Line*.

"Hey man. Can I get a light?" Pill Line asked.

Convict Jones reached in his top left pocket, pulled out his cigarette lighter, and handed it to Pill Line. Pill Line grabbed the lighter then reached down to the ground and picked up a smoked cigarette duck and put it in his mouth. The cigarette duck stuck two inches out of his lips. Pill Line turned his head to the side, striked the lighter, and placed the flame on the two-inch cigarette duck. The flame of the lighter burned Pill Lines uneven mustache. After what seemed like five minutes of Pill Line burning up his mustache and Convict Jones' lighter, Convict Jones requested his lighter back. Convict Jones then went inside of his pocket, gave Pill Line three loose cigarettes, and informed him to throw the duck down. He later found out that giving Pill Line those three cigarettes may have been the worst thing that he had ever done because every time Pill

Line needed a cigarette, for some odd reason, Pill Line was knocking on Convict Jones' cell door.

On the way to his cell he stopped by the wall phones again and checked to see if his phone pin number had been activated. He picked the phone up off the receiver and dialed his number. Convict Jones was shocked to see that his phone pin number had been activated. After the directions from the phone operator, warning about three way calls, and a bunch of other instructions, his phone call was processed. After about forty seconds, Convict Jones heard a click followed by a soft female voice.

"Hey baby," Convict Jones' fiancé answered the phone.

"What's poppin', ma?" Convict Jones asked, sounding hardcore just the way she liked it.

"Why in the hell have you not called me? I've been worried sick about you. Are you alright?" she asked.

"Baby, I don't know where the hell I am at, but they say the institution is called Evans. Baby, I have a story to tell you," Convict Jones informed his fiancé whose name was Kemmiko Davis whom everybody called Kim.

"Are you alright?" she asked again concerned about her man. "I've been calling everywhere looking for you," she informed Convict Jones, and then giggled for no reason at all.

"Yeah, I'm straight." He quickly replied then asked, "What you giggling for?"

"Nothing baby. You need some money?" she asked, knowing that Convict Jones loved her, but he also loved money.

"I'm cool. You need some?" he asked laughing, but by no means did he forget that she had just shifted the conversation of why she giggled for no reason.

"When can I come see you?" she asked, yawning in the phone.

"I don't know yet. Let me find out what's going on around here, and I will call you back later with the four-one-one," he replied, looking across the rock area at two prisoners arguing about a spades card game.

"Alright baby, make sure you get the directions to the prison as well."

Convict Jones and Kim talked on the phone for another five minutes before the operator interrupted their conversation, informing them that they had forty-five seconds left before the phone call would be terminated. The two wrapped up their conversation with kisses, smooches, and I love you's then phone went dead..

CHAPTER 20

As Convict Jones walked back to his cell, he heard the Muslim's calling the Adhan. Looking to his right, he noticed Mo on the top rail trying to get his attention without anybody else knowing what he was doing. Mo tapped the rail five times, allowing Convict Jones to know that he had a sell for five bags of marijuana. Convict Jones turned around in his tracks and headed towards an empty dayroom where prisoners play cards and board games. Convict Jones stepped into the empty dayroom and dropped five bags of marijuana on the ground then left back out. After Convict Jones left the dayroom, Mo entered the dayroom and picked the five bags of marijuana up off the ground. When Mo came out of the dayroom, Convict Jones had already gone back to his cell. Ten minutes later, Mo slid into Convict Jones' cell and dropped twenty-five dollars cash money on Convict Jones' bed. Convict Jones gave Mo the remaining three bags of weed he had and informed Mo that he should sell all of them for canteen, and he would look out for him later. Mo then exited the cell to go handle his business, while Convict Jones kicked off his shoes and lay back on his bed enjoying the killer buzz he had.

Two minutes later, Smith entered the cell and asked Convict Jones, "Are you going out to the large recreation field?"

Smith did not get a reply.

After fifteen seconds of not saying anything, Convict Jones thought that it would be better to communicate with Smith, being that he was hustling and did not want Smith to drop a note to the prison guards informing them of his activities.

"Yeah, I'm going out there to holla at my partner."

The large recreational field is where two or maybe three units out of the five units on the compound gather for recreational activities and exercise. However, you have to have a trained eye to see the other activities that go on by the prisoners when the guards are not looking. Everything from drugs being sold, to fights, and murder occur on the large recreational field. It was established that Unit Two would be released to the large recreational field at one o'clock on the dot. The prisoners lined up and were escorted to the large recreational field. The prisoners went through four different gates with six different locks to get on the field. If Convict Jones knew what type of shit was about to go down, surely he would have brought his blade with him to even the score.

The recreational field was very large. It had four full basketball courts, two big baseball fields, four handball courts, and one big race track that surrounded all the courts. Patches of grass grew through the uneven rocky dirt field. Four prison guards from each corner of the field stood watching with either twelve gauge pump shotguns or thirty aux rifles. These guns would be used in case a riot or a fight breaks out. Prisoners separated into groups upon entering the field. Blacks hung with blacks, whites hung with whites, and Mexicans hung with Mexicans. Each set of prisoners had games they wanted to play, but the majority of the prisoners either stood around or walked around the large recreational field track talking or making transactions.

"Major Riley, you have a call on line three," a female prison guard informed him.

"Please tell them I will return their call at my earliest convenience," Major Riley replied.

The female prison guard went back to the phone and informed the caller of what Major Riley stated.

Thirty seconds later, the female prison guard returned back to Major Riley's office, and said, "The caller said it was an emergency, and that's it urgent that he speaks with you."

Major Riley looked at the female prison guard and thought to himself, *Stupid bitch, you don't know how to follow instructions too well.*

Then he told the female prison guard, "Please inform the caller that I am in a meeting."

Major Riley looked back into the newspaper he was reading.

The female prison guard returned back to the phone with the message only to return fifteen seconds later stating, "Major, I hate to inform you, but the caller insisted that I come back and inform you that it's Mr. Rico Cross on the phone."

Major Riley immediately spilled some of the coffee from his cup he was drinking at the mention of Rico Cross' name. He also burned his lip, which resulted in a few curse words as coffee spilled on his paperwork.

"Hold that call!" he yelled, trying to clean up the coffee spill.

The female prison guard informed Major Riley that the caller was on line three and returned to her workstation. After cleaning the coffee up, Major Riley took a deep breath then answered the phone.

"Didn't I tell you to not call my job?" Major Riley shouted angrily.

"Hey buddy," Rico replied politely then he flipped the script. "Look here old fucker. I call when I feel like calling, and watch your tone of voice when you speak to me, nigga," Rico blasted on Major Riley.

"What do you want, Rico?" Major Riley asked politely while looking at his door, making sure that no one was ear hustling his conversation.

"You know what the fuck I want. Don't ask me no stupid ass shit like that. When are you going to have my money for that lick I pulled for you?"

Rico got straight to the point about what he was calling for.

"How many times do I have to tell you about talking over the phone like that? Please don't make me hang up on you," he stated with authority.

"You do, and I will see you sooner than you think. Now play with it," Rico replied sharply, and Major Riley knew he spoke the truth.

"Hey, meet me after I get off work at the *Cocktail Lounge*. Of course you do know where that is at smart-ass. I will have some of your money then," Major Riley informed Rico then he was ready to hang up the phone.

"What do you mean some of my money? I need all my damn money and not a penny less!" he shouted into the phone.

"We'll see," Major Riley responded, wanting to get Rico off the phone.

"We'll see my ass. Have my bread when I get there!" Rico demanded, becoming further frustrated.

"Alright. I'll see you when I get there," Major Riley replied, slamming the phone down on the receiver causing more coffee to spill on the paperwork on his desk.

When the phone hung up on Rico, he looked at the phone in his hand and stated to himself, "This motherfucker is trying to play me for my paper. I know what I'm going to do to this fake G.I. Joe ass motherfucker." Rico walked away talking to himself while getting in a vehicle. "I'm going to leave that motherfucker slumped over right there in the Cocktail Lounge."

Rico then tucked his .357 Magnum filled with hollow point tips into the waistline of his pants, and placed his shirt over it to conceal it. Rico then pulled off in his brand new convertible BMW.

CHAPTER 21

Convict Jones walked over towards the basketball court and stood around watching a full court game in play.

"Who got the rise?" Convict Jones asked and only two other prisoners spoke up so Convict Jones continued. "I got third rise."

He began to stretch his legs.

One of the teams on the court had won the last three games in a row. The winning team players were talking crazy shit to the opposite team's players. For some reason, which was not a smart one, Convict Jones felt he wanted to shut their mouths up and show them their game was not all that.

Convict Jones' rise finally came up. However, another prisoner said that he had the rise, so to stop any and all confusion before it started the prisoner and Convict Jones ran together on the same team. Convict Jones picked three more players who he thought had basic basketball skills. The very first game Convict Jones' team knocked off the winning team by three points. The second team came up, which was really the same team except there was only one different player. The second game was also won by Convict Jones' team. The third team they played was the same team they played at first. During the course of the third game, the score was eight to seven with Convict Jones' team leading. The game was going to ten points. Due to several mix matches on the court, the team opposite of Convict Jones' team began arguing with each other.

"Nigga, you can't hold him!" the bigger player yelled at his teammate.

"You guard your man, I got mine."

On one of the plays, the basketball rolled out of bounds. Convict Jones took advantage of the ball rolling out of bounds by calling his team into a quick huddle.

"It's time to take it to them clowns," Convict Jones instructed his team.

"Yeah!" his teammates yelled and broke the huddle.

Convict Jones could tell by the hard fouls the opposite team was delivering that the game was turning into a black top game. Convict Jones was a fine player, but if black top is what they wanted then black top is what he would give them.

"Fuck nigga, do it again!" one of the players on the opposite team from Convict Jones screamed at him.

He was named Pat Cleveland and everybody called him *Lil' Pat*.

Lil' Pat was a small black kid but quick as a mouse. He had dark wavy hair, and you couldn't tell him he wasn't the next Allen Iverson. Lil' Pat loved to show off his dribbling skills. The player from the opposite team was mad because Lil' Pat cut him off and stole the ball during a pass without touching him.

"Do it again nigga and I'm going to fuck you up."

Oohs and ahhhs could be heard throughout the crowd.

The very next play after the dude had threatened Lil' Pat, the dude from the opposite team intentionally elbowed Lil' Pat in the face. Immediately tension filled the air. You could see gang sets gathering up. Lil' Pat raised his hands to some of his homies, allowing them to know he was alright. The game then continued without a fight or someone getting killed.

The score being eight to seven with Convict Jones' team leading in score, the ball was passed in from the sideline. Convict Jones' team was in possession of the ball. The ball was passed to Convict Jones and he dribbled the ball to the center of the court. A guy from the opposite team came running up on Convict Jones all crazy and wild. Convict Jones stopped, faked, and pulled back, shaking the guy out his shoe with a half crossover and stop. Convict Jones then passed the ball to one of his big men. This particular player was Moose. Moose stood standing under the goal by himself. Two defenders attacked him, and he passed the ball back out to Lil' Pat. Lil' Pat immediately passed the ball to Convict Jones while he was breaking to the hole. Convict Jones had a clean layup by himself when out of nowhere, and from behind, the same guy who elbowed Lil' Pat in the face pushed Convict Jones in the back while he was in the air. Convict Jones hit the ground hard and just lay there. The only thing that was going through Convict Jones' mind was the cat's blood on his shank. Convict Jones immediately jumped up from the ground ready to attack, but patience being the key to everything.

Convict Jones looked at the guy, and said, "Good foul and point, nigga."

Convict Jones took off running back down the court to catch up with his team.

Convict Jones also made a mental note to later handle the guy on some real life shit. Convict Jones thoughts were broken by laughter coming from the stands. It was clear the guy was laughing at the fact that he got pushed out the air. Other prisoners standing with the guy also joined in with him. You could tell they only laughed with him because they wanted to be down with whatever he had going on. Other than that, they could give a fuck about him.

The laughing voice then appeared out the crowd of prisoners as if he was watching a Richard Pryor movie or something. Convict Jones could feel the hate vibe coming from the familiar face. It was the same cat they called O-Dog who watched him all morning in the cafeteria. The basketball was thrown inbounds. The score now nine to seven with Convict Jones' team winning. The next attempted basket by Convict Jones' team member he was fouled hard and knocked to the pavement. When the player got up his lip was busted and you could hear the laughter coming from the crowd O-Dog was in. Convict Jones looked up in the stands and locked eyes with O-Dog. Convict Jones then smiled and went back to playing basketball.

"Oh y'all playing like that, huh?" Convict Jones asked.

"Yeah nigga ain't no need in crying. Play ball nigga. You know what it is," the guy who fouled Lil' Pat and pushed Convict Jones while he was in the air stated.

The ball was inbound again. Convict Jones grabbed the ball and noticed out the side of his vision one of the players from the opposite team coming his way fast. Big Bo, one of Convict Jones teammates also saw the guy coming and threw a hard pick, knocking the guy on his ass. Big Bo was bigger than Moose, and they did not call him Big Bo for nothing. Big Bo stood at 6'3" and weighed in at two hundred and seventy pounds solid. Big Bo was strong as a mountain bull but quiet as a roach. Although Big Bo was humble as a dove, he was also wise as a serpent. It was rumored to never get him upset.

CHAPTER 22

Big Bo, born Brian Boston, was serving a fifteen year prison sentence under the eighty-five percent law for armed robbery. He had already served five years on his sentence and was praying and hoping that he got out the jam he now found himself in.

It was one night five years earlier that Big Bo had got with the wrong type of guys from his school. These guys were young black males who lived for the drama of the streets. Big Bo, on the other hand, was well-known throughout his county and several surrounding counties as a very good football player. Big Bo had been invited to the Governor's Mansion on many occasions where banquets and parties were held in his honor. He also attended seminars and several other conventions. He was a member of the Big Brother and Big Sister program, where he helped the unfortunate street kids come off the street. Big Bo was also on his way to college. The only problem with that was choosing between five schools who wanted him.

This particular night, once again Big Bo scored the winning touchdown that beat their rival team. After the game, Big Bo hooked up with some old friends from his school and neighborhood. Big Bo and his friends partied, celebrating his victory. They drank beer and smoked weed. However, Big Bo refused the weed, but he did not turn down not one beer or liquor bottle. About two hours later, Big Bo was heavily intoxicated. He was falling all over the backseat and bumping into everybody.

"Hey guys, take me home," Big Bo told his friends. "I've overdone myself," he said as he was falling on one of his friend's shoulders, passing out drunk.

"Nigga, you alright," the driver of the vehicle whose name was Rod Aulston stated. "We ain't gonna let nothing happen to you, champ."

As a passed out Big Bo and his friends rode around drinking and smoking, they ran out of beer and marijuana. They guys stopped by a couple of other spots, which were to no avail in coming up with more money to get beer and weed. The guys then pulled up into a 7-Eleven convenience store.

While they sat in the car, one of the guys whose name was Charles Acker, said, "Let's lick this spot."

He pulled out a .38 snub nose.

"What about Big Bo?" Willie Yergin asked, concerned for his friend because he had known Big Bo the longest out of all the guys.

"He'll be alright," Charlie Acker said.

The three friends exited the vehicle, leaving Big Bo passed out drunk in the backseat of the car. The three guys entered the store, and Charles immediately pulled out the .38 snub nose.

Charlie yelled, "This is a stick up! Don't nobody move!"

He was waving the gun around.

After the three men finished robbing the place, coming up with a total of seventy-five dollar and a case of beer, they ran back to the car, jumped in, and pulled off. During the time of the robbery, the store clerk had already pushed the silent alarm. She pressed the alarm when the three guys entered the store due to the way they looked.

They were coming down the main open road in the middle of the night, passing a patrol car. The blue lights began flashing. Instead of pulling over or jumping out and running, Rod, Charles, and Willie decided to take the police on a high-speed chase. Two miles down the road, Rod tried to make a quick right, mistimed it, and the vehicle flipped and hit a telephone pole.

Rod, Willie, and Charles exited the car on foot, and took off running leaving a passed out Big Bo in the backseat. Within seconds, the vehicle was surrounded and Big Bo was dragged from the backseat of the car, while guns were drawn down on him. Big Bo had no idea what was going on, while being drug from the vehicle and beat with a Billy club and walkie-talkies. Big Bo was then thrown in the back of a police cruiser with hands cuffed behind his back.

Once at the police station, Big Bo was charged with armed robbery, although the store clerk said that he was not one of the guys that robbed the store. The weapon was also never found, and because Big Bo would not tell on his friends, the state wanted to make an example out of Big Bo by destroying his life. Although Big Bo made bond, eight months later he was forced into an involuntary *guilty plea by the advice of a public defender or pretender. He was sentenced to fifteen years under the eighty-five percent law for armed robbery.*

Back to the game, Convict Jones was on the move and heading for another clean layup by himself, when he saw out of the corner of his eye, the same guy coming his way, the one who pushed him out of the air last time. Another player from the opposite team also picked up the rear, forcing Convict Jones to slow down and rethink his move. By this time, Big Bo shot to the inside, and posted up. Big Bo had a small player on him. Convict Jones stopped in play and just dribbled the ball, looking around at his teammates move around. Big Bo dominated the hole and was taking position with the small guy on his back. He yelled for the ball. Convict Jones faked a shot, and did a behind the back pass to Big Bo in the middle of the hole. Once Big Bo got the ball in the paint, another defender went over to help his teammate, used his weight on a drop step, taking a hard foul and scored the winning basket.

"Yeahhhhhh," Convict Jones' teammates yelled while the opposite team began cursing.

O-Dog stood to his feet watching with a snarl on his face. He could not keep his eyes off of Convict Jones. Every step Convict Jones took O-Dog was on him. He stared Convict Jones down long and hard. Convict Jones had to rub the back of his neck thinking to himself, *What is wrong with this nigga. I hope I don't have to kill 'em.* He was walking off the basketball court.

The opposite team wanted another chance for bragging rights, but Convict Jones refused the challenge. He knew that shit was about to get out of hand. Faking like he was tired, Convict Jones handed his rise over to the next player. Convict Jones then noticed Mo throwing signs trying to get his attention. Mo threw up three fingers, followed by eight allowing Convict Jones to know he needed some work. Convict Jones informed Mo to walk around the large recreational field.

During the walk around the track Mo said, "I got one hundred and fifty dollars from one cat, and another thirty dollars from another cat."

He showed Convict Jones the money.

"I'll talk back with you in the dorm," Convict Jones informed Mo who was walking off in a different direction while O-Dog sat watching from a far.

CHAPTER 23

Convict Jones was sitting on some bleachers watching the prisoner going to and fro when he noticed O-Dog and a couple of prisoners walking towards his direction. One of the prisoners with O-Dog was the same person who was playing on the opposite team Convict Jones was playing on. In fact, it was the same cat that pushed Convict Jones out of the air when he had a clean lay up to the basket. Convict Jones gritted his teeth, but he knew he had to keep his composure. He knew the odds were stacked against him, but he wondered why and when would a move be made against him.

Convict Jones got up off the bleachers and began walking towards O-Dog and his crew. Convict Jones was a true believer of rolling up on your enemy before they ran up on you. This way you can control the situation better. Approaching O-Dog and his crew, Convict Jones prepared himself for whatever because he was also a believer that anything could happen in these last few days. Watching O-Dog and his crew were passing a Black and Mild cigar back and forth between the three of them. Convict Jones noticed that O-Dog disrespected one of his partners by blowing smoke in his face and laughed about his actions.

The other prisoner yelled, "Man, what I tell you about blowing that smoke in my face. I don't smoke," his partner stated whose name was Shawn Brown.

"Shut the fuck up, bitch," O-Dog replied, disrespecting his homeboy verbally.

Convict Jones then said to himself, "This cat O-Dog don't have respect for his own crew, so how can he have respect for anybody else."

That made the situation that much more serious to Convict Jones.

Coming upon O-Dog and his crew, he locked eyes with O-Dog and asked himself, "Where in the hell did I see this nigga before?"

He remembered O-Dog's face and eyes. Convict Jones then peeped Shawn passing O-Dog a shiny object. Convict Jones had to think fast. As they came within five feet, Convict Jones had already placed his shirt in his hand for a defense against a blade if it went down right there on the spot.

To prevent an attack, Convict Jones had to use his wits, when he said, "Peace black brothers."

They were looking at O-Dog's hand wrapped in a shirt.

"How are y'all doing today?" Convict Jones asked, staying to O-Dog's right since he was carrying the blade in his right hand. Convict Jones then continued, "Jesus the Christ our Lord loves you brothers. Can I share my testimony with you for a few seconds about how he saved my life?"

Convict Jones laid the Christianity on thick. When Convict Jones made those statements, O-Dog and his crew looked at him dumbfounded and confused.

Dirty Dee, who was the third person with O-Dog and Shawn turned towards O-Dog, and asked, "What the fuck you and Major Riley trying to do?"

He was asking about Major Riley and O-Dog's plans against Convict Jones.

O-Dog and Dirty Dee argued concerning Major Riley and O-Dog's plans for Convict Jones. Convict Jones continued to walk on, being they were ignoring him anyway. However, Shawn was looking back and forth at Convict Jones and O-Dog. He was confused as to why O-Dog had said nothing to him or done nothing to him. Convict Jones walked over to another set of benches, sat down, and watched his surroundings.

After ten minutes, Convict Jones noticed that O-Dog and his crew were sitting down on some more bleachers twenty feet away, staring at him. Convict Jones made it his business to allow O-Dog to know that he knew they were watching him. Convict Jones then watched Dirty Dee and O-Dog get to arguing again. He then witnessed Dirty Dee push O-Dog down, whereby Shawn immediately went to O-Dog's aid.

Later on Convict Jones found out that the reason for O-Dog and Dirty Dee's argument was about him. Dirty Dee was against Major Riley and O-Dog's plan to hurt a Christian brother, which Convict Jones pretended to be when he passed them. Dirty Dee was from a deeply rooted Christian family, and it was unheard of when it came to transgressing against another Christian brethren.

Convict Jones got up from the bleachers when he noticed the prison guards were calling for the recreational field to be closed. As he walked off the field, Convict Jones would not allow anyone to creep up on him. It had to be a different type of brother to get that close without being seen by Convict Jones. He quickly turned around prepared for war.

Convict Jones looked in the eyes of the person who tapped him on the shoulder. For a few seconds, Convict Jones had to figure out who the person was. Slowly, a smile appeared on Convict Jones face when he saw an old friend.

"Willie Ham!" Convict Jones shouted, excited to see an old friend from a county over.

"What's happening little brother?" Willie Ham asked, watching his surroundings.

"How long has it been?" Convict Jones asked because it was over ten years since he last saw his friend. "Last time I saw your old dusty ass they were locking you up for spitting on the warden."

Convict Jones laughed, remembering how real Willie Ham was.

"And I'll spit on that bitch again if they get out of line," Willie Ham informed Convict Jones.

The look in Willie Ham's eyes assured Convict Jones that he meant every word he said.

Convict Jones then said, "Damn! Well, I thought you already got out."

He was watching a couple of prisoners horseplay.

"Hell no!" Willie Ham replied, moving two steps to Convict Jones' left. "Them stankin' motherfuckers gave me ten more years for spitting on that bitch ass warden."

Curse words were falling out of his mouth like a drunken sailor.

"So when do you get out?" Convict Jones asked concerned for his friend.

Convict Jones really wanted to know the answer, because he wanted to know like all other prisoners if the next man would get out before them.

"Shit, I got three more years to wrap this bid up." He replied and continued, "You know I got the life sentence off me due to newly discovered evidence. They cut the life sentence to thirty years."

"Beautiful baby," Convict Jones replied, happy for Willie Ham. "They finally showed some love."

He was wishing that the court system would have showed him some love too.

William Ham had already put in twenty-one years day-for-day on the life sentence. If he had not caught the ten years for spitting on the warden, consolidated with the good time they took from him by having the life sentence cut to thirty years, he would have already been released from prison. Because of the ten years, he now had three more years to serve before he completed his sentence.

Convict Jones looked at William Ham, and noticed that he was getting up in age. He remembered when him and Willie Ham used to sit on the yard under the shed drinking wine and smoking marijuana, which was before the control movement policy and the yards being closed down. Convict Jones remembered when Willie Ham shared the reason why he came to prison. This is one of the reasons why Willie Ham does what he does. He feels like he should have never been in prison, and truth be told if what he said was true, then he should have never been there. Convict Jones remembered the story as Willie Ham told it to him.

CHAPTER 24

It was June 3rd, 1986, when Willie Ham came to prison for rape and murder after pleading not guilty and being convicted by an all-white jury, beside one lone black woman who thought she was white. An old white woman, named Mrs. Linda B. Turner, was the alleged victim in Willie Ham's case. The state claims that Willie Ham had broken into Mrs. Turner's house and raped, robbed, and murdered her.

Testimony came in at trial that Mrs. Turner was asleep when Willie Ham broke in the house. She woke up during the robbery and caught Willie Ham in the act so he murdered her. Willie Ham said that the state produced nothing but lies to find him guilty. Willie Ham said that he did go in the house, and like all the other times Mrs. Turner pretended to be asleep and he pretended to be robbing her.

Mrs. Turner would roll over, wake up, and say, "Stop! Please don't take this old wet pussy."

She would open her bed coat and bust her legs open.

Willie Ham, like always, played stunned then moved in slowly towards the bed while watching Mrs. Turner rub up and down on her pussy lips.

"Don't leave without sticking that big black dick in this hot, pink pussy."

Willie Ham dropped the alleged stolen goods on the floor, and slid up on the bed with Mrs. Turner. Willie Ham came out of his overalls. Mrs. Turner immediately reached out, grabbed Willie Ham's penis, and began stroking it. Willie Ham's penis became semi-hard and Mrs. Turner took him into her mouth. As she gave Willie Ham a blowjob, he fuck her old white lips.

"Hmmmm," she moaned as Willie Ham's dick got harder.

She then reached down and began softly rubbing his balls while deep throating him.

"Ohhhhh," Willie Ham let out a groan. "I'm about to cum."

He started jerking.

Willie Ham began pumping his hips back and forth as he grabbed Mrs. Turner's long, silky gray hair. Mrs. Turner realizing that Willie Ham was about to cum, grabbed his ass cheeks, and swallowed his entire dick as Willie Ham began shooting off.

"Ahhhh," Willie Ham moaned, releasing his semen in Mrs. Turner's mouth.

Mrs. Turner then brought her mouth off of Willie Ham's dick and stopped to bless the head of his penis.

"Ohhhhh," was all he could moan while she brought his dick back to life.

She continued to drain Willie Ham of his seeds, while at the same time keeping him hard as a cement block. Then she got up and turned around. Willie Ham immediately entered the old woman from the back. Upon Willie Ham entering her, she let out a low howl as he broke through her walls.

"Ohhhh, Willie!" she screamed as he drove harder into her, grabbing both of her ass cheeks.

With access to nothing but pussy, Willie Ham pounded her.

"Fuck me, fuck me," she demanded, throwing the pussy back.

For the next three minutes, William Ham beat the pussy until Mrs. Turner began shaking and cumming at the same time.

"Don't stop, please!" she yelled while her love juices spilled all over Willie Ham's penis. "It's coming! It's coming!"

Willie Ham then pushed all of himself into her as she came all over him. With the last stroke, Mrs. Turner's entire body just collapsed as her pussy walls opened up wider along with her bowels, getting her last and final orgasm.

Mrs. Turner was no longer moving, while Willie fucked her until he got his third nut off. He finally realized that not only was Mrs. Turner no longer moving, but she had also defecated on herself due to the smell. Willie Ham pulled out of her and shook her.

"Baby, baby, what's wrong."

He was shaking her when she began to go into convulsions. Laying over her in shock, he jumped from the bed and watched her not knowing what to do. When he realized what was going on, Willie Ham panicked and ran out the house the same way he would come in every day.

The very next day Mrs. Turner was found dead in her house by her granddaughter. The medical records indicated that Mrs. Turner died from a massive heart attack. However, because Willie Ham was seen leaving the house by the next-door neighbor and semen of his found in her, coupled by the fact he was black, Willie Ham was charged with the crime. The next-door neighbors had informed the police that Willie Ham had been going in and out of Mrs. Turner's house for over six months.

CHAPTER 25

Convict Jones was brought out of his daydream by Willie Ham getting his attention.

"You got an admirer," Willie Ham told him, glancing at O-Dog standing over by a fence with some new faces.

"What the fuck is up with this young ass nigga?" Convict Jones asked no one in particular.

"All inmates, recreation is closed. Report to your assigned unit," the Institutional P.A. intercom announced.

Several prison guards then appeared on the field to escort the prisoners back to their dorms.

Convict Jones and Willie Ham began walking away towards Convict Jones' unit when Willie Ham said, "Boy, they told me that you had got out."

"A lie don't care who tells it long as it gets told," Convict Jones denied the accusation.

The two convicts never stopped moving, but kept their eyes on their surroundings.

"What's up with that young O-Boy?" Convict Jones asked, fishing for more information.

"Them little young bitches better stay in their place before somebody sends them home to their mammy," Willie Ham replied with a dislike for not only O-Dog, but young cats in particular. "But to answer your question, ain't nothing to that young bitch. He just trying to get a name for himself. You remember how you used to be, same thing," Willie Ham explained, smiling.

Convict Jones immediately thought back to how he used to be when he came into the system. One would define him as off the meat rack.

Convict Jones then said to himself, "I got some drama coming my way."

That was due to the fact Convict Jones knew how his heart was when he was younger. He was cold blooded and consolidated with a young state of mind. KRS-One couldn't have said it any clearer, *Self-Destruction*.

"You don't have no beef with them cats?" Willie Ham asked, giving Convict Jones a strange look. "Please say yeah so I can get some recreation."

Willie Ham was wanting to let the beast out.

"Truthfully, I don't know. I don't even know this young nigga, but since I hit the yard the young cat been watching me and grilling me."

Convict Jones hoped that Willie Ham didn't just set it off because he knew he would. Being way out of their region, Willie Ham would not spare no off brand nigga unless you were a real true brother. Willie Ham also still thought that he was still nineteen years old, refusing to face the fact that it was time to hang his boots up.

"Check this, I'll look into the matter. In the meantime just lay low. You know what I mean?"

"Nah, I don't know what you mean, but I'll spare a nigga, if they don't get out of line or they going to have to do me. You know the drill," Convict Jones replied.

"I feel ya. Also, before I leave let me get two of them bags of weed?" William Ham asked with his hand out.

Convict Jones and Willie Ham immediately began laughing.

"What the fuck you talking about?" Convict Jones asked, acting stupid.

"Don't play no games nigga. I'm a convict. I watch everything that goes on around me. If some asshole is sold on this yard, I know who is buying it and who is selling it. Just like it ain't hard to put one-and-one together to know that you got Mo running around slanging," Willie Ham informed Convict Jones as they both began laughing again.

"I'll holla at you in the dorm before I go meet my man at Jummah," Convict Jones stated.

"Oh, you Muslim now, no more dope game," Willie Ham replied, singing 2 Pac's verse of the song, *I Ain't Mad At Cha.*

Convict Jones did not have to tell Willie Ham nothing because a true convict already knows what's going on. Convicts know what to look for, and know how to read between the lines. This is a true convict's art to survival. Its a part of their nature.

Convict Jones and William Ham went their separate ways. Convict Jones continued to the side of his unit thinking about everything going down around him. When he looked up, he saw the same old man who was by the medical facility grooming the flowerbed and staring at him. Convict Jones locked eyes with the old man for a few seconds. The old man's eyes then traveled over to O-Dog, who was standing several feet away from Convict Jones. Convict Jones followed the old man's eyes, and his eyes landed on O-Dog who was now clowning for his homeboys. Convict Jones looked back at the old man, and then the old man eyes traveled to another prisoner which was Dirty Dee. At that very moment, Convict Jones thought to himself, *What the fuck is going on? Convict Jones immediately put some pep in his step,* He thought to himself.

"Once I get in the unit, I got to cop me two blades," he said to himself so that he would be prepared for anything.

Convict Jones intended to stay strapped for the rest of the time he was at that yard, or any yard due to shit being crazy. He refused to be a victim to the unknown. If he died he wanted to know what he was being killed for. Even if he died, he would more than likely die with his eyes open from all the shit he had seen. Convict Jones hurried into the unit so he could go take a shower, and meet one of his homeboys at Jummah.

CHAPTER 26

Agent Johnson and Agent Williams sat in a blue Ford pickup truck staking out a *Motel 6* room.

"I have not seen one person go to that room or leave yet," Agent Johnson stated, yawning.

"Patience partner. Casper will show," Agent Williams replied, hoping that his confidential informant's information was solid as usual.

"Hey man, I'm going over there to the gas station to get some coffee. Do you want anything while I'm over there?" Agent Johnson asked his partner who was leaned over on the truck door.

"Yeah, donuts and coffee, and make sure my coffee is all the way black."

He looked up at the motel room they were casing.

Agent Johnson got out of the truck and walked across the street to get the coffee and donuts. While watching from the truck, Agent Williams noticed a honey colored chromed out convertible BMW with blue specks in the paint job, reflecting off the baby blue interior inside the vehicle. A slim, built young black male jumped out of the vehicle. Agent Williams looked down at the photo in his hand then back at the person. He did another quick glance at the photo again and then back at the person again. Agent Williams then squinted his eyes and looked at the photo again.

"It's him!" Agent Williams shouted to himself. "I got you now, Casper!"

He reached for his police issued .45.

Agent Williams slowly opened the truck door, which squeaked a little, drawing the attention of the suspect, Casper. Rico could not help but feel the presence of the police. He hated pigs, and much worse he hated fake ass pig, like Major Riley's prison guard ass. Immediately Rico pulled from under his Gucci sweater a Mini Mac-11 and let off a five round spurt at Agent Williams, knocking one of the side rearview mirrors off the truck.

"Shit!" Agent Williams shouted.

Hearing the gunfire from across the street, Agent Johnson dropped everything in his hands, and took off running from across the street while pulling his weapon. Arriving back at their truck, he found Agent Williams pinned down by gunfire. Agent Johnson let off two rounds. Rico ran in the motel room, grabbed a bag, and came back out blasting. Agent Johnson and Agent Williams ducked for cover. Rico ran down the hallway of the motel and out a side fence where a black van was sitting awaiting his arrival. Agent Williams and Agent Johnson were back on their feet and in pursuit of Rico. The two agents saw Rico get into the back of the black van. Agent Williams went around the left side of the van, while Agent Johnson covered the right front side of the van. The van was actually surrounded by a two-man stand down.

"Come out with your hands raised high!" Agent Johnson shouted as he kicked the van with his nine shot Beretta drawn and ready to fire.

Silence filled the air. If they didn't see Rico going into the van, you would have never known that he was in there.

"This is your last warning! Come out with your hands up!" Agent Williams yelled, while Agent Johnson moved in closer to the van's back double doors.

Inside the van, which was bullet proof, Rico laughed at their remarks. He also mocked them.

"Come out with your hands up."

He sounded like a little girl.

The agents outside the van could hear him mocking them and became frustrated. All the while, Rico was reloading his Mini Mac-11 reversible fifty round clip. He already had on his black matching helmet to the 750 Honda motorcycle he was now sitting on. Rico hit the switch on the motorcycle. Due to the switch installed in the motorcycle, the agents outside the van did not hear the bike start up.

"Come out withhhhhhhh—" Agent Williams words were caught in his mouth as he dove to the side.

Rico came out the back of the van on the motorcycle at the speed of thirty miles per hour within thirty seconds, letting off rounds from his weapon.

"Oh shit!" Agent Johnson also dove to the side ducking a bullet.

Rico stopped the motorcycle about thirty feet away from the agents. He watched them get back to their feet. Actually, he could have killed them right there like he normally would have, but with the plans he had he didn't need that type of heat on him. Once the agents were back in control of themselves, Rico stuck his middle finger up at the agents, did a donut, and fish tailed it for ten feet before disappearing into thin air.

"Motherfucker!" Agent Williams shouted

Agent Johnson shouted, "Shit!"

He slammed his hat to the ground.

"We'll get that ass," Agent Williams stated, turning around going back to their truck, only to find two tires shot out along with the front windshield.

"Shit! If it's the last thing we do," Agent Johnson added to Agent Williams earlier statement.

"Verily all praises is due to Allah. We praise him, seek his help, and ask for forgiveness. We seek refuge in Allah (SWT) from the evils of our own souls and bad actions whom so ever Allah guides, there is no one that can lead him astray and whomever Allah lead astray, theirs no one that can guide him. I bear witness there's no God but Allah, and I bear witness that Muhammad is his last and final messenger (may Allah bless him and give him peace with his family and companions). O you who believe Allah (SWT) says in the Qur'an the honorable book. O you who believe, fear Allah as he should be feared and do not die except in the state of a Muslim and O mankind, fear your Lord who has created you from one single soul, and its mate, which spread forth from them, many men and women and fear Allah through whom you demand your mutual rights and do not cut the ties of relationship with your kin. Verily Allah is a watcher over you," The Iman (eman) of the Muslim's who sat in the middle of the floor in ranks tuned into every word he spoke.

The Iman's name was Rafee. Rafee was a young white brother, well versed in Islamic matters. He spoke Arabic fluently, and walked the walk because he talked the talk. Rafee raised his hands in the air and continued to address Allah's Umma.

"O you believe, fear Allah and always speak the truth. Allah will direct you towards the righteous deeds and forgive you your sins. He who that has obeyed Allah and Allah's messenger has indeed achieved the greatest reward and achievements. The best of speech is the book of Allah and, the best of guidance is the guidance of Muhammad. The worst of matters are newly invented matters in the dean of Islam, and in every newly invented matters is an error, and every error is misguidance, and every misguidance is the hell fire and weak seek refuge from that," Rafee paused to allow the words to sink into his Muslim brothers.

Rafee loved his Muslim brothers for the sake of Allah. He wanted for his brother what he wanted for himself. He wanted paradise, and he wanted his brother to not only have the same but want the same. Rafee focused back on Allah's Umma and continued to teach.

"O yeah who believe Allah (SWT) says in the Qur'an the honorable book. O you who believe when the call is made for Salahtul Jumr'ah, haste into the remembrance of Allah and leave off all your business and trades, that is better for you, if you only knew but when the prayer is over go out into the land and seek the bounties of Allah and remember Allah much that you may be successful," Rafee spoke to Allah's Umma.

After Jummah was over, Rafee shook hands with visitors and other Muslims. He looked in Convict Jones' direction and nodded his head. Convict Jones replied in the same manner. Ten minutes later, while Convict Jones was exiting the chapel where they held the Jummah, Rafee grabbed Convict Jones by the arm.

"Peace brother."

"Shalom brother," Convict Jones replied.

"When are you going to come on in?" Rafee asked. "Before the sun set from the wrong side."

He was smiling a pretty smile.

"Soon brother," Convict Jones replied because it seemed like the right thing to say, knowing all the while he didn't know what Rafee was talking about.

Rafee and Convict Jones said their peace and went their separate ways. Convict Jones went back to his unit.

CHAPTER 27

The very next day, Convict Jones was sitting in his cell eating a jack mack set up with fried corn.

Two prison guards appeared at his cell door, and one shouted, "Jones!" he was shouting like he was not standing in Convict Jones' face. "Major Riley wants to see you."

They were standing at attention like they were actually in the Army.

The two guards were members of the welcome committee. Convict Jones slowly got up off his bunk, watching the guards and praying they didn't try anything slick. Convict Jones walked over to the sink to wash his hands to get the fish smell off of him before going to the meeting.

The two prison guards shouted, "Right now!"

They were yelling like they were crazy.

Actually, Convict Jones was just testing the waters with the two prison guards, like he would sharks in shallow waters. If the guards were down for an altercation, which Convict Jones knew they were, he decided to stay silent and follow orders. Convict Jones was escorted to Major Riley's office.

Once inside the office, Major Riley stood to his feet, pointed at Convict Jones, and yelled, "Son of a bitch, it don't take you too long to get started does it?" he asked.

Convict Jones replied, "Whatever do you mean, sir?"

He sounded like he was from France.

"Wise ass, huh?" Moving around the desk towards Convict Jones direction with fire in his eyes. "Say what!"

He scared the dog shit out of Convict Jones as he brought his fist down on the desk.

Convict Jones thought to himself, *This is one crazy ass motherfucker here.*

He kept his eyes on his surroundings then stated, "No sir. Its just that if you lack in knowledge of a thing, how can one provide a correct reply. I have no idea what you are speaking about."

He was actually believing the bullshit game he was preaching.

Silence filled the office quick, along with tension. The two prison guards, coupled by one that was in the office when Convict Jones got there, began coming closer to him. For the next two minutes silence filled the air again.

Convict Jones tried to diffuse the ill feeling by stating, "Major Riley sir, what is all this about?"

He really wanted to know, but like always Major Riley took it a different way.

"Who told you to talk, bitch?" Major Riley shouted, grabbing Convict Jones' arm, squeezing it, and penetrating his flesh with his nails. "Answer me damn it!" he shouted, snatching Convict Jones up close to him until they were eye-to-eye.

For thirty second not one word was said as they stared into each other eyes.

Convict Jones whispered, "Here we go again with the bullshit."

Major Riley walked back around to his desk and sat down. He then looked down at some papers on his desk and back up at Convict Jones.

"I hear that you have that bomb weed on my yard," Major Riley was asking a question and answering it all in one sentence.

Convict Jones damn near shit his pants.

He caught his breath, and answered, "Sir, you told me to follow your rules, and I have been doing just that. I will continue to do just that unless you want to hit me with a package or something," Convict Jones stated, playing his cards close to his chest.

"Don't bullshit me. I'm going to give you enough rope to hang yourself."

He was smiling, thinking about when Convict Jones did fuck up, he was going to nail him to the wall.

"Rope has never been an issue to Tarzan, I'm just swinging with the flow baby."

He was playing the ass kicking line real close.

"Whatever that means I don't know, but I'll bet it was some of that up north slick back talk shit from a big city," he said as he changed his voice to sound like he was from the deep country. "But just in case it was," he stopped talking and looked at one of the guards.

The guard then struck Convict Jones in the side of the ribs with a nightstick.

"Huhhhhh," Convict Jones grunted while Major Riley continued.

"We can do this all day long," Major Riley meaning every word. "But I have a meeting so stop playing games with me."

"I don't know what you're talking about," Convict Jones replied, throwing his hands up in case a blow was coming.

Major Riley stood to his feet and waved the guards off. One of the guards escorted Convict Jones out the office and back to his unit. Convict Jones was now even more confused, especially why they just stopped everything they were just doing and just took him back to the unit.

CHAPTER 28

Rico pulled into a hole in the wall on the left side of the abandoned building on his 750 Honda motorcycle. After shutting the bike down and putting the kick stand down, he glanced at his watch and realized that it was almost time to go meet Major Riley to get his money. Once Rico got all his money from Major Riley, he could put one slug in his head, and then leave the country like he planned to do. The reason he wanted to kill Major Riley was not only personal, but also because he wanted to clean up all his tracks of involvement with him. Rico, due to earlier encounters with the federal government, now knew that they were on his trail. He couldn't figure out how they knew anything about him because he was very careful when it came to concealing his identity.

Rico dropped a box of cop killer's ammunition on his desk, and reached over and grabbed his favorite weapon the Mini Mac-11. He released the half-empty reversible fifty round clip and began reloading it. Rico then glanced over at the TV monitors he had installed and stationed around the building. As he continued to load his weapon, and thought about Major Riley.

"Rotten motherfucker," Rico spoke to himself, thinking about something Major Riley had done in the past.

Rico glanced back up at the TV monitors and noticed a ten year old child playing around the back of the building in an open field filled with garbage. He got up from the desk, walked over to the wall, and pressed a button. The pressing of the button released his three trained pitbulls named Demon, Angel, and Preacher. The three dogs all looked identical because they were all from the same bitch. Rico was the only one who could tell them apart by the way he had their tails snipped. He had trained the dogs himself. The dogs obeyed his every command, except for Angel. Sometimes she got out of hand and had to be put back in her place. Rico dismissed putting Angel down because he understood the emotions of a bitch pitbull. However, no man should try to put one hand on Rico when she was around.

Rico glanced back at his watch, and said to himself, "Showtime!"

He jumped from his desk and grabbed his keys to another vehicle parked a street over.

Convict Jones walked into the unit they had him assigned to after leaving the meeting with Major Riley. Convict Jones looked at his watch and realized that an hour had passed by. The unit was lining up for dinner when he walked in, which was the last meal of the day. Reading the time on his clock which was 4:30 P.M., Convict Jones decided he would walk to the kitchen to meet up with Willie Ham. Once in the kitchen, Willie Ham appeared out of thin air and approached Convict Jones from his left. Convict Jones peeped the whole move and sat down at a table, awaiting Willie Ham to join him.

"What's up, homie?" Willie Ham asked.

"Shit! Just keeping my eyes open for incoming hits," Convict Jones said with a smile as his eyes traveled around the cafeteria. Convict Jones then rearranged the icepick he had under his shirt, and said, "Boy, I bet you won't believe where I just came from?" Convict Jones asked but before Willie Ham could answer Convict Jones continued, "They had me in the Majors office."

"For what!" Willie Ham wanted to know.

"Talking about he knew I had weed on his yard, but he was going to allow me enough room to hang myself."

He laughed because he found finding it funny, while Willie Ham thought different.

"That's why I had to flush the little half ounce I had brought with me to be on the safe side," Convict Jones said, running game.

"Some foul shit is going on around here," Willie Ham replied, looking across the cafeteria at two prisoners talking and looking in his direction.

"Ain't that the truth," Convict Jones agreed, looking at the prison guard watching him.

Convict Jones continued to inform Willie Ham about what was going on. He knew that all good things come to an end because Allah gives and Allah takes.

"I'll get back up with you later. I have to go handle some business right quick," Willie Ham stated, walking off in the direction where he watched the two prisoners looking in his direction.

Three minutes later Willie Ham returned, and stated, "Yeah, I forgot to tell you. Your boy O-Dog does have some kind of beef with you. Something about his mother or something like that. Dirty Dee didn't go into details, but you have to watch Dirty Dee too."

Convict Jones took the warning and planned to use it.

Willie Ham then walked off again as Convict Jones stood up from the table. As Convict Jones waked back to the unit he thought to himself, *This cat can be no more than twenty to twenty-three years old, coupled by the fact, aren't not even from the same county or city. Then I have been in prison for the last fourteen years, so what kind of beef could he have with me, or how does this you boy even know me?* Convict Jones then thought, *Perhaps I'm his father.* He laughed to himself, while other prisoners looked at him like he was crazy.

Convict Jones would like to think that he was an international player due to the fact he played up and down the East coast in the early eighties. Maybe O-Dog witnessed Convict Jones play and break his mother's heart some twelve to thirteen years ago, which would make O-Dog around the age of ten or twelve. Convict Jones' daydreaming ended quickly as he stepped back into the unit.

"Dice!" someone yelled from over by the dayroom.

Convict Jones walked over to the dayroom where Mo was standing smoking a cigarette.

"What's jumping baby boy?" Convict Jones asked.

"Nothing much." He watched Convict Jones trying to figure out his motive being on the yard then he continued, "I heard that the police came and got you earlier."

"Yeah, something like that," Convict Jones replied, and then he explained the meeting with Major Riley.

Convict Jones immediately began his process of elimination by removing certain individuals who he had been dealing with or had knowledge of him having his hands in dealing marijuana since his arrival on the compound. Only two people knew that Convict Jones had weed. Those two people were Mo and Willie Ham. Someone was running their mouth and knew too much about Convict Jones' business.

Convict Jones decided to fold his hands, and let things die down before he resurfaced and smashed the game with the exception of making moves in silence and under the radar.

Little did Convict Jones know Mo nor Willie Ham were not the ones ratting on him, but it was someone else who had knowledge of Convict Jones' participation in dealing drugs in the prison system. Convict Jones walked towards his cell and noticed his roommate Smith standing on the top steps watching his every move. When Convict Jones looked up at him, he turned his head and walked off. Convict Jones later found out how the prison officials knew that he was participating in selling drugs on the compound.

CHAPTER 29

The very same night at around 5:30 P.M., Convict Jones heard the Adan being called. Muslims came out of everywhere to worship their Lord. Convict Jones followed to watch the Muslims as they gathered together, greeting each other in peace. The Muslims picked each other's lint off their clothing.

From a young dumb mind, one would automatically say, "That's some punk shit."

However, they just lacked the knowledge in the action in and of itself.

For some reason the Iman Rafee was in Unit Two that night and leading the prayer for the Muslims. Convict Jones stood from the sideline watching and learning. After the prayer was over the Muslims disappeared around corners, and most wouldn't be seen until next prayer time. Convict Jones walked on down the corridor of the prison when he saw a younger prisoner walking his way.

"What's good partner?" Convict Jones asked.

"What's happening? Where you from?" the young cat asked.

"G-ville. Why, what's good?" Convict Jones asked, looking the young cat directly in the eye.

"Homeboy," the young cat said and started smiling.

"What's your name, and what hood you from?"
Convict Jones asked.

"Fieldcrest."

"Brick City. I know y'all mad they tore it down," Convict Jones kept the conversation moving.

"Yeah, but it look good now," the young kid named Kevin stated. "You know Shelly Ann?"

"Yeah, from the bricks."

"Yeah, that's my mother," Kevin informed Convict Jones, looking past him.

"Say word. Me and your mother go way back," Convict Jones replied, thinking about the time him and Shelly Ann pulled a lick on a white man.

Convict Jones and Kevin conversed for a few more minutes then Kevin began talking about a guy named Rico.

"You talking about Kemmiko's brother?" Convict Jones asked.

"Yeah."

Convict Jones then began talking to Kevin like he just knew of Kemmiko and Rico that the fact that they were actually engaged to be married soon.

"So what Kemmiko doing out there?"

"She doing good. She go with that dude with the dreads from Mississippi."

That statement tore a hole in Convict Jones' heart, but he wouldn't allow hearsay be the final fact.

"What about Rico?" Convict Jones asked now really distracted.

"He doing alright, married to some girl from the country. Making babies," he replied, laughing.

Convict Jones and Kevin conversed for a few more minutes then parted ways. Convict Jones went directly to the wall phones and dialed Kim's number.

"Institutional roll call count in fifteen minutes," the Institutional PA intercom announced to the prisoners.

Prisoners began moving to and fro around the unit, preparing to go to their cells for the remainder of the night. Convict Jones walked in his cell and saw that Smith was on the top bunk reading a book. Convict Jones already considered that since he had to be in the cell with Smith, they had to have a common ground to stand on.

Once the prison officials made their rounds counting the prisoners, Convict Jones opened the conversation with, "Roll up."

Convict Jones informed Smith, tossing four bags of marijuana and two blunts on his top bunk.

Smith looked at Convict Jones then the marijuana and smiled.

"Hell ya!" Smith responded excited.

The reason Convict Jones had Smith to roll up two different blunts was because he didn't believe in smoking behind homosexuals, although Smith informed Convict Jones that he was a bi-sexual, which was the same thing to him. However, Convict Jones was relieved when Smith allowed him to know that he was not his type.

While smoking the blunts, Smith allowed Convict Jones to know a little bit about his life, particularly how he got caught for the crime he was now serving his sentence on. Smith informed Convict

Jones that he was originally from Ohio, but moved to South Carolina following his white girlfriend, Pam Turner.

Pam had to come to South Carolina to take care of her grandmother who seemed to be prone to slight strokes and heart attacks. Later, Pam's grandmother passed away, leaving her the house she died in. However, Pam was originally from Macon, Georgia. She was only in Ohio on business. Pam would travel all over the United States robbing and conning big insurance companies. She would rather con the companies or people she came across, but if it came down to armed robbery, so be it.

Pam was not an ugly woman at all, in fact, she looked something like a runway model. She was the best at what she did when it came to her hustle. Convict Jones listened to Smith tell his story, although he did not trust one word that came out of his mouth. Later, Convict Jones found out that what Smith told him was the truth. In prison, all types of prisoners who are also individuals have hidden motives, and to remove the veil from their hidden agenda proves that you will never ever be able to judge a book by its cover, and for sure not this book.

CHAPTER 30

Convict Jones dreamt for a few seconds to his past life fourteen years earlier. He couldn't help but to think about his son and baby's mother. His baby's mother's name was Stephanie Adams. He had not seen her and his son in years. The reason Convict Jones and Stephanie never hit it off like they were supposed to was because Convict Jones had been hurt deeply by another woman prior to her. Consolidated with the fact that he was falling in love with her, and the best way to protect his and her heart was to back up off her. He couldn't risk the chance of being hurt again.

Convict Jones and Stephanie never got into arguments. Every time they came in contact with each other they couldn't keep their hands off one another. This was a couple that should have been together. However, due to Convict Jones catching a thirty year prison sentence it was another assault against the love they had for each other. As Convict Jones thought, his son came to mind.

Although he didn't spend too much time with his son when they were on the street, he loved him and cherished every moment they spent together as a little boy. Convict Jones always promised himself that if he ever came in contact with them again, he had some serious apologizing to do. Smith then called Convict Jones' name bringing him out of his daydream.

"Dicey."

Convict Jones was now paying attention to him and replied, "Yeah, what's good?"

"I was just telling you about how I got in here," Smith replied, sucking his teeth just like a girl.

"Yeah, go ahead. I'm listening," he stated, giving Smith his undivided attention.

Smith told Convict Jones that the crime that he got bagged on was because of Pam's alleged mistakes made during the commission of the crime. Pam, who always happened to be in possession of some form of blueprint to an insurance company, presented it to Smith. The blueprints to the insurance company that Pam came in possession of showed the ins and outs of the foundation of the insurance building. It showed where the alarms were stationed in the building along with the cameras. It also gave the information on how to disarm the alarms. The blueprints also showed where three different safes were located with the security code to get in each and every last one of them.

The blueprint cost Pam a pretty penny. She gave up ten thousand dollars and a shot of pussy for the blueprint. According to Smith, this was the biggest that he himself had ever pulled off. The safes in the insurance company building, consolidated together, held well over four hundred thousand dollars. The information provided to Pam was that they had to enter the building through the side using a radar scanner to disconnect the silent alarms.

Pam and Smith were dressed in all black. Once in the building they started on the second floor where the first safe was at. Then they worked their way down to the first floor, where the second safe was at, and then to the basement where the largest safe was at. Pam and Smith had to go in that same identical rotation, due to the sections in the blueprint that read opening any other safe outside that order would override the alarm system and reactivate them. However, in the basement after emptying the last and final safe, Pam turned on a light switch, which should have been the first sign that something was seriously wrong with her. Smith overlooked and dismissed it as a simple mistake, especially when it wasn't what got him busted by the police.

Pam and Smith pulled off the job successfully is what he thought until he was arrested for the criminal act. The mistakes that Smith noticed Pam had done, he found out later that they were not mistakes at all. In fact, they were all a part of her plan. What got Smith's name in the police's mouth was the fact that when Smith and Pam were leaving the building the same way they came in, Pam intentionally dropped his picture ID card, making sure that the police would catch him. She also used to her advantage that Smith was a stand-up guy. Smith would not snitch on anybody, especially her, due to all the dreams she sold and would continue to sell him.

Immediately after leaving the insurance company building, Pam and Smith went to a house that she informed Smith she had grew up in. This was another one of the many lies that Pam had told to get her plan to work in her favor. Actually, the house that Pam and Smith were in was a house that Pam rented for the sole purpose of deceiving Smith. Once Smith was caught by the police, the house would be evacuated, and Pam would no longer be heard from, but only after covering the odd ends of the plan. Inside this house, Smith and Pam began counting the money they pulled from the robbery of the insurance building. Pam and Smith made passionate love on top of the money for hours. After having sex the following morning, they woke up and packaged the money, which amounted to six hundred and seventy-five thousand dollars. Pam had already counted on Smith trying to be the man in control and suggested that they put the money up somewhere safe.

Pam was a master manipulator. She also suggested that they do not spend any of the money until everything blew over. Just as she planned, he followed her every instruction to a tee. Smith and Pam put the money away at her alleged grandmother's house deep in the country in Gray Court, South Carolina. This house was also rented for six months, which was a part of the plan.

Smith being in the streets all his life, he was not just stupid enough to put the money at the house. Smith decided that wherever she went he would be there. He would not allow her to leave his eyesight. However, Pam was much smarter than that, and she had already planned on him smothering her. She considered all men predictable. Her total belief in life was that pussy ruled everything. That is what she would always state to herself and old girlfriends that she went to school with.

"If I say the man is going to shit at 3:45 P.M. on the dot, you can bet your last dollar, he will shit at 3:45 P.M. on the dot."

There was laughter after every time she made that statement.

Three days later, the house that Pam and him were living in was raided and he was taken to jail. While Smith sat in jail, Pam moved the money and began tying up all the loose ends. It wasn't that Smith wasn't a real brother, it was just that he was a stupid nigga. It seemed like he got stupider and stupider day-by-day. Especially when he allowed Pam to manipulate him later after being in jail without a bond to enter a guilty plea for one year with an attorney that she hired.

Pam informed Smith that she would be there for him and hold him down. You couldn't tell him that Pam was not his soulmate and ride or die chick. However, Smith kept his eyes and ears open to the streets behind the fence, and the day finally came when that big one eyed monster they call TV allowed Smith to know where Pam was at. The last thing he heard, which was a year and a half ago, was that Pam was a millionaire and married to a famous basketball player.

CHAPTER 31

Kemmiko lay in her bed staring at the ceiling, but she was not alone. Another man lay beside her as they both cuddled. Although, they did not have physical sex with one another, they were mentally fucking one another.

"You know I am here for you," the guy named Tyrone informed Convict Jones' fiancé.

"It's just been so long. I have been waiting on him for over ten years. I'm tired."

Tyrone reached over and wrapped his hands around her.

As Kemmiko lay in Tyrone's arms, her phone began to ring. She looked at the caller ID and noticed that it was Convict Jones. She turned over and allowed it to ring without answering it.

"Yo Dee, go get Shawn and tell him we about to move on that cat," O-Dog stated, placing two icepicks in his waistline.

Dirty Dee immediately went to Shawn's cell, got him, and informed him about what was going down. When Dirty Dee got to Shawn's cell, Shawn was also strapping up with a blade.

"Come on nigga, we rolling!" Dirty Dee shouted and turned around and walked back towards O-Dog's cell to see if he was ready.

Shawn followed behind Dirty Dee and they met up with O-Dog.

"Look, Major Riley has informed me that it is now head hunting season. We got the green light on that fuck nigga."

Dirty Dee grabbed two large master locks and placed them inside a pair of socks. Willie Ham who stayed getting up before the sun rose, sat on the rock watching the early morning world news, when he noticed O-Dog and his crew were on the move. He didn't know what was going down, but due to recent events he figured that it had something to do with his friend due to the homework he had done.

Willie Ham, who did not have to go get a blade because he stayed strapped, walked towards the entrance of the unit door. He intended to go straight to Convict Jones' dorm instead of the cafeteria. Once the unit doors opened, Willie Ham went to Unit Two where Convict Jones lived while O-Dog and his crew went to the mess hall to where they expected to see Convict Jones. Convict Jones' dorm released their prisoners, and Willie Ham caught him at the door and informed him what was going down.

"I owe you one partner," Convict Jones informed Willie Ham and continued. "Fuck that shit.

Let's go eat." Moving his ten-inch shank around his waistline. "Them faggot ass niggas can't do me nothing."

He was allowing the weed to think for him.

Convict Jones, Willie Ham, Mo, and Smith then all walked towards the mess hall to eat.

Coming back from eating breakfast, Convict Jones, Mo, and Smith proceeded to Unit Two. Convict Jones had noticed while he was in the cafeteria, O-Dog and his crew staring at him. Every member in O-Dog's crew was wearing coats, which automatically allowed Convict Jones to know that something was going down. That coupled by the information he received from Willie Ham. It was too damn hot for coats in the middle of summer.

Willie Ham had gone back to his unit to avoid an out of place disciplinary infraction. Willie Ham had also thought, like Convict Jones, that O-Dog and his crew returned to their unit because they left before Convict Jones and his friends. As the prisoners of Unit Two headed back to their dorm, the Institutional PA intercom system announced that roll call count would be conducted in fifteen minutes.

Coming into the unit, Convict Jones immediately saw O-Dog and his crew standing by his cell door. Smith immediately saw what was going down and went in the opposite direction, wanting no part of the incident. That was despite the fact that earlier he was stating that he was down with Convict Jones for whatever. Convict Jones thought to himself studying his surroundings, *It's going down*. Thinking fast and arranging his shank in his waistline to be ready for action.

Convict Jones walked over towards the cat they called Shawn, and asked, "Yo partner, you got a light?"

He produced a cigarette.

Shawn just stood like a deer caught in headlights, not saying nothing with his face screwed up in disbelief that Convict Jones would ask him for anything.

"What's good black man?" Convict Jones asked then continued. "You got a light? I got one for you too."

Shawn looked him up and down with a frown on his face.

"Get the fuck out my face, bitch!" Shawn spat back in a nasty disrespectful tone.

At that very statement, Convict Jones snapped in raw reflex and slapped the shit out of Shawn. Shawn hit the floor like a bag of potatoes and began bleeding from the nose. In Convict Jones' younger days he could not stand nor afford to have someone disrespect him because if he let someone get away with it, it becomes an open invitation for others to disrespect him. Convict Jones stayed in fights because of this similar disrespect because somebody else did not know how to hold their tongue.

As a result of Convict Jones bombing first, Shawn jumped off the floor then Convict Jones hit him with a two-piece. The two prisoners began fighting. He knocked Shawn out cold, and then all hell broke loose. Dirty Dee immediately pulled his blade and attacked Convict Jones.

He was stopped in his tracks when Mo stepped in the middle of the two, and said, "Hold up partner! It ain't going down like that."

O-Dog began sneaking and circling around Mo.

Mo was prepared to ride or die. Mo quickly turned and caught O-Dog sneaking, where by O-Dog stopped dead in his tracks. By this time, Convict

Jones was fully ready for war with two blades in his hands. For a brief moment, everything stopped and the only thing that seemed to be working between the prisoners were their eyes as they watched their surroundings. O-Dog and Dirty Dee then backed up and looked over at their other comrade and saw that Shawn was knocked the fuck out. Dirty Dee and O-Dog rushed over to Shawn.

They picked him up as soon as the Institutional intercom said, "Five minutes to Institutional roll call count."

The two prisoners toted Shawn out of Unit Two and headed back to their unit. Convict Jones and Mo then went to their cell for standing roll call count. Once inside the cell, Convict Jones placed two toothbrushes in the cell door so that it could not be opened from the outside. Convict Jones then looked at his roommate and shook his head. Convict Jones went over to his bed and laid down trying to get some sleep but was unable to due to the incident that had just taken place. Thirty minutes later, sleep found its way to Convict Jones.

CHAPTER 32

Kemmiko sat on her couch watching *Sponge Bob*. As she watched, her mind drifted back to the time she had called Convict Jones' baby's mother Stephanie.

"Look, there is no need for you to call him anymore, and you know that is not his child. We are married now. Leave me and my husband alone," Kemmiko told Convict Jones' baby's mother, making sure that she had Convict Jones all to herself.

Kemmiko's mind was brought back as her front door shut. As she looked up, she saw Tyrone. She looked into his eyes and he returned her stare. She knew she had made solid promises to Convict Jones, but she began another relationship with Tyrone, thinking that she could handle two men at one time. However, like anything else you cannot serve two masters.

"What's wrong, baby?" Tyrone asked, noticing a worried look on her face.

"Nothing, why you ask?" she replied.

"Nothing. I love you," he informed her.

Just as the phone hung up, she replied, "I love you too."

She looked over at the phone and saw that it was Convict Jones.

"Damn!" was all she could say.

Tyrone asked, "Who is it?"

They both stared at each other in silence.

Tyrone already knowing, sucked his teeth, turned around, and exited the house. Kemmiko began shedding tears for lost love.

Convict Jones' drug dealer dreams and federal nightmares always would start out the same way. The nightmare was as close to reality as it would get, except for the added little thing that Convict Jones' wished would have happened that did not occur. Most of the time when he had the dream it was just as it had happened that night five people were murdered in a drug deal gone bad. During that night, out of the five people that were murdered, two of the people were Convict Jones' closest friends whose names were Nick Madderson and Robert Bryant.

It was September 17th, 1988, when Convict Jones, Robert, and Nick had met up with two guys out of Atlanta, Georgia. Convict Jones and Nick had already been dealing with these two guys who they knew by *Donnie* and *Rent*. Prior to the meeting with Donnie and Rent, Convict Jones and Nick had been purchasing two kilos every week from them. Every time Convict Jones and Nick made the trip to Atlanta, they would meet Donnie and Rent on I-85 at a rest stop where they would make their transaction. However, Convict Jones and his crew were making a much bigger purchase this go around because money was being made at a faster pace, coupled by the 1988 drought had come through Greenville, South Carolina where they were from.

Convict Jones and his crew were buying two and a half more bricks, making it four and a half brick with a side order of firearms. As always Convict Jones would meet Rent and Donnie off I-85 at a rest stop. From there they would go to a nearby *I-Hop*, where Rent and Donnie would pick up the drugs. Convict Jones and his crew would then follow Rent and Donnie to another rest stop where they would make the transaction.

However, this night, everything was different from the very start beginning with the meeting with Rent and Donnie. First, only Rent was there and Donnie was nowhere to be found. Rent had another cat with him that Convict Jones or Nick did not know. Alarms immediately began ringing because the transaction was going against the grain. Second, the location to pick up the drugs had changed. Convict Jones, going against his better judgment, disregarded the two most important facts due to the money was blinding his eyes. He went along with the plan to handle it a different way. Convict Jones figured that because there was more money, drugs, and guns involved was the reason why the location changed, and why another guy was there instead of Donnie.

The new guy that Rent brought with him said his name was Rico, who played the role as the big supplier. Although Convict Jones' vibes were telling him that something was wrong, he went along with the deal because Nick and Rent insisted that everything would be alright. Convict Jones thought to himself, *We will be in and out of there in five minutes.* He was watching his rearview for any undercover cops and glancing at his back up in the Ford Taurus by Robert.

He was following Rico and Rent up I-85, where they bypassed the rest stop they normally handled their transaction at. After passing the rest stop, they rode for another ten minutes and pulled off on exit ramp 53. They followed the two men down a country road for two miles and made a quick right and then a left, and entered a small neighborhood.

The neighborhood was not run down, but you could tell that it was hood. There were about twenty people walking the streets. Convict Jones pulled up behind Rent and Rico who were pushing a convertible money green BMW dripping in chrome with BBS on the wheels. The system they had in the car could be heard for blocks. After Convict Jones parked his 1986 Fairway Ford with crystals in the metallic flip flop candy paint job, sitting on 1991 Roosters on Bulldog tires with a kit, Nick and him stepped out of the vehicle. Convict Jones looked around and noticed that Robert had parked up the street and was watching their every move without being noticed by Rent or Rico. Nobody walking the street ever noticed Robert sitting idle in the vehicle.

Robert then watched his friends along with Rent and Rico enter a ground level apartment building complex. Inside the apartment, Convict Jones immediately realized that it was a trap house and got on alert. A beanbag sat in the corner with a jam box beside it. A table with four chairs sat in the middle of the living room, but there was no more furniture in the apartment. Convict Jones also noticed that two of the chairs in the apartment were pulled out. Convict Jones immediately sat down in one of the pulled out chairs, and knew that there were more people in the apartment due to the heat radiating from the chair. Convict Jones knew that someone had just been sitting in the chair.

"Ain't nobody else here?" Convict Jones asked.

"Nah!" Rico replied then cut his eyes towards the backroom, making Convict Jones uncomfortable.

"Well, let me use the bathroom before we get started," Convict Jones said, really wanting to check the rest of the apartment out. "I been holding this piss for an hour."

He stood up and prepared to go to the bathroom.

"We will handle business first," Rico replied sternly, "then you can use the bathroom."

Rico was talking to Convict Jones like he was a child.

"Hold up partner. I'm not doing shit until I use the bathroom nigga," Convict Jones corrected Rico with authority in his voice.

At that very moment, two cats with black mask and gloves came busting out the bathroom with nine millimeters drawn and ready to squeeze.

"Hold!" Convict Jones shouted, raising his hand up.

Convict Jones then turned towards Rent, and yelled, "What the fuck is this nigga?"

Convict Jones was staring him dead in the eyes.

Rent replied, "You know what it is nigga. Now shut the fuck up."

All in one motion, Nick reached and pulled his Russia Ruger handgun. He was cut down by Rico before he could even get a shot off.

Rico then turned towards Convict Jones, and asked, "Where is the money, bitch?"

He as pointing the gun at Convict Jones.

"You just killed the only man that can tell you where the money is at. I'm just one of his do boys," Convict Jones informed him.

Rico informed the two masked men to go check Convict Jones and Nick's vehicle for the money, while Rent just stared in disbelief to what was going on.

CHAPTER 33

Attorney and counselor at Law, Debra Butler walked across the courtroom floor towards the jury box.

"The state wants you to believe that my client was the person who murdered Mr. Achillies. My client's fingerprints are nowhere to be found. No one can identify him as being responsible for committing the crime, and the only person that places him at the scene of the crime is his alleged codefendant Mr. Johnson who openly admitted today during trial that he was not at the crime scene. If this is true then how can he identify my client as the shooter?"

Ms. Butler walked back around the defendant's table and picked up a piece of paper.

After the closing arguments from Ms. Butler and the State, the jury deliberated for approximately twenty-five minutes then came back with a not guilty verdict for her client. This made Ms. Butler record eight straight wins in the last two years.

Outside, Robert sat up the street looking at the apartment Convict Jones and Nick entered. As he watched, he noticed the door open and two people coming out who he thought would be Convict Jones and Nick. The gunshot inside the house Robert heard, but he thought that it was a car backfiring because they shot Nick, and the guys forgot to take off their mask, coupled by the fact they were still holding their guns in their hands. The two men walked to the vehicle, opened the doors, and began searching the car. Robert pulled out his chrome .45 Magnum and checked the clip. He then opened his car door slowly without making any noise and slid out of the vehicle.

Once outside the vehicle, he pushed the door close and began moving while bent down towards the guys searching Convict Jones' car. When he got within five feet of Convict Jones' vehicle, Robert realized that the masked men were not the same two men he had seen at the rest stop that Convict Jones and Nick normally met due to the build and shape of their bodies.

While the masked men searched the car, Robert walked up on one of them standing outside by the trunk of the car trying to get it open, and asked, "Hey man, you got a light?"

He produced a cigarette.

"Nah, get the fuck out of here," he told Robert, and then continued to talk to the guy in the car. "Pop the trunk, nigga."

He took his attention off Robert. The guy in the car was halfway in the car under the seat looking for the money, while the guy by the trunk's attention was focused back on Robert who locked eyes with the masked man. Robert, by this time, was raising his weapon and blazing. He sent the masked man falling and tripping backwards over the side of the car. The gunfire alerted everyone in the area. People began running, while the other guy in the car began shooting without having a target to fire on. Bullets were going everywhere. Robert ducked and slid up the side of the vehicle where he noticed the gunfire stopped. Robert knew that the masked man in the car had run out of ammo. Robert hopped to his feet, ran to the car door where the guy was half way in the car, and dumped three rounds in his face, killing him instantly.

Inside the apartment, Rent yelled, "Man, I don't have nothing to do with this!"

He was trying to explain to Convict Jones who stared him in his eyes.

"This is not the time for that now," Convict Jones replied, kicking his leg under the table while Rent was peeping out the window.

Everyone in the apartment heard the gunshots outside and Rico was waiting for his partners to bring the money so they could go. Convict Jones already knew what was going on outside. He knew that Robert was putting work in. That was one of the reasons he placed Robert as look out. He knew without a doubt, Robert would bust that gun, coupled by the fact Robert was trustworthy. Rico peeped out the window again. While he was looking out the window, Convict Jones was making a move for his .40 Caliber under his Pelle Pelle sweatshirt. Rico immediately turned around, feeling something was wrong.

With his gun pointed he stated, "Don't even think about it nigga!" he was walking towards them. "I should kill you for just attempting some dumb shit like that."

Boom! Boom! Boom!

Gunshots rang out as the window to the apartment shattered. Next, the door came crashing in, which sent Rico diving for cover. He was aiming his Glock and letting off shots. He hit Robert in the chest and throat area. Rico rolled up on his knees, while Convict Jones was now letting off thunderous shots from the .40 Caliber, which sent Rico running and jumping out the window. Rico landed in a bush beside the apartment. Glass cuts were all over his face and arms. Convict Jones and Rent moved quickly. They were bent low, and dodging stray bullets. Outside, next door to the apartment, a young black woman named Mechelle with her ten year old son was getting into her car. Rico looked around for a way out and found none until he turned around and saw Mechelle getting in her car.

Rico thought to himself, *Bingo*. He started moving on impulse. Rico ran up on Mechelle, not paying attention to her son. He put the gun to her head and demanded her keys to her car.

Mechelle being straight ghetto said, "I ain't giving you shit, nigga!"

She was looking Rico in the eyes.

Rico without argument let off a single shot, knocking half of her wig off. Blood flew everywhere, even on her son, as her body collapsed on her son. Rico snatched the keys out of Mechelle's death grip, jumped in the car, and pulled off. As Rico turned one corner at the top of the street, eight police cars with more on the way turned on the street down the block. The entire neighborhood was surrounded.

Convict Jones ran to the window and looked out. He then looked at his friend lying dead in the apartment. He looked at Rent and squinted his eyes. He then ran over to the window, peeped out, and then looked back at Rent.

"We trapped. Damn!" he shouted as he tried to think of a way out. "Any drugs in here?" Convict Jones asked Rent.

"I guess so. I don't know man," he answered, panicking.

Rent dropped his head to his chest, shook it, and then in a low tone of voice said, "Man, I didn't know this was going to happen, for real."

Rico was sounding sincere and Convict Jones believed him.

Trapped with no way out, Convict Jones and Rent were arrested. Rent immediately got diarrhea in the mouth, while Convict Jones refused to talk to the police with the exception of asking for a bail and his attorney. However, Convict Jones was eventually charged with five counts of murder, even though the weapon he had did not match the bullets that killed his two friends, the female outside of the apartment, or the two guys that were with Rico.

The police were everywhere when Rent and Convict Jones were brought out the apartment in handcuffs. Convict Jones was covered in Robert and Nick's blood due to trying to save them, but to no avail. Coming out of the apartment in cuffs, soaked in his friend's blood all over his Pelle Pelle sweat suit, in which Rico had on an identical sweat suit, except his was all black, Convict Jones stopped and looked around. He witnessed a little ten year old holding on to a body lying in the street and crying. The person he was holding on to looked to be dead. The police tried to remove the little boy's tight grip, but that was to no avail. However, when they did finally break his grip, the little boy looked up and saw Convict Jones being escorted out of the apartment in cuffs and soaked in blood. You couldn't tell the little boy that the police didn't have the right person who killed his mother.

Convict Jones looked away for a brief moment and studied his surroundings. When he looked back in the little boy's direction, he noticed the little boy's lips and eyes began to change, showing hate. Convict Jones paid little attention because he was ready to get to jail, get a shower, and get out of the blood soaked clothing. However, the little boy did not feel any kind of relief, even though he felt they had caught the man who killed his mama.

The little ten year old boy's mother's name was Mechelle Johnson. She was the daughter of a Toni Johnson, a prostitute, who had been married to a pimp named Youngblood Johnson in New York City. The two were separated by incarceration when Toni had Mechelle. Unfortunately, Mechelle's mother, Toni, never saw Youngblood Johnson again, but carried his seed Mechelle Johnson. Mechelle Johnson gave birth to Terry Johnson, the ten year old boy who watched his mother get murdered.

After Mechelle's death, Terry was shipped to different group homes and eventually ended up in juvenile prison. Terry had become a product of his environment. He also joined gangs at the tender age of thirteen looking for his mother's love. These actions led to Terry committing carjacking, robberies, stealing, and many other crimes. After so long Terry would become a product of the South Carolina Department of Corrections, when he stepped over the state lines looking for his mother's killer.

"This Casper guy is going to make a mistake, and when he does, we are going to be there." Agent Williams said to his partner.

Agent Johnson replied, "Let's just hope he makes that mistake real soon because the clock is ticking."

Agent Johnson was looking at the paperwork as they drove down a highway.

"He wasn't going back to that motel. I'm positive he left a clue behind. I'm pretty sure a clue was left behind which will give us a clue as to his next move." Agent William stated, making a right turn.

"I don't see anything wrong with that," Agent Williams immediately made a U-turn in the middle of the street.

The agents knew that the trail was cold, and they were praying for anything to fall out the sky to give them some form of knowledge that would put them on the right path to catching Casper. The agents were heading south on I-85, back to the last spot they'd had a run in with Casper as the agents would call him.

Pulling up to the Motel 6, the BMW and black van were in the same spot they had left it in.

"There's the van right there," Agent Williams stated, looking around for the BMW.

The agents stepped out of their vehicle and looked around the area of the motel. The two agents walked to the lobby of the motel and requested to see the manager. After talking with manager for a few seconds and flashing their federal badges, the agents were allowed access to the motel room Rico had rented out. Once inside room 202, the agents began a search in hopes that they would find something that would allow them to know Rico or Casper's next move. Agent Johnson then looked inside a trashcan and found a piece of paper with the name of a cocktail lounge on it.

"Williams!" Agent Johnson shouted excitedly. "I believe we have found our break."

"What you got there?" Agent Williams asked, walking over towards his partner to examine the object.

"It's just a location of a lounge that our boy may be going to or has been to." Agent Johnson said, smiling ear-to-ear.

"Well, let's stake the place out and see what we come up with," Agent Williams replied.

The two agents then exited the motel room and headed back to their vehicle. Once inside the vehicle, Agent Williams immediately called the federal building head office and asked for the location of the cocktail lounge. When the information came back to Williams there were four different listings of a cocktail lounge in the area with that name, which made it impossible to stake out each one of them.

The agents decided not to stress their brain and decided to pick the closest cocktail lounge to the Motel 6. The agents headed to the lounge and sat watching for several hours. Finding no signs of Casper, the agents staked out the next cocktail lounge. After sitting six hours at that lounge and nothing happened, the agents started back to their vehicle. They headed back to their head office in Atlanta, which was less than a half a mile from the abandoned building where Rico's hide out was at.

CHAPTER 34

"Mail call!" a prison official yelled.

Prisoners came from everywhere circling the prison guard waiting for their mail. A letter was one of the most important things to a prisoner. It allows him to know that he is loved by at least someone. Other prisoners who don't receive mail or have the opportunity to call a loved one are like a person dropped off on the planet Earth and told to survive. Some prisoners just don't have any family members at all, and have to depend on themselves for everything they do.

Convict Jones' name was called. The prisoner official handed Convict Jones his mail. Convict Jones grabbed his mail and returned to his cell. Once in his cell, he sat down on his bed, looked at the letter, and saw that it had come from his future wife. He opened the letter and began reading.

10-08-09/ 2:45 A.M.

Hi Dyson,

Yes, I was disappointed in you not making parole, but our Father in Heaven has his reasons not to question. You know I really need a friend or someone who I could really talk to who really cares or who is really willing to take time out and help someone. It seems no one loves anybody anymore, but I love everybody in the world and will do and give my last to help someone. However, when I need that no one's around, but they can look at you and smile but behind your back it's another thing. It's okay though. I'll have to go through this alone which is good. I'm not mad. I'll go through and keep my mouth shut. Dyson, I don't know if you and I will make it. Sometimes I feel like I've wasted time waiting! I should have lived. When you come home you'll be 40 or 41. I'll be 50 or 51. You're not going to want an older woman. You're gonna want someone younger and prettier, which I don't blame you. Don't try and tell me different. I know better. I'll be your friend and help you until you get on your feet, but marrying and all that I don't know. I'd love to have a young handsome Dyson, but I can't give you what you've already missed, like kids. I'm not as pretty as I was. You know what I mean, so if you already have someone cool, but be for real about it to me. You know I stay to myself. I go to my room, close the door, and sometimes just take a sleeping pill. I sleep except when I'm working.

Yes, Jerry is still staying with me, but I told him I'm ready for him to move. Hopefully, it will be anytime now. Tyrone comes by and checks on me. He's a real friend. Jerry doesn't want to move and sometimes he acts like does, but I don't care. I'm ready to be alone and get myself together to where

I don't have to answer my door or phone, not even for family. They're not there either and I don't think if you were here you would be here either. Its shit like that, but you fuss, you this you that, whatever, if I didn't have a man, I wouldn't be going through this here.

I told you this is the reason I didn't want a man in my life. You're never here for me and then the explaining. Then people talking behind my back and not doing anything to help or even reach out a hand to help. I'm sorry to be revealing all this to you, but I got to hear your response.

I've lost everything. No car, no bank account, look bad, no friends, no phone, no nothing, but I thank God for my job. I'm starting over and don't need nobody around to even think they can say they've helped because no one but God is here for me. He's the only one I owe. I don't owe nobody but God, and I'm thankful for him. So much for this right now.

The company received your book. She called and will call and let me know something later on. No, I haven't heard from anyone. I'm sending a package off the 3rd week in October. You can call Mechiko next month. I will let you know after two to three weeks. I love you, and I am here for you always. Take care of yourself.

Love you,
Kemmiko

Convict Jones finished reading the letter, lay back on the bed, and placed his hands behind his head. He placed the letter down beside him and made a prayer that everything was alright but little did Convict Jones know, he was slowly but surely losing his woman.

We going to get that fuck nigga!" O-Dog shouted, swinging his fist and hitting the wall locker.

"Hey Shawn, you all right man?" Dirty Dee asked, holding him up from falling.

"Nigga, fuck that! You not all right. We going to get that nigga," O-Dog said, insisting on revenge.

O-Dog was now pacing the floor back and forth.

"Man, the major wants to see us as soon as counts clear. I believe he has already heard what went down," Dirty Dee informed O-Dog.

"How you know, nigga?"

"Because Sergeant Jackson informed me right before lockdown," Dirty Dee replied, standing up and looking into the mirror over the toilet.

"Man, I don't want to hear shit out of that motherfucker!" O-Dog shouted with his mouth twisted.

"Well, Sergeant Jackson stated that it was very important that the major see us so he might not know what the fuck went down."

Shawn rose up, weaving from side-to-side. and stated, "Hey man, can you get me some Tylenols?"

Shawn was holding his head.

"Yeah, I got you man," Dirty Dee said, showing compassion for his friend.

"Man, don't get that nigga shit! He let that punk motherfucker knock his ass out!"

"Chill out man, damn!" Dirty Dee replied.

"Man, fuck this shit. I'm out," O-Dog replied, walking out the cell and sneaking back to his cell since they were the only prisoners with doors left open.

Once O-Dog got inside of his cell, he opened his locker, pulled out a creamer of homemade wine, and a sack of marijuana provided to him by Major Riley, and got high and drunk.

CHAPTER 35

Convict Jones was lying back on his bed when L.C. Floyd knocked on his cell door.

Smith looked up, and said, "The door for you roomy."

Ever since the fight, Convict Jones had not said two words to Smith because of the cowardly act he pulled. Convict Jones got up from his bed and went to let L.C. Floyd in the cell by removing the two brushes out of the door. The dream he had earlier weighed heavy on his mind, but due to everything that was going on around him he had no time for sleeping.

First, O-Dog and his crew wanted to kill him for something, and he had no idea what he had done to them. Second, his future wife is talking crazy, coupled by the fact, the young dude he had ran into earlier said that Kemmiko was dealing with another man. Once L.C. Floyd entered the cell, he immediately handed Convict Jones two twin nine-inch icepicks. Ice picks would cause internal bleeding, which will kill a man slowly. The icepicks also had rubber handles on them.

"I heard O-Dog and his crew was planning to roll on you in the cafeteria," L.C. Floyd said, looking around the cell.

"What meal?" Convict Jones immediately asked, checking out the icepicks.

"I don't know, but I brought these babies just in case, feel me?" L.C. Floyd smiled that devilish grin he was known for.

"Yeah, true that, true that," Convict Jones said, walking back over towards his bed and sitting down.

While Convict Jones and L.C. Floyd were conversing, Mo came to the cell door and informed Convict Jones that some dudes wanted him out front.

"Who is it, Mo?" Convict Jones asked.

"I don't know, but they say they're you're homeboys," Mo replied.

"Tell them I will be out in one minute."

He placed the two icepicks under his shirt, while Mo left out the cell door.

"Want me to roll with you?" L.C. Floyd asked.

"Nah, I'm good. I'll see you later," Convict Jones replied, as L.C. Floyd got up and exited the cell.

Convict Jones walked out of his cell and exited Unit Two building. He was immediately met by three other prisoners also known as convicts. These prisoners were also from Greenville, South Carolina, but represented different hoods, except for one, who went by the name of *Pig Sty*. Pig Sty and Convict Jones were from the same neighborhood. The other two live wires were named Rodney Pitts and Black Nuk.

"What's up, nigga?" Convict Jones yelled excitedly because he had not seen his homeboys in over seven years.

Pig Sty immediately ran up on Convict Jones, grabbed him, and hugged him showing love. The two neighborhood homies, back in the day, had put work in together kicking up dirt. However, Rodney Pitts, on the other hand, Convict Jones and him were beefing in the streets. Once they entered the belly of the beast, the street beef immediately came to an end. All Greenville niggas represented for their home team and watched each other's back, especially when they are out of their region or jurisdiction. Black Nuk and Convict Jones would also get together sometimes and down cases of Coors Light Extra Gold-Beer when they were free. Still it was all love between the home team, and they were happy to see one another.

"Nigga, we heard you was on the yard through one of your loyal supporters," Rodney stated.

"Who?"

"Your boy Raw Raw," Rodney informed Convict Jones, looking around and checking his surroundings while Black Nuk placed his back up against the wall.

"Has he got off of lockup yet?" Convict Jones asked, showing slight concern for his little partner.

"I believe so, but I am not for sure. I heard that they transferred him just this morning," Rodney replied, moving a blade from around in his pants.

Black Nuk then interrupted the conversation, and said, "Yo, what's up with them fuck niggas, O-Dog and his crew?"

Black Nuk was grilling him a mean mug like something smelled awful.

"Shit! Just this morning I knocked one of them bitches out cold. I believe his name was Shawn. At least that was the information that came back to me," Convict Jones informed his homies thinking about the incident.

"Yeah, I know that nigga," Pig Sty added to the conservation.

"For some reason O-Dog and his crew got beef with me, and I don't even know why. Shit, I don't even know them niggas. They must think I'm an easy lick," Convict Jones stated then began laughing.

"Let me look into the matter, and get to the bottom of it. When I've finished my investigation I'll let you know what's real baby boy," Pig Sty stated, really thinking on another level.

"Yeah, you do that brother befo' I catch a triple life sentence in this bitch!" Convict Jones stated, meaning every word he said because he was getting tired of everything that was going on in his life.

"Boy, we been meaning to get over here and see you, but you know how it is when you on your fucking grind to come up," Black Nuk stated.

"Yeah, I feel you," Convict Jones replied, watching the shakedown team coming down the sidewalk towards his dorm.

"More than likely we wouldn't be here now if we didn't hear through some associates that there was a hit on your ass," Rodney stated, laughing.

"What nigga!" Convict Jones replied in shock.

"Yeah nigga, somebody wants you dead! Dead! Dead!" Black Nuk stated also laughing.

"Well, many have tried and failed baby boy."

Convict Jones then went down in his boxers, removed a twenty cent piece of marijuana, and handed it to the three homies.

"That should brighten your day," Convict Jones stated really wanting to get the marijuana off him now that the shakedown team was in his unit.

"Good lookin' out, nigga," Rodney stated. Rodney was a true live weed head. "Boy, you still crazy as hell," Rodney stated, grabbing the weed and putting it up.

"Nah, I'm just real, you know the drill." Convict Jones said, meaning every word.

"True, true, true," Rodney replied, ready to go get the high.

"Well, I'm ready to roll on them niggas anytime you ready," Black Nuk stated while Rodney agreed with him.

"So they carrying out the hit, huh? We need to find out who placed the hit."

Convict Jones' mind began racing.

"Hold up, let Pig Sty find out what he can find out? What the beef or the hit is about?" Pig Sty asked, talking in the third person, something he liked to do. "They may have you fucked up with someone else."

Convict Jones did want a peaceful resolution, instead of an all-out war where blood would be shed over something that might have been talked about.

"Well, whatever you choose to do nigga. You know we Greenville Riders. We with the team, nigga," Rodney informed Convict Jones, meaning every word he said.

The prisoners then began giving each other pounds and hugs, and agreed upon a pack that if they went down, they went down together. The prisoners then broke the circle and went their separate ways.

"Major, your boys tried to take inmate Convict Jones out and failed," Sergeant Jackson informed Major Riley.

"Those little punks can't do nothing right. They always say, if you want something done right you have to do it yourself," Major Riley stated, pissed off.

Major Riley then thought about his up and coming meeting with Rico which made him even madder.

"Sergeant, please cancel that meeting with Terry and his crew because I have a very important meeting I have to attend to," Major Riley informed Sergeant Jackson.

"Yes sir, done yesterday," Sergeant Jackson stated, walking out of Major Riley's office to carry out the order.

Major Riley then sat in his office at his desk and thought about the meeting he would be having with Rico. He had three hours left and it would take him every bit of one hour and forty-five minutes to get to Atlanta to attend that meeting. He jumped up from his seat, grabbed his jacket off the back of his chair, and rushed out of his office looking at his watch. Once outside of the institution, he got into his dark blue Dodge Ford truck, and drove off going to meet his son.

CHAPTER 36

The very next day Convict Jones was heading towards the multipurpose building to watch a basketball game between Unit Two and Unit Four.

As Convict Jones neared the multipurpose building, Rafee, the Iman for the Muslim community, approached Convict Jones, and said, "Peace brother."

He spoke while looking Convict Jones directly in the eyes.

"Peace brother," Convict Jones replied, shaking Rafee's hand.

Releasing Rafee's hand, Rafee stated, "Do you know that the Qu'ran states that the rib the woman was created from is crooked? If you try to straighten it out or correct it, it will break so take care of it, love it, but do not obey the rib."

Rafee was smiling as he put his hand on Convict Jones' shoulder.

"Why are you telling me this?" Convict Jones asked.

"It's something that came to me, and I felt I had to relay the message," Rafee replied, patting his back.

"Thank you uuhhh?" Convict Jones was searching for his name.

"Rafee, brother."

"Rafee," Convict Jones repeated his name while smiling ear-to-ear.

"You coming to Jummah Friday?" he asked Convict Jones.

"Hopefully, if I'm not dead," Convict Jones replied.

"Ishaallaah!" Rafee replied, meaning if it was the creators will.

"Okay, let me get over here and handle this business," Convict Jones informed Rafee.

"Take care of yourself," Rafee replied and walked off, greeting six to seven more Muslims that were coming in his direction.

Just as Pig Sty informed Convict Jones he began looking into the matter, and headed over to O-Dog and his crew's dorm. Upon arriving in their unit, the first person that Pig Sty saw was Dirty Dee.

"What's up, dawg?" Pig Sty greeted Dirty Dee with a pound.

"Shit, ain't nothing moving," he replied, but kept it moving because he did not have time to stop and politic.

"I heard some cats got to fighting over in Unit Two this morning," Pig Sty said as if he didn't know what was going on.

"Yeah, we had to handle some business over there," Dirty Dee stated, sounding like they had actually handled Convict Jones accordingly.

Dirty Dee was also known for providing information he should not provide, especially to a prisoner like Pig Sty. Pig Sty was well known for stabbing other prisoners and putting the extortion down on other prisoners, whether they were soft or hardcore. Pig Sty barred none. Dirty Dee should have known something was wrong when Pig Sty asked certain questions about his business.

"Shit, I heard Shawn got knocked the fuck out," Pig Sty replied, which should have been enough evidence for Dirty Dee to shut his mouth.

"Yeah, the cat got a lucky punch off," Dirty Dee replied, sounding as if he was not really trusting his own words.

"What's the beef about?" Pig Sty asked straight out.

"Shit, I don't know. That's my little man's beef. Where he go, I follow."

He allowed Pig Sty to know that he would ride or die with O-Dog.

Actually, Dirty Dee was tired of following O-Dog because O-Dog always had them in some stupid little boy shit. O-Dog would start fights, and the next thing Dirty Dee knew was that he was also fighting. A couple of times Dirty Dee felt as if he could have lost his life dealing with O-Dog, but by the grace of Allah he was spared.

"I feel ya," Pig Sty replied, thinking that Dirty Dee could get it too.

"Check this. I got to make a move right quick. I'll holla at you later," Dirty Dee stated, stepping off and turning a corner to his left.

Pig Sty immediately went to the dayroom where a bunch of prisoners were playing cards. Certain prisoners knew of Pig Sty, and also knew he was out of place. The only time Pig Sty would go out of place was to carry out a hit on other prisoners or to pick up money from another prisoner he had the time down on. When Pig Sty entered the dayroom, he saw Shawn sitting at a table with three other prisoners playing spades.

"What's poppin', Shawn?" Pig Sty asked with his hand out for a pound.

The pound was not returned.

"Yeah, what's up nigga," Shawn replied in a salty tone because truthfully he didn't like Pig Sty.

"I need to speak with you for a second."

His request sounded more like a demand to Shawn, which also placed him on defense.

"Yeah, give me one minute. Let me finish this hand."

After Shawn finished the hand, he got up from the table and walked with Pig Sty over in a corner to get some privacy.

"Yo Shawn," Pig Sty began, "what's up with that beef between O-Dog and that kid in Unit Two?"

Pig Sty was all in their business.

"Fuck that nigga," Shawn sharply replied feeling ill due to Convict Jones knocking him out.

"You don't even know what the beef is about?" he asked a question, trying to get him to answer then continued all in the same statement. "And you rushing up into shit and don't know what's going on."

He started giggling because he knew he was getting to Shawn.

"Don't make no difference. Fuck that bitch ass nigga. He's a dead man walking."

He was clearly informing Pig Sty that they were going to kill Convict Jones.

Shawn then began thinking about why was Pig Sty asking so many questions about something that he did not have nothing to do with.

"However, you feel partner."

"I'm not your partner first off, and why the fuck you asking all these motherfucking questions. You done turned police or something?" Shawn spat back with rage, offending Pig Sty's gangsta status.

"You getting beside yourself, youngin'. Hold your dick sucker with that police shit, bitch," Pig Sty replied disrespectfully because really that was all he wanted to do in the first place.

He wanted to set it off.

"Fuck you, nigga!" Shawn shouted, looking him up and down.

"No, fuck you nigga. You'll get lesser dick bitch."

Pig Sty's eyes got big as his blood began to pump.

"What's up then, nigga?" Shawn asked, feeling he had to get some redress off someone due to getting knocked out earlier.

Enough said, and Pig Sty set it off with a sucker punch to Shawn's mouth, reopening the stitches of his split upper lip. Immediately after that Pig Sty went up under him and dumped Shawn on his neck and head.

"Uhhhhhhhh!" Shawn grunted upon making contact with the hard brick floor.

Pig Sty began stomping and kicking Shawn, busting his eye back open and breaking his nose. The other prisoners that were playing cards with Shawn began to grab Pig Sty and break up the fight. Shawn attempted to get off the ground, only to fall back down due to that fact that he was dazed. Once he did get off the ground, he slowly walked to the door with blood running from his mouth, nose, and eye.

Shawn turned around, looked Pig Sty in the eye, and said, "I got your number, nigga."

Pig Sty replied to the threat by pulling out two shanks and running at Shawn, who took off running in the other direction. Once Shawn had gotten away by running to the prison guard area, Pig Sty disappeared into the crowd of prisoners and left O-Dog and his crew's unit.

CHAPTER 37

Debra Butler walked to her dark blue BMW, got in, and pulled off. She had to be at the courthouse for a guilty plea agreement. She had informed her client that if he took it to trial she would beat it. However, because her client was familiar with the legal justice system her client took the seven years non-violent rather than to risk catching fifteen years violent. Debra pulled up to the courthouse, grabbed her briefcase, and exited the vehicle. Once she got in the courthouse, she went to courtroom three. Upon entering the courtroom, the States attorney was sitting at the table talking to her client. She walked up and intervened.

"What I tell you about talking to him. I am your attorney, and I'll do all the talking for you. You paid me to do a job, and I will do my job to the best of my ability."

She stared in her client's eyes as he dropped his head.

"Ms. Butler, we were just going over the plea agreement," the solicitor replied.

"I tell you what. We decided to go to trial because you and I both know that you have nothing. The evidence is weak, and furthermore, second hand, not to mention coercive."

She began to get loud, and started gaining the attention of the trial judge.

"Calm down, Ms. Butler. Look," the solicitor stated and looked around to make sure nobody was watching or listening to what they were saying, "I decided that we will cut the seven year plea agreement to two years suspended and six month's probation. Will you agree to those stipulations?"

He knew that he did not have a case, but he needed a conviction.

"I don't know. Let me talk to my client."

Debra and her client stepped to the side and immediately came to the conclusion to accept the plea agreement. Actually, that was all Debra wanted in the first place. She knew that the solicitor didn't have a case, and he knew she knew, so she used that to her advantage to get her client the lowest time she could get him. Debra and her client went back to the solicitor then immediately before the judge and accepted the plea. Debra rushed out of the courthouse and back to her vehicle so that she could get to a meeting she had with another client.

At the same time that Pig Sty was kicking Shawn's ass, across the yard in the multipurpose building, O-Dog, Dirty Dee, and three other prisoners who were down with O-Dog were in a cipher discussing their plan of attack. From the bleachers in the multipurpose building, O-Dog and his crew were being watched by Rodney and Black Nuk.

"What you think they talking about?" Rodney asked, keeping his eyes on their every move.

"You know what time it is. We need to warn Dyson," Black Nuk replied as both prisoners stood to their feet.

As O-Dog and his crew held their meeting, Shawn came running into the multipurpose building and busting through the cipher. Shawn said a couple of words, and O-Dog and his team immediately took off running out the door. The entire time Black Nuk and Rodney watched, and immediately followed behind them. Black Nuk and Rodney headed to Unit Two where Convict Jones lived and O-Dog and his crew went to their unit to get their weapons. When Black Nuk and Rodney got to Convict Jones' cell they found Pig Sty was also there informing Convict Jones about what went down between him and Shawn.

"That nigga luck bad as a motherfucker," Rodney stated, laughing.

Black Nuk added, "Two ass cuttings in one day, damn!"

All of them began to laugh.

Rodney and Black Nuk then informed Pig Sty and Convict Jones what they had seen. They also stated that they believed O-Dog and his crew were going to get strapped up, and what was once a three-man team turned into a six man team.

"They will be over here in a minute," Rodney stated, looking out the window of Convict Jones' cell.

"Everybody got their shit with them?" Convict Jones asked as he pulled out the two rubber grip icepicks.

"Never leave home without it," Pig Sty replied also pulling out two blades.

"Okay, let's go smash these young ass niggas," Convict Jones stated while gritting his teeth.

As the four convicts came out of Convict Jones' cell, there stood O-Dog with his six-man crew all strapped with knives. Convict Jones and his crew were outnumbered six to four.

Out of nowhere a large image appeared with a deep heavy voice stating, "Hold up, O-Dog! It's not going down like that!"

He was standing with a sock with two cans of Jack Mack in them.

"Johnson!" Agent Williams shouted. "Come look at this."

He showed him a fax sheet.

"Hmmm, it looks and sounds like the work of Casper doesn't it?" Agent Johnson replied, staring at the sheet of paper that was just faxed from their subdivision office.

At the same time the agents were reviewing the report, Rico a.k.a. Casper was leaving out of his hiding spot three blocks away from the federal building going to the cocktail lounge to meet Major Riley.

"I believe we need to check out another one of them cocktail lounges. We might get lucky, and catch this son of a bitch," Agent Johnson informed his partner, standing up from a desk.

"I'm game," Agent Williams replied.

The two agents busted out laughing and left the federal building heading to the cocktail lounge on the other side of town.

CHAPTER 38

Major Riley sat in his Ford pickup truck between two other trucks, watching the parking lot of the cocktail lounge. He noticed a money green 5.0 whip in the parking lot. Major Riley squinted his eyes as the vehicle parked and the car door opened. He watched Rico get out of the vehicle.

"Gotcha you son of a bitch," he said, cocking his .38 bulldog special handgun and placing it into his jacket coat.

Major Riley slowly opened the door as he watched Rico walk towards the cocktail lounge. When Rico entered the cocktail lounge, Major Riley walked over to Rico's vehicle, opened the door, and got in. After ten minutes, Rico returned to his vehicle thinking that Major Riley had stood him up. He had already promised himself that on eye contact he would blast Major Riley for standing him up.

As Rico walked to his car, he noticed a dark blue Range Rover pulling into the parking lot as well. As he watched the vehicle, he noticed a familiar face. It was one of the agents he had seen at the Motel 6 and he would bet bottom dollar that the other agent was on the other side of the vehicle. The two agents did not see Rico because he began moving up beside different vehicles, staying out of their sight. Paying little attention to his vehicle, Rico ran and jumped into his car.

Once he closed the door and started the car, Major Riley who occupied the backseat stuck the .38 special to Rico's head, and said, "Don't try nothing stupid boy."

He shoved the pistol hard into the back of Rico's neck.

Rico began laughing, not because he didn't take the situation seriously, but because he couldn't believe he let the old man catch him slipping.

Rico then said, "You got my money, nigga?"

Rico was asking questions while looking through the rearview mirror.

The two agents then walked past the vehicle that Major Riley and Rico were sitting in, but did not pay attention.

"I should turn your ass in to the police," Major Riley informed Rico, laughing. "Get the reward money."

Rico looked at Major Riley through the rearview mirror hard as if he was talking in a different language.

"I don't have time for this bullshit. Where the fuck is my money, nigga."

Rico blew out a sigh of breath, tired of the bullshit.

"I'm not giving you shit, young punk. You better worry about what's about to happen to your ass. Now start the fucking car!" Major Riley demanded, having the upper hand on Rico.

Inside the cocktail lounge, Agent Williams and Agent Johnson stood at the bar talking with the bartender. Agent Johnson then went into his jacket pocket and produced a picture along with his badge and slapped it down on the bar counter.

"Have you seen this guy?" Agent Johnson asked as Agent Williams looked around the premises.

"He was just in here," the bartender stated.

Agent Johnson immediately turned around and began looking.

"Where did he go?" Agent Johnson asked the bartender.

"He walked out the door a couple of seconds before you two walked in," the bartender replied, pointing at the front door.

The two agents immediately took off running towards the front door. Once outside the lounge, the two agents began looking for Rico.

"You see him?" Agent Williams asked.

"Go that way, and I'll go this way," Agent Johnson ordered, tasting victory in his mouth.

Rico was just backing out of the parking space that he occupied when Agent Williams spotted the car.

"There he goes right there!" Agent Williams yelled to Agent Johnson, pointing at the car.

The two agents ran towards the car, drawing their weapons. The agents wanted to take Rico in alive, but they had no problem bringing him in dead. For a brief second, going towards Rico's vehicle, sliding through different vehicles in the parking lot to surround the car, the agents lost view of the vehicle for eight seconds at the most.

Once they surrounded the vehicle, Agent Williams shouted with his gun drawn, "Stop the car now!"

He was pointing his gun at the windshield, ready to unload his entire clip.

Agent Johnson slid up from the other side of the car, also with his gun drawn and aimed ready to fire. The car stopped immediately.

"Take the keys out of the ignition and toss them out the window," Agent Williams demanded then continued, "Take your right hand and open the car door from the outside."

The driver followed the instructions.

Once the car door opened, they immediately closed in on the vehicle as a figure began stepping out of the car. The two agents grabbed the driver and slammed him down hard on the gravel.

"What the fuck is wrong with you people?" Major Riley yelled with his South Carolina Department of Corrections uniform on, looking up at the federal agents.

"This is not him!" Agent Johnson yelled, looking around the parking lot. "Where did he go?"

They were both surprised that it was not Casper.

"He was in this car! Where did he go? I saw him!" Agent Williams yelled to no one in particular.

"Who are you talking about?" Major Riley stated from the ground.

The two agents looked around dumbfounded as Rico pulled out of the parking lot in Major Riley's Ford truck.

CHAPTER 39

There he stood, two hundred and seventy pounds solid with two cans of Jack Mack in a sock.

"What's up, nigga?" O-Dog shouted as if he knew Black Nuk was calling.

From the blindside, Dirty Dee caught a right hook from Black Nuk, and was knocked out cold. The blow immediately broke his jaw because Black Nuk also had a heavy object in his hand. This blow also set off a mini-war. A mini-war that after ten minutes of straight brawling resulted in busted lips, heads, and noses, and a couple of stabbings. Convict Jones was cut on the wrist, while trying to disarm one of O-Dog's crewmembers, blocking a swinging blade intended for his gut to cause internal bleeding. O-Dog had been stabbed twice, once in the ribs and the other in the shoulder. Dirty Dee lay knocked out, while Rodney and Pig Sty tried to stomp and kick him into a coma. Another one of O-Dog's crewmembers stabbed Big Bo six times before Rodney left Pig Sty to go assist Big Bo. Big Bo and Rodney cornered the member of O-Dog's crew, which also resulted in him being stabbed twelve times.

O-Dog's crew was rumored to have received wounds, but they all departed from the mini-war when shit got hot. Pig Sty was drenched in blood with a stab wound in the back and a broken nose. His head was also busted. Black Nuk was later seen laughing with two black eyes, which you could barely tell due to how black he was but the missing tooth was another story.

It took no time for the prison guards to show up on the scene. There were twenty-three prison guards in all. They all were in riot gear with mase canisters and billy clubs. Everybody with wounds or blood on them was immediately handcuffed and taken to lockup. Even prisoners that were not involved, which had blood on them went to lockup. They were ready to snitch to save their own ass.

"I am going to tell him just give me some more time!" Kemmiko yelled at Tyrone.

"You been saying that for the last year," Tyrone snapped back and continued. "I take care of you. I pay these bills. That nigga ain't here for you. More than likely he don't give a flying fuck about you because if he did he wouldn't be in prison," Tyrone spat. "Soon as he gets out he won't even come this way, and you sitting up here sending him all that damn money."

He told her as he was walking into another room of the house.

"Where you going?" Kemmiko asked Tyrone. Tyrone refused to reply, therefore Kemmiko feeling insecure yelled, "I'm getting ready to write the letter right now!"

She pulled out a pen and pad and wrote the letter. When she finished writing the letter, she gave it to Tyrone and informed him to mail it for her. Tyrone walked out the door with the letter, leaving Kemmiko alone thinking about what she was doing. She then began cursing and talking to herself.

"He's got to understand that I am out here by myself. I'm tired of waiting. I've been waiting on him for the last umpteenth years. Shit!"

She began crying, but quickly wiped the tears away. She reached over and grabbed the crack pipe that Tyrone introduced her to. She then picked up a piece of crack, placed it on the pipe, and smoked it. Blowing out the smoke and now high, she forgot all about what she was doing to Convict Jones or what Convict Jones had done for her. Convict Jones no longer existed in her mind and heart.

Imprisonment by whatever name it is called is a harsh thing and the discipline that must be exercised over human beings in close confinement can never be wholly agreeable to those subjected to it. When an attempt is made to hide the harsh reality of criminal justice behind euphemistic descriptions a corrupting irony may be introduced into ordinary speed that is fully as frightening as Orwell's Newpeak.

Prison is a complex of physical arrangement and measures, all wholly governmental; all wholly performed by agents of government, which determines the total existence of certain human beings except perhaps in the realms of the spirit and inevitably there as well. From sunup to sundown, sleeping, waking, speaking, working, playing, viewing, eating, voiding, vending, along, with others, it is not so with members of the general adult populations to rise at a certain hour, retire at a certain hour, eat at a certain hour, live for a period with no companionship whatsoever, wear certain clothing, or submit to oral and anal searches after or before visiting hours, nor have state governments undertaken steps to prohibit numbers of the general adult population from speaking to one another, wearing beads, embracing their spouses or corresponding with their lovers.

However, prisoners are people whom most of us would rather not think about, banished from everyday sight. They exist in a shadow world that only dimly enters our awareness. They are members of a *total institution* that controls their daily existence in a way that few of us can imagine.

CHAPTER 40

Convict Jones was once again on lockup for the fight with O-Dog and his crew. While on lockup for the second day, you could hear several prisoners dry snitching, yelling to see the Major in an attempt to tell something they saw in order to be released back to prison population. While Convict Jones was washing his face, a prison guard came by and slid a letter under his cell door. Convict Jones picked up the letter and smiled when he saw his fiancée's name. This was his relief. He opened the letter and began reading:

Hello baby,
You've been on my mind for a while now, just haven't took time to write you besides the other day to tell you how much I love you and miss you. I've been having some dreams about you lately. Nothing bad, just wondering where they are coming from. Went to court on the 2nd of February. Stayed all day and didn't get seen, but me, Cheko, Mechiko, and Ms. Ann, this lady I live with, we tripped out. You

know Cheko been out of work about three months. It's her eyesight. She can't see too good out of her one eye. She can't drive or go anywhere by herself. Supposed to go back to court in three weeks. Judge Miller is cool. He gave nobody time and the ones that were in jail he let them out. He's really nice. I think every things cool. All I want is a fine. No probation, but I'll take it if I have to. Hopefully it gets thrown out. I'll send you something on my birthday. Not putting anything in anyone else's name. I'm getting ¹a card and sending it to you 'cause it makes me think crazy and from me not hearing from you is making me think somebody has moved in my place. Have they? No matter what, I own you, your mine, seriously. My sim card in my phone is no good so my phone isn't working. I'm trying to get another service so that you can call me. Give me a minute. Sorry can't send you money like I used too. It's all my fault, but after this year things will be better. I'm taking my time. Jerry moved into a motel with his girlfriend. Him and my friend Tyrone can't get along. They don't want me talking to each of them. You probably don't remember Tyrone. Before all this happened with me he used to be over at the house, then he went to do fed time for two years. You've talked to him on the phone before. He's real good people. No, nothing has happened between us, but he did tell me that if you didn't act right when you came home that I was gonna be his lady. He said right now he's giving you respect. Now that's a real man. He don't try anything. He's 52 and he's cool. I wanna see you Dyson, and I wonder are we gonna make it. I really and truly hope so, if God's willing. Well, I'll write you Thursday night. I love you and can't wait 'til you get home. Got to go to the doctor on my birthday.

I'll be 50 years old. Can you believe it? I feel good, baby. Feels like I'm 35, and it's a blessing to me. I thank God after all I been through. I know you're disappointed in me, but I'm coming around slowly, but it's happening. I'll be right when you come home. Jerry got a 2000 black Cadillac. He's gonna take me out to eat on my birthday. Him and his girl Kesha then Tyrone, me, and Ann going out to eat Friday or Saturday. Mechiko is baking me a cake. All I want to be is loved, and I am very thankful. Send me some love Dyson. Real love, damn I miss you and I want you. Are you mine? I'm all yours.

Love your Kemmiko

Convict Jones placed the letter down on the bed beside him. The last two letters clearly told him what was going on. The broken communication between Convict Jones and Kemmiko was becoming the cause for their separation. First, the visitation privileges were suspended indefinitely, and then the phone calls were cut off. Convict Jones had heard from Kemmiko herself as well as people in the streets, that she was on drugs bad and losing everything that the both of them worked for. The love Convict Jones had for Kemmiko would not allow him to accept the fact that the love of his life was in darkness, and that she could do no wrong. Convict Jones would say to himself, *She'll get back.*

Convict Jones got up from the bed, lifted the mat, and began writing a letter back to her hoping that she would be able to overcome any and all things. Convict Jones wrote the following letter, at the same time trying to stay focused on when the next attack may come.

My dearest Kemmiko,

It is very important for me to express to you how much you really mean to me. I wish I could do this in person, while holding you in my arms and gazing into your lovely eyes. Since we are physically separated by miles of emptiness, this expression must come in the form of a letter such as this.

Kemmiko, I know it is difficult for you, as it is for me, to be separated for so long. Hold on baby, and be strong. I am on my way home. Life seems to be full of trials of this type, which test our inner strength, and more importantly, our devotion and love for one another. After all, it is said that true love is boundless and immeasurable and overcomes all forms of adversity. In truth, if it is genuine, it will grow stronger with each assault upon its existence.

Kemmiko, our love has been assaulted many times before. Talking about my partner Timmy and all those other guys you seeked to find love from, but was to no avail, because I am the only one for you. Therefore, I am convinced that our love is true, because I am the only one for you. Therefore, I am convinced that our love is true, because the longer I am away from you, the greater is my yearning to be with you again. You are my princess, and I am your devoted prince.

I cherished any thought of you, prize any memory of you which arises from the depth of my mind and live for the day when our physical separation will no longer be.

Until that moment arrives, I send to you across the many empty miles, my tender love, my warm embrace, and my most passionate kiss. I love you always and forever.

NTP OG Dyson

CHAPTER 41

The next day two prison guards came to Convict Jones' cell at approximately two o'clock in the morning. Convict Jones was immediately awakened by the prison guard's keys banging against the cell bars.

"Jones?" one of the prison guards yelled.

"Yeah."

He was paying close attention to their movements.

"Get dressed. You going to medical for a checkup," the guard replied.

Convict Jones immediately knew that some shit was going down because not one prisoner on the compound would go to medical at two o'clock in the morning. The prison officials escorted Convict Jones past medical and the multipurpose building. Walking into the gym area of the multipurpose building, Convict Jones was informed to walk to the middle of the basketball court where a figure stood. Convict Jones could not identify the figure because it was dark in the gym. As Convict Jones approached the middle of the floor, he recognized it to be Major Riley. Major Riley stood there working out with long tight spandex jogging pants on. He also had on a Golds Gym tank top.

"Inmate Jones, did I not tell you that I would give you enough rope to hang yourself? And what do you do, go acting like Tarzan, or should I say George of the Jungle, because you crashed right into a tree," Major Riley said with a laugh, and then began doing crunches.

"Sir, I say this with the utmost respect. What is going on?" he was really wanting to know because he had no idea what the beef was about.

"Inmate, you cannot be that damn stupid, or maybe you are. You know what goes around also comes around. If you live by the gun, you sure as hell will die by the gun, just like your partner Reginald Harris," Major Riley stated as if he was teaching a class.

Reginald Harris was a name that Convict Jones had heard, but he couldn't remember where he had heard the name. The name rung bells like church was beginning to start service on an early Sunday morning. Reginald Harris was an inmate who had got murdered or overkilled is how the newspaper reported the slaughter. It was one year prior to Convict Jones' arrival at Evans that Reginald Harris was killed by several prison guards from Evans Correctional Institution. Reginald Harris's death was known statewide, as well as being discussed in surrounding states, for instance, North Carolina, Georgia, and even Florida. The newspaper talked about Reginald Harris' murder for over six months. The prison officials involved in the incident said that Reginald Harris tried to escape. He was later caught in a wooded area miles away from the prison. Prison guards said that he had obtained a gun and knife from somewhere. The prison officials, who were well over ten guards, said that they had to defend themselves and the people surrounding the area from Reginald Harris. Reginald Harris was first beat to death, and then shot with over twenty bullets.

Although, Convict Jones remembered the name Reginald Harris, he had no idea that Reginald Harris was Rent, his codefendant. Convict Jones thoughts were then interrupted by a loud shout.

"Do you understand, boy!" Major Riley yelled.

"I didn't get the last thing you said, sir," Convict Jones replied, not knowing what he said.

"Yeah, you are one stupid son of a bitch," Major Riley replied, looking at the doorway of the gym.

"What is this all about?" Convict Jones asked, getting frustrated with all the bullshit from Major Riley.

Major Riley just began laughing, and stated, "You will find out soon enough. Hopefully, you'll get to live to tell about it."

He was snarling and glaring down on Convict Jones with sweat dripping off his body from his workout.

Convict Jones then noticed two figures out of the corner of his eyes standing over by the back entrance of the gym. Shawn and O-Dog appeared out of the darkness with arm braces and slings holding their arms in place. You could see that Shawn was really messed up because he could barely walk. His face looked like it belonged to someone else.

"Inmate Jones, I would like you to meet Shawn and Terry Johnson, in which you know as O-Dog and Shawn," he said while laughing like Convict Jones didn't see this coming. "Ever since I lost my wife, Mechelle, I and my stepson Terry here have made a pact to never rest until we put the killer to death."

Tears were now running down Major Riley's eyes.

"Well, what the fuck do I have to do with that, Major?" Convict Jones spat back.

"As I said inmate, what you put out there in the universe is what you get back. However, because I got some important business to attend to this morning, you get to live another day and breath another night," Major Riley stated while O-Dog, Shawn, and him turned around and left the gym.

Convict Jones was then rushed, provided a couple cheap blows, and taken back to lockup.

Rico sat in his hideout thinking about the meeting between him and Major Riley. He then thought about the federal agents who also showed up at the cocktail lounge.

"I wonder if that old motherfucker was trying to set me up." Rico asked himself, thinking about Major Riley.

Rico immediately erased that thought because if it wasn't for Major Riley allowing Rico to use his truck then he may have gotten jammed up in the lounge parking lot.

"Why would he let me use his truck to get away, when he had a gun on me? Plus, owe me money," Rico racked his brain with questions.

Unable to come to a conclusion about Major Riley's motives, Rico went back to cleaning his weapon. As Rico cleaned his weapons, his mind drifted back to three years earlier when he faked his death. He was in Tampa Bay, Florida at the time. It was warm as usual. Rico stood on the beachfront with a dark Cuban guy named Joe.

Joe was a drug lord who owed Rico a favor for a hit Rico pulled for him. The reason Rico faked his death was because the federal government was on his ass. At that time, Rico went by the name of Chris Taylor who earned the name *Nightmare*. Snapping back out of his daydream due to a fly landing on his arm, Rico placed the Mini Mack-11 down on the desk and stood to his feet. He walked over to the wall beside the safe, pressed in a six-digit code, and a silent alarm was turned on. He then pressed another four-digit code in and laser beams ran across the bottom of all the doors in the building.

Rico then locked the door where he had placed his dogs prior to setting the alarms. He grabbed his .45 Magnum with the silencer and injected a clip into it. He then walked over to his futon, lied down, and drifted off to sleep with one eye open.

CHAPTER 42

Convict Jones was released from lockup two weeks later on a Friday. He was sent back to Unit Two but in a different cell. When Convict Jones entered the unit silence filled the air. Mo looked up and walked over to Convict Jones.

"What's up, partner?"

"Shit, ain't nothing happening," Convict Jones replied, watching his surroundings and watching Smith's cell.

"Your old room dog been running around smoking weed with everybody, and talking about getting transferred," Mo stated while looking Convict Jones in the eyes.

"Where is he at right now?" Convict Jones asked, walking off towards Smith's cell as Mo followed.

"He around here somewhere," Mo stated with a serious look on his face.

For two weeks Smith had been smoking and selling Convict Jones' marijuana. Mo was tight about the ordeal because Smith did not give anything to him. Smith looked out for all his homeboys and everybody else, except Mo. Mo was heated about that and wanted Convict Jones to beat Smith's ass. Convict Jones approached Smith's cell. Smith was standing with his back to the door, not paying attention to his surroundings. For all he knew, Convict Jones could have been the police rolling on his ass. Convict Jones opened the door and stepped into the cell. Smith turned halfway around with his hands in his pants, fumbling around with something. Smith looked at Convict Jones and his eyes got big as golf balls.

"Whhhat's shaken, roomey?" he asked stuttering.

"Nothing much. You?" Convict Jones dryly asked and continued by asking, "Where is my shit at?"

He moved in closer to him as Mo blocked any room for escape.

"Hold up ddddice. Calm down, baby. I got you right here, man," Smith replied with fear coming out of his voice as he moved closer to the wall.

Smith began pulling money and marijuana out of his pants. He then went to his locker, opened it, and pulled more money out.

"Here's one hundred and fifty dollars right here," Smith stated, handing Convict Jones the money. "And here is ten bags of weed. I'll send the rest of the money to your account, and write you a hundred dollar list for the canteen," Smith stated also opening his locker and handing Convict Jones three boxes of black and mild cigars.

"Boy, I don't know why you went through my shit!" Convict Jones yelled, thinking about doubling up the payment on him just because he did something that he was not supposed to do. "All I asked you to do is hold it nigga."

Convict Jones was faking like he was mad, but he was actually relieved to know that Smith did get some money with it because he had took it as a loss.

If it wasn't for Major Riley and O-Dog and his crew plotting to take his life, Convict Jones would more than likely still be on lockup. Convict Jones now knew that in order for Major Riley to have him killed it had to be done on the yard and by a prisoner because Major Riley couldn't afford for it to get back to the head office in Columbia or to the federal government.

Convict Jones immediately stated to himself after taking in all the facts and concerns to Major Riley, "Rule two, always put protection around yourself."

He started thinking that he had to get to the phone and call Kemmiko so that she can contact some people he knew.

"Man, I could not hold that shit in here like that. Plus, I thought you had been shipped to another Institution so I did what I had to do and what anybody else would have done and got my hustle on."

Smith looked Convict Jones eye-to-eye like a man, which Convict Jones couldn't do anything but respect it.

"You good, dawg," Convict Jones informed him while Mo got a smirk on his face. "Just have me fifty dollars canteen store day, and you keep the other fifty dollars worth of canteen," Convict Jones stated as he was counting money in his head.

"Boy, you a real nigga," Smith stated, excitedly giving Convict Jones a pound.

"Yeah, that's only because I am looking out for you."

Knowing that Smith looked out for him, he felt it only right to pay him for his worth.

Convict Jones then asked Smith did he have some cigars. Smith reached into his locker and pulled out two cigars.

"I need three of them," Convict Jones informed Smith as he got another cigar out his locker. "Everybody roll their own troubles," Convict Jones stated with a laugh as he gave Mo and Smith three bags a piece.

The three prisoners sat around and smoked their blunts to the head. Five minutes later, Mo, Smith, and Convict Jones were high as ten bags of jelly donuts in *Krispy Kream* on the top shelf. Convict Jones and Mo left Smith in his cell. As Convict Jones and Mo walked to the middle of the rock area, Willie Ham appeared out of nowhere. He informed Convict Jones that he had just seen O-Dog and Shawn coming down from lockup. Actually, O-Dog and Shawn were not even on the compound, when everybody thought they were in lockup. Shawn and O-Dog were at Major Riley's house living it up, but only to return to prison to serve the rest of their time.

Convict Jones rearranged the two rusty icepicks around in his pants, which were replacements for the rubber grip icepicks he lost in the mini-war. He then proceeded to the phone to get some protection around himself. Once at the phone, Convict Jones dialed Kemmiko's number. The phone rung three times before a male voice answered.

"Hello."

"Who the fuck is this?" Convict Jones shouted into the phone.

Convict Jones could hear the male figure giving Kemmiko the phone.

"Hello," she answered.

"Who the fuck was that?"

"Look, don't be calling here asking all them damn questions," Kemmiko stated, sucking her teeth and blowing out her breath.

"Who you talking to like that?" Convict Jones asked, not believing she was going off on him like that.

"I don't have time for this," she dryly stated, blowing out her breath.

Silence filled the phone conversation, except for the voice of the guy in the background of the phone call. Convict Jones immediately knew that Kemmiko had jumped ship. He could not save her and himself at the same time. He figured self-preservation is the best preservation. Convict Jones got himself together and spoke back into the receiver.

"You must be having a bad day. I'll talk to you later," Convict Jones spoke softly.

"Whatever," Kemmiko replied, hanging the phone up, leaving Convict Jones looking at the receiver.

Convict Jones left the phone hanging from the wall as he headed to Mo's cell. Approaching Mo's cell, he saw the old timer that was up by the medical facility who seemed to always say or do something crazy. Convict Jones also realized that this old man was in some way related to everything that had been going down. Convict Jones' concerns with the matter were whether the old timer was for him or against him. At present, Convict Jones couldn't trust anyone but Allah. Convict Jones approached the old timer.

"What's shaken, pop's?" he asked.

"What's going little Mike Jones," the old timer replied whose name was David Bell.

Convict Jones just looked at the old timer, wondering where he knew that name from. Convict Jones knew then that he had to be very careful. Someone was too deep in his life, and he did not like it one bit.

"You know me from somewhere?" he asked speaking directly to the old timer.

"I know everybody youngblood and especially you. I used to change your diapers when you were a young whipper snapper in Harlem," the old timer stated, smiling ear-to-ear.

The old timer had to be at least twenty-five years older than Convict Jones, and he looked kind of familiar. Convict Jones stared at him, but he couldn't place where he'd seen the face at. He needed a name to go with the face.

"Hold up old man. Who the fuck are you?" Convict Jones asked, getting tired of the small talk.

"A good friend of you father and now a good friend of yours. My name is David Bell."

CHAPTER 43

David Bell was not an unfamiliar name to Convict Jones. In fact, at one time, in Convict Jones' household the name David Bell was mentioned more than Jesus' name was mentioned in a Christian household. David and Convict Jones' father were like brothers, even though Convict Jones' father, whose name was Mike, was ten years David's senior. Mike had taught David damn near everything he knew about the game when David arrived in Harlem, New York back in the early sixties. David was loyal to Mike and missed Mike just as much as Convict Jones did since Mike passed away some years back.

The word throughout the East coast was that David was gangster as well as a killer. In the early eighties, David had caught a prison sentence for five counts of conspiracy to commit murder and drug trafficking. Mike informed his son that David had taken a plea to fifty years to save the entire family from going to prison. That was David's contribution to the family's survival. In turn, David was taking care of for years by Mike. Convict Jones remembered Mike sending David a hundred to two hundred dollars every other week, even though the agreement was to give David Bell one hundred dollars a month. That was despite the fact that he was given thirty grand when he started his prison sentence, coupled by the fact that David's immediate family would also be taken care of. On birthdays and holidays, David's children received presents and money from Mike. Mike loved David with all his heart and David felt the same way.

"I know you man. What's up, unc?" Convict Jones stated, smiling ear-to-ear and knowing he had a real brother in his corner who would do him no harm.

"I'm sure you do," he replied also smiling.

As both men stared at each other, tears formed in their eyes.

"You look just like your father," David informed Convict Jones.

"Yeah, I miss him too," Convict Jones replied, already knowing David's thoughts.

"Listen," David stated, grabbing Convict Jones attention, "we need to talk."

"Yeah, I'm pretty sure we do. With all this shit going on around here, I don't know what's going on," Convict Jones said, meaning every word.

"You don't know the other half. These are some sick people around here. You have to be very careful when you are in the mouth of the lion with sharp teeth. You got to ease out this motherfucker,"

David dropped the same jewels on Convict Jones that Mike used to drop on Convict Jones and David.

The story that David was about to tell Convict Jones, would not only prove that the world is a small place, but also shocking. As David began telling the story, Convict Jones' thoughts went back to what Major Riley told him.

What you put out there in the universe will always come back, Convict Jones thought of as he tuned back in to what David was telling him.

"Think back to the night of September 17th, 1988, and what you were doing?" David informed and asked all in one statement.

Convict Jones began thinking for a minute, and then said, "That was the night that I got knocked for this time I'm doing right now."

"Good, we are on the right page. Let me tell you what I know," David said before he began providing untold information. "The night of the murders that you now find yourself doing time for, the guy who killed your friends, Robert Bryant and Nick Madderson, was the same guy who killed Stacy Jones. This same guy also killed a woman that night named Mechelle Johnson. That was the woman that got car jacked—"

David was stating when he was cut off by Convict Jones stating, "Yeah, I remember that."

"Well, this guy was named Chris Taylor, better known as Nightmare up and down the East coast. I got knowledge of the cat through investigating Stacy's death. Word was that he was the next me," David stated, laughing then continued. "After further investigation, I found out that this guy, Nightmare had no solid location where he could be caught slipping. First, I heard he was from Atlanta, then I heard he was from Ohio, then I heard he was from South Carolina, and the list goes on-and-on-and-on." David stopped for a second, watched a couple of prisoners walk by, and then continued. "My investigation proved that the guy was on the run from the federal government. The feds were looking to burn his ass. He was labeled number one on the world's most dangerous criminal list, clearly out doing any work I ever put in. This cat was a loose cannon."

"Okay," Convict Jones stated, impatiently listening and wanting to do something about it.

"Listen and pay attention Dyson. This guy got bodies lined up from New York to Florida. As you can see this cat got around."

"What you mean *got around*. Where is he now?" Convict Jones asked, listening closely to David's every word.

"Well, three weeks after the murder of your friends, the woman, and Stacy, my investigation people said that this guy was found in Tampa Bay, Florida with his dick cut off and shoved in his ass. They say a dog dick was also cut off and stuck in his mouth," David said as he started laughing.

"What he do, snitch?"

"The word on the street was that Nightmare, as they called him, tried some fuck shit with some Cubans from across the waters. It was said that these Cubans were responsible for the majority of the cocaine coming into Florida. It was also said that Chris had robbed one of the Cubans and pistol-whipped him within inches of his life. Chris had come off with over three hundred thousand dollars and several bricks of raw cocaine. Instead of Nightmare leaving town immediately, his balls got too big, and he went to the bottom of Miami, Florida and set up shot selling bricks for the low-low. The Cubans found it to not only be disrespectful but also a challenge. They say the following week, Chris' motel door got kicked in by three Cubans. A motel clerk who was present and also disappeared after the incident informed the police that he saw a man, which was Chris, screaming while being dragged by his feet to the trunk of a brown 500 Benz. Chris' body was found in Atlanta three days later in the front yard of his people's house," David stated, looking around as several prisoners walked in a straight line to the cafeteria.

"That's all good, but what does this have to do with me?" Convict Jones asked, not connecting the dots.

"You still don't see what's going on? Let me explain in detail what you have to do with this," David said as he sat down, getting comfortable on a brick wall. "The night of your crime a lot of people got killed, and you and your boy Reginald Harris whom became indirectly involved just like you, some people want to hold you responsible for those death, even though neither one of you fired a shot."

"What does this cat Reginald Harris got to do with me, and who is he?" Convict Jones asked because over the years he left the past in the past in order to move on with his life.

"Little Mike Reginald Harris is your boy Rent," David informed Convict Jones flat out.

Convict Jones' mouth dropped to the floor in surprise as his brain began working.

David then said, "That night that Nightmare killed that woman Mechelle Johnson for no reason at all in front of her ten year old son whose name was Terry, she was getting ready to get married to a man named Joe Major Riley." David was talking as Convict Jones' brain turned at an alarming pace. "Joe Major Riley is the Major and Terry Johnson is known as O-Dog," David finished and wrapped it up in one big nutshell.

"Oh shit!" That was all Convict Jones could say as he visualized the little boy's face on that night. He whispered to himself, "O-Dog."

CHAPTER 44

David watched Convict Jones as he took in all the information.

"Yeah, I know," David said, smiling like a Cheshire cat.

All the bullshit that Convict Jones had been going through for the last two months had come to a close. Everything began to make sense.

"David," Convict Jones stated, "if they know that I or Rent didn't kill this woman named Mechelle then why did they kill Rent, and why do they want to kill me?" Convict Jones asked logical questions.

"Because Rent lied on you and said that you were the trigger man, which Major Riley knew was a lie. Rent begged for his life before they killed him, and none of the truth made any difference to Major Riley. He was on some military M.P. law type shit, feeling like the hands of one are the hands of all, and they consider your hands involved in this mess," David informed Convict Jones with a serious face.

Convict Jones took all the information in, but something was missing. He had to get to the bottom of this ordeal. First, he had to get protection around himself, and then he had to go to Jummah to meet a friend.

"Hey David, I got to go sort something out. I will talk with you later," Convict Jones told him as he was looking around and checking his surroundings.

"Yeah, little Mike. Be careful and keep your eyes open at all times," David stated, turning on his heel, walking off, and disappearing into the cafeteria.

Convict Jones proceeded back to Unit Two. As soon as he walked into the unit, he headed towards the phones on the wall. He picked up the receiver and dialed Kemmiko's phone number.

The phone rang twice and she answered it, "Hello."

"What's happening, baby?" Convict Jones asked.

Silence filled the phone for a few minutes until Convict Jones said, "What's going on?"

He had the feeling something was wrong.

"Look, I'm not allowed to talk to you anymore," she replied.

"Say what?"

He was shocked that she would even say some shit like that to him.

"I have moved on with my life. I am tired of waiting on you. Please don't call my phone no more," she said, sounding distracted as she spoke.

"Kemmiko, what the fuck are you talking about?" Convict Jones asked, not understanding what she was talking about.

"Leave me alone," she replied and hung the phone up.

Although Convict Jones was hurting bad, there were bigger fish to fry. He had to get protection around himself. Convict Jones began walking back to his cell when he saw Mo. He waved Mo over.

"Check this out. I need to get out on a jack," Convict Jones stated, talking about a cell phone.

"Old dude be renting his cell phone for three dollars for every thirty minutes," Mo informed Convict Jones.

"Canteen or what?"

"Don't make no difference," Mo replied, looking up towards the prisoner's cell.

"Okay, follow me to my cell," Convict Jones stated, walking off as Mo followed.

Once in his cell, Convict Jones pulled twelve dollars out of his locker and gave it to Mo.

Mo took the money to the prisoner with the cell phone and returned in ten minutes with it, and said, "He said you got till twelve o'clock." He looked out the window door, and then said, "I'll stand out here and watch for you while you use it."

Mo stepped out the door.

For the next hour and a half Convict Jones dialed several numbers and talked to several people but was unable to get in contact with the person he was looking for. Just as Convict Jones was about to give up, one of his homies from Brick City, better known as Jesse Jackson Town Homes which everybody knows as Fieldcrest, called him back.

"Yo partner," Bey Bey stated, "I found her on Facebook, son."

"True, what's her information, and do you have a phone number where she could be reached at?" Convict Jones asked, smiling glad that he found her.

"Yeah, I handled that. You got a pen?" Bey Bey asked ready to relay the information.

"Yeah, I'm good."

"The number is eight-six-four-two-three-two-two-five-two-five."

"Thanks homie. I will call you later if I get the chance," Convict Jones stated, watching the phone number.

"Come home nigga. We love and miss you, man," Bey Bey said, allowing Convict Jones to know how he and his wife felt about him.

"Love you too. I'm out."

"NTP for life," Bey Bey said and then ended the conversation.

After Convict Jones hung the phone up, he immediately began dialing the number he got from Bey Bey.

The phone rang twice, and a female voice answered, "Hello."

She sounded sweet like she always did.

"Stephanie!" Convict Jones shouted excitedly.

"Who's this?" she asked, not knowing who was on the other line.

It had been over ten years since the two of them spoke with one another. Stephanie was the mother of his only son. The two of them never got in arguments or anything. It would have seemed that the two of them were meant for one another, but because of Convict Jones' selfish ways back in the days he wanted everything. It didn't matter to him who would get hurt.

"Your baby daddy," Convict Jones replied.

Silence filled the phone because what Convict Jones stated sent thoughts through Stephanie's head, not really knowing who was on the other line due to some crazy shit she did back in her day, when she told another man that her son was his, instead of Convict Jones' son.

"Who?" she asked.

Not having time to play games, Convict Jones stated, "It's Dyson baby."

"Oh my God. My world. Where have you been, baby?" she asked, not knowing that Convict Jones knew she had been married and divorced.

"Right now I need you," Convict Jones informed her in a serious tone, which she knew it was important.

"Anything baby," she replied, not thinking one time to turn him down due to she also contributed to their separation.

Convict Jones informed her of everything that was going on, and how his life was in danger.

"Don't worry, baby. I got some people that can handle it," she informed him, giving him some relief.

"Well, handle that. When I come back from Jummah, I'll call you on the wall phone," Convict Jones informed her.

"True, baby, true," she said, hanging up the phone with Convict Jones on her heart and mind.

Convict Jones looked at his watch and realized that it was time to go to Jummah to meet his friend, but little did he know he was also going to meet Allah.

CHAPTER 45

Convict Jones walked into the Chaplin's office where Jummah was being held. Muslims were everywhere.

"As-salamu Alaikum," one Muslim said to another Muslim named Hakeem.

He returned the greeting saying, "Wa-lakum sadlam and eid Mubarak!"

He was smiling ear-to-ear, while shaking several other Muslim brother's hand as he entered the Chaplin.

Convict Jones walked through the doorway and entered the area where Muslims were sitting on the floor in ranks. Very low whispering could be heard, while other Muslims performed two Rakat prayers. After fifteen minutes, Rafee entered the area and another Muslim stood to his feet and began harmonizing the Adhan. After the Adhan was complete no one was allowed to say a word while Rafee held the Kubar.

"All praise is due to Allah for allowing us to see another Jummah Friday. Everything was created on this day, and everything will also be destroyed on this day," Rafee stated, going in his back pocket for his mini Qu'ran.

Rafee opened the Qu'ran and flipped through a couple of pages then stopped on a Surah and began reading.

"Bish ma la, hear rock man near ra heem," he spoke in Arabic, stating in the name of Allah, the most gracious, the most merciful.

All the Muslims were paying close attention as Rafee looked at each Muslim, and then began reading from the Qu'ran.

"All praise is due to Allah the Lord of the universe; the beneficent; the merciful; Lord of the day of judgment. You alone we worship, and to you alone we turn for help. Guide us to the straight path: the path of those you have blessed; not of those who have incurred your wrath, nor of those who have gone astray."

He was looking at the Muslim community which is called the Umma.

Rafee cleared his throat, and further stated, "We quote this Surah every day, five times a day to be in fact, and sometimes more. Why are we not doing what we are supposed to be doing? You say, in Allah you place your trust, then why do you not trust him. As long as members of this Ummah continue to indulge in the forbidden things contrary to Islam, you will continue to live a life of hardship." His voice getting louder as he continued to say, "There are some who say we believe in Allah and in the last day, yet they are not believers. They seek to deceive Allah and the believers, but they only deceive themselves, thou they do not realize it." Rafee laughed a little, and continued, "Allah is Ackbar. The greatest. Praise and put your Lord before all things, because without your Lord is you're nothing. The prophet Muhammad, peace and blessing be unto him, said worship Allah, and worship him alone without any partners. Allah is one God, and there is none else like him, or behind him, beside him, or in front of him, and Prophet Jesus, Esua. Peace and blessing be unto him as well, clearly told you that our Lord, is one God," Rafee stated when two prison guards stepped into the room and silence filled the air.

"We need to do a recount," one of the guards said as all the prison Muslims and guest began lining up on the wall to be counted.

After the recount, Rafee continued his Kubar until he was finished.

Once the Kubar was over, Rafee came up to Convict Jones, and said, "Here take this and read it."

Rafee walked off smiling.

Convict Jones looked at the object in his hand and saw that it was a small Qu'ran.

Convict Jones then looked up and saw Rafee leaving out the door, and yelled, "Thank you."

Rafee stuck his right thumb up and smiled then kept it moving. Convict Jones then saw the friend he came to see. They held a discussion about his friend buying some marijuana, but for some reason Convict Jones did not feel like indulging. Convict Jones informed his friend that he would get with him later.

As Convict Jones went back to his unit, he couldn't help but feel different. All he could do was think about what Rafee said in the Kubar, and how nothing happens without the approval of Allah.

Convict Jones entered back into his unit and went directly to his cell. Although he was thinking about the word of Allah, he did not slip on thinking about what Major Riley and his boys wanted to do with him. He now knew the real meaning behind the statement that in order to change the conditions of your surroundings, you first had to change the conditions of yourself. Convict Jones planned to do just that, change the conditions of himself, but first he had to put safety around himself.

CHAPTER 46

When Convict Jones made it back to his cell, he sat down on his bunk and began thinking to himself. Convict Jones knew firsthand how it felt to be a victim, and had made a pact with himself some years back that he would never become a victim again. In fact, he told himself that he would be the aggressor in any situation that might occur. Convict Jones stood back up and headed out of Unit Two. A female prison guard tried to get his attention and stop him from leaving the unit, but Convict Jones ignored her. She picked up her radio and called for backup as Convict Jones continued walking, paying her no mind. Several yard officers came running full speed across the yard as if the President of the United States was being murdered. Convict Jones, now in the middle of the yard heading towards operations, was stopped by one of the prison guards. Convict Jones recognized the prison guard as being one of the members of the welcome committee.

"Where is your pass to be on the yard?" the officer asked, moving in close.

By no means was Convict Jones taking another ass kicking by the officer without a fight, and they were going to have to kill him or get killed. Convict Jones was all in. He had too much shit going on in his life. The stress could kill him by itself.

"I have important business with Major Riley," Convict Jones replied, not thinking about what the guard was talking about.

"Return back to your unit!" the guard demanded while two more prison guards came to assist him in restraining Convict Jones.

"That will not do, sir."

"Are you disobeying a direct order, inmate?" the guard shouted, getting mad.

"Whatever you want to call it. This information I have must be given to Major Riley immediately," Convict Jones informed the guard who paid no real attention to what he said.

There was nothing Convict Jones could state to the prison guards to persuade them to allow him to go see Major Riley, in fact, these prison guards had already been informed to keep Convict Jones stationary in one area, and that area was Unit Two.

"Return to your unit, inmate," another demand was given from the guard who now sounded like a robot.

"Fuck that shit!" Convict Jones yelled, ready for whatever.

The prison guards immediately began to pull their mace canisters from their belts and circling Convict Jones. One guard was shaking the canister and released a burst towards Convict Jones' face. However, Convict Jones leaned sideways, dodging the burst. The burst found its way, due to the wind blowing, into one of the prison guard's face. Convict Jones was then rushed and football tackled to the ground. He was beat with walkie-talkies, feet, and fist. Although he tried to fight back, it was to no avail. Convict Jones was then dragged by his feet to the holding cell in operations that was referred to as the *shit hole*. That is where they planned to continue their assault on him without any prisoner being witness.

"Yo Pig Sty, I seen your boy getting dragged by his feet to operations," another prisoner stated, laughing.

"Who you talking about?" Pig Sty asked.

The guy explained who he was talking about, in which Pig Sty knew who he was talking about. Pig Sty then became angry because as the prisoner talked, he kept cracking jokes and laughing about how Convict Jones was being handled by prison guards.

"What you find so funny about that?" Pig Sty asked.

"Shit, the nigga stupid. He keeps fucking with them officers," the prisoner remarked, sounding just like a stagnated house nigga.

"Get the fuck out my face nigga, before I put my dick in your mouth."

Pig Sty blatantly disrespected the prisoner.

The prisoner, just like a bitch, dropped his head to his chest and walked off. Pig Sty immediately sent word to Rodney and Black Nuk. Ten minutes later, Black Nuk and Rodney showed up with more Greenville representers to discuss a plan to get Convict Jones out of the jam he was in.

Stephanie had been calling around, trying to get somebody to listen to her, but everybody was too busy with their own lives to worry about what a prisoner was going through. Stephanie even called the South Carolina Department of Corrections head office, only to be told that they would check into the matter. Nothing seemed sincere to Stephanie. As Stephanie made those phone calls to no avail she began to think about Convict Jones. She wondered how is it that she was still moving on his call, and she had not seen him in over ten years. She had to admit to herself that she truly loved him. She then began thinking about why had she not heard from him in over ten years. The conversation she had with Kemmiko came to mind.

Stephanie then asked herself, "Why would she tell me they were married?" With no answer to the question, she then asked herself, "Where is she at and why isn't doing this leg work for him, if she truly loved him and they were married?"

None of the questions had an answer, but common sense told her that if Convict Jones and Kemmiko were married and she loved him, then she would be doing what she found herself doing.

She knew that something was not right and said to herself, "I got you, baby." Thinking about Convict Jones, she went on to say, "I told you that bitch wasn't shit."

She was talking to herself as she reached to pick up the phone.

Stephanie had one last person to call. She didn't know if the name was right because it had been many years ago. It was a lawyer named Debra Butler. She had actually met Debra through Convict Jones' father one day when she came to Convict Jones' house to drop him off. She was knocking on the door when a blue Benz pulled up in Convict Jones driveway. At the same time Convict Jones' father, Mike, answered the door thinking that it was Debra. Stephanie remembered the day vividly because it was a Thursday, and she had plans on going to a meeting and needed Convict Jones to keep his son.

"Stephanie," Mike said, opening the door.

"Hey," she replied as Debra came walking up the driveway.

"Stephanie, this is Debra. She is a lawyer. If you ever need her services she's good, real good," Mike stated, laughing as Debra and him hugged one another.

"I'll keep that in mind, but I don't think I will ever get in trouble," Stephanie replied, smiling.

"You never know," Debra added to the conversation and continued. "People will do anything, and it might just affect you or this little handsome man right here."

She grab Convict Jones' son and picked him up.

After the introduction between Debra and Stephanie through Convict Jones' father Mike, Stephanie had used Debra in two criminal cases she caught for beating two girls up and a civil matter where Debra got Stephanie a settlement for forty thousand dollars for a slip and fall. Stephanie was brought back to the present where her phone rang and scared her.

"Hello," she answered.

"Is Mark there?" a male voice asked.

"I'm sorry, you have the wrong number."

"Okay, sorry to bother you," the male caller stated and hung up the phone.

Stephanie then dialed Debra Butler, Attorney and Counselor at Law's phone number. The phone rang three times and a female voice answered.

CHAPTER 47

O-Dog sat in his cell staring at the wall. He had already slapped his cellmate and kicked him out of the cell. O-Dog wanted Convict Jones dead. He could taste Convict Jones' blood in his mouth, he wanted him dead so bad. Although O-Dog was banged up with two stab wounds, he was not going to allow that to stand in his way of killing Convict Jones. He promised that the next time he saw Convict Jones, no matter where it was at, he would die by his hands. O-Dog stood to his feet and staggered a little. He then reached down, grabbed the creamer of wine, and turned it up to his lips.

"Ahhhhh!" he grunted after taking a long, big swallow.

Intoxicated, angry, frustrated, mad, and violent all balled up into one was O-Dog. He wanted what he wanted, and murder was the thing he wanted. He walked to his locker, reached in, and grabbed his shank. He put it on his waistline and stepped out of his cell, going to Dirty Dee's cell.

"Hello, *Butler and Associates Law Firm*," a receptionist named Tammy answered the phone.

"May I please speak with Debra? It's very important!" Stephanie yelled into the receiver.

"I'm sorry. She is in a very important meeting at this moment. Would you like to leave a message?" Tammy asked Stephanie. "I'm sure she will return your call."

Stephanie hung the phone up and began thinking how she could get to speak to Debra. She knew that Mike had passed so she couldn't use him.

"Think, Steph, think," she spoke to herself.

Stephanie then called her best friend, Anita. Anita and Convict Jones were originally supposed to hook up, but Stephanie and Convict Jones' attraction to one another was much stronger. Anita saw their attraction for one another and stepped to the side for their happiness. Anita was neither hurt nor upset, frankly because Convict Jones and Anita had just met two days prior at a club.

Anita answered the phone, and said, "Hello."

She sound very sluggish.

"Wake your ass up, girl," Stephanie stated, laughing.

"I'm up," Stephanie said, sitting up on the couch. "What's up, girl?" she asked while yawning.

"I need you to get me in touch with Debra Butler, the attorney. She still doing your lawsuit, right?" Stephanie asked

"Yeah," Anita answered.

"Give me her cellphone number," Stephanie demanded.

"What's going on, and why do you need her cellphone number?" Anita asked as she began getting up off the couch because she was truly concerned about her friend.

"I don't have time to explain right now. I need that cell number,"

She allowed Anita to know that she was serious.

"Damn girl! Let me go get it," Anita stated, sucking her teeth and stomping to her backroom.

Anita returned back to the phone after five minutes had passed.

"Yeah," Anita said into the phone.

"What took you so long? Damn!" Stephanie said impatiently.

"I had to find the number. Slow your roll, girl," Anita stated, laughing. "The number is eight-six-four-two-four-two-four-four-four-four."

"Thank you. I'll call you later," Stephanie replied, hanging up the phone in Anita's ear.

Stephanie immediately dialed Debra's cellphone. The phone rang three times before a female voice answered the phone.

"Hello, who is this calling my phone?" Debra asked, sounding salty.

"Is this Debra Butler?" Stephanie asked.

"Yes, this is Debra. May I help you?" Debra asked, wondering how she got her private cellphone number.

Stephanie explained to Debra the reason for calling her. She informed Debra that it was a life and death situation. She provided Debra with who she was, which Debra began thinking back.

Debra then asked, "Is this Stephanie Adams who used to be my client?"

"Yes."

"How are you doing?" Debra began conversing a little better.

Stephanie cut her off stating, "No disrespect Ms. Butler, but you have to handle this now before they kill him."

"Kill who?"

"Dyson."

"Please tell me you're not talking about Mike Jones' son?" Debra asked, thinking about the man who taught her everything except law.

"Yes," Stephanie said urgently.

Stephanie explained everything that Convict Jones had told her.

Debra then stated, "Okay, I am right on it. I will call you back as soon as I get some information."

"Thank you, Ms. Butler," Stephanie stated as she hung up the phone and waited for Convict Jones to call so she could tell him the good news.

CHAPTER 48

Debra sat at her marble brown desk at the same time Convict Jones' homies were holding a meeting to help him out of the situation he was in. Debra pressed a button on her intercom, Tammy her receptionist, immediately came into her office.

"Yes ma'am."

"Cancel all my meeting for today and get me the phone number to the South Carolina Department of Corrections head office in Columbia," she ordered. As Tammy walked out the door, Debra stopped her in her tracks and gave her another order. "Tammy baby, please get me all information on a one Dyson Michael Jones. He is an inmate at SCDC. His prison number is two-one-five-seven-five-seven."

Tammy pulled out a pen and wrote down everything that Debra requested her to get.

Twenty minutes later, Tammy had all the information that Debra requested.

"Thank you, Tammy. Wouldn't know what to do without you," Debra said as she was taking the information from Tammy.

"No problem at all, boss lady," Tammy replied, smiling.

Debra looked at the information then reached over her desk and picked up the phone.

She dialed the number and the phone rang three times before a female voice answered the phone stating, "Evans Correctional Institution."

Debra Butler was an attorney who had been in the legal field for the last fifteen years. When she first passed the Bar in Greenville, South Carolina, she made a lot of mistakes making a name for herself. For the sake of justice, she had decided that she would try with all her heart to win all of her client's cases, despite what the *good old boy system* wanted her to do. Debra refused to be like all the other attorneys in Greenville who sold their souls, as well as their client's souls, such as attorneys like Dorothy A. Manigault and Theo W. Mitchelle.

Debra won a majority of her post-conviction relief and habeas corpus cases on the state court level. Many of the white men in the thirteenth judicial system wanted her to join them in their good old boy system, but she rejected them, which caused her to be treated unjustifiable. She pushed on through whatever storm she encountered with them. Debra had graduated from Harvard University at the top of her class. Convict Jones' father, Mike, is the one who paid her way through school. He had found her on fallen Broad, known as Broad Street, trying to hang out with the gangsters and hustlers. Mike could tell she was out of place immediately and placed her under his wing.

Mike was every bit of ten years older than Debra. Mike took Debra to several functions run by the *Sterlin Tiger Organization*, which she later became a member. She was introduced to Lottie Gibson, County Counsel of Greenville, Duke Ackered, a retired educator and judge, and several more black leaders. Mike and Debra had many conversations every Thursday at the same time at a café on Main Street. This was their time to spend together, no matter what else was going on in the world.

Mike talked to her about all his problems, even his son's incarceration, and she did the same. Although the two had sex a couple of times, they mostly enjoyed each other's company and intellect. It wasn't all about sex, and Debra was a bad mama jama. Most of their conversation were developed around the communities in Greenville taking a stand for justice for the black folks. With blood, sweat, and hard work, they intended to better the community for the black folks. Debra looked at Mike as a strong black man, and even gave a speech at his funeral, which was the hardest day of her life. Everybody called the piece beautiful because it identified Mike Jones down to the tee. She missed Mike with all her heart.

Debra had already received some information on Convict Jones through Tammy calling the South Carolina Department of Corrections head office in Columbia, South Carolina. While looking over the information, Tammy came across some familiar information, especially Convict Jones' full name.

Tammy took the information to Debra, and said, "You need to take a look at this."

Tammy handed her the paperwork.

"What am I looking for?"

Tammy replied, "Well, I was looking at this paper, and that name right there reminded me of that case we worked on some years back for that old lady, Mrs. Harris, out of Atlanta, Georgia, but moved to Sumter, South Carolina. Her son was killed by the prison guards at the same institution that this new client, Convict Jones, is at now. Also, that guy that got killed was also Convict Jones' codefendant or involved with the guy who got killed in this case, see?"

Tammy was pointing out the name to Debra.

Debra looked at the name Reginald Harris, and then at Convict Jones' name.

"Strange," she said, not really seeing anything wrong with it. "Small world," she continued, and then she thought about what Stephanie had told her. She said, "Something is just not right. Get me the number to the Federal Bureau of Investigation just in case we might need them."

She closed the file.

Debra stood to her feet, grabbed the file, and walked out of her office with Tammy following her and asking a million and one questions. As Debra walked out of her office, she pulled out her cellphone and gave it to Tammy.

"Call Evans Correctional Institution again,"

The last time she called they gave her the run around about talking with the Warden.

Tammy sat on the passenger' side of the vehicle, and dialed the number while Debra began driving.

The phone rang twice and a female voice answered the phone saying, "Evans Correctional Institution."

"May I speak with the Warden of the institution?" Debra asked, preparing herself for the bullshit.

"He's not in at the time, but if you would like to leave a message—" The female prison guard was stating when she was cut off by Debra.

"I don't think you understand. I am not asking for the Warden. I am demanding that you go get him because I know that he is there sitting on his lazy ass. Now, if you want to keep your job you'll do just as I ask, officer," Debra stated, requesting her name while Tammy sat on the passenger's side smiling.

"There she goes," Tammy stated as Debra looked at her and smiled back.

"Do you understand?" Debra asked as she continued to talk into the cellphone.

"Yes ma'am. I will see what I can do. Please hold for one second," the female prison official stated, clicking over to a clear line.

CHAPTER 49

The silent alarm went off in the abandoned building that was Rico's hidden spot.

"What the fuck!"

He rose out of his sleep with the Mini Mack-11 in his hand. The three pitbulls, at the sound of a short whistle from Rico, stood at attention and were prepared to die defending their master's life. Rico with his weapon in hand ran to the TV monitors and saw nothing moving. As he was clicking the switch on the monitors to show different locations of the building, his cellphone began to rang.

"What now?" he shouted, grabbing the cellphone off his belt and walking back over to the wall to reset the alarm. Rico then walked over to his desk, and hit star 69 to redial the phone number that just called.

The phone rang twice and a male voice answered, and said, "Hello."

"Who called this number?" Rico asked immediately.

"Your time is up," Agent Johnson stated, while ordering his team of agents to circle the building by using hand signals.

Rico didn't know that the federal agents had the building surrounded, but calculated that if they ever did he would also have a way out for that. Rico not only had an escape plan, he also had the entire building booby-trapped. Rico ran back to the TV monitors and stared at the screen. He then began to see agents moving from out of their hidden spots.

"Shit!" he yelled to himself, holding up the Mini Mack-11 in his hand and checking the clip. He then ran over to the corner of the room and grabbed his backpack, which contained several reversible clips for the MAC-11 and three grenades he bought from a military corporal with an unfavorable discharge. He already had his 750 motorcycle with a small rack on the front it downstairs. This rack was used to hold two baby machine guns close to the handlebars on the bike with a red button that you could press to fire the guns. He then placed the .40 caliber in his waistline and a .25 automatic in his ankle holster.

"How in the fuck did they find me?" he shouted.

What he didn't know was that he slipped in a very bad way. The black van that he left at the Motel 6 in the parking lot was impounded. Inside the van Rico had dropped an old cell phone. Although the cell phone was a throw away TracFone, the cell phone had a bill that was ran into the cellphone that Rico currently had in his possession. The agents decided to follow the second phone by doing a GPS trace, which lead them to the abandoned building several days earlier. That's where Agent Johnson and Agent Williams watched his every move.

"That motherfucker!" Rico shouted, thinking that Major Riley had put the federal government on his ass.

Agent Williams lead the second six man team of agents up the back flight of stairs of the abandoned building while Agent Johnson lead his seven man team through the front door of the building. As the first man went through the door of the abandoned building, his leg was removed from the ankle down due to the invisible laser beam Rico had installed as a booby trap. He had bought this device from the same military corporal who sold him the grenades and other weapons.

"Pull back, pull back!" Agent Johnson yelled as his men retreated.

An explosion went off in the back of the building where Agent Williams was leading his men.

"Ahhhhhhhh!" you heard an agent scream at the top of his lungs.

All of Agent Williams men were killed in the explosion, and Agent Williams was the first man through the door leading them to a false victory. As the smoke cleared in the back entrance of the building where the explosion was at, coming through the smoke doing a wheelie was Rico on his motorcycle with the extended rack of machine guns. As he passed Agent Johnson, who was now coming around to the back of the building to investigate the explosion, Rico dropped two mini grenades. As soon as the bike's front wheels hit the ground, he pushed the red button on the handle bar connected to the machine guns and began blasting.

"Watch out!" Agent Johnson screamed, diving to the side, avoiding gunfire.

Three agents immediately hit the ground dead. Agent Johnson immediately rolled to his feet and began letting off shots at Rico. Agent Johnson then signaled to two other agents that were part of his team to take cover and fall back as he watched Rico turn a corner and was gone. Agent Johnson radioed Agent Williams but didn't receive an answer. He tried again and began looking around. He didn't see Agent Williams or any of Agent Williams' team anywhere. Agent Johnson and the rest of his men then went further around to the back of the building where they saw several body parts laying around everywhere due to the explosion.

Agent Johnson's attention was drawn to a shiny glare from his side view. He walked over to a pile of rummage and moved some out of the way. He reached down, picked up the shiny object, and rubbed the dirt and dust off of it. It was Agent Williams' badge with blood mixed with dirt on it.

Tears immediately began falling from Agent Johnson's eyes as he stated to himself, "I'll get that bastard, Will. If it's the last thing I do."

He placed the badge around his neck with his badge.

CHAPTER 50

She wrapped her legs around his back as he went up into her with all the passion he had in his being for her. Her walls opened up to allow him all the access to her womanhood that he could possibly get from her. Anything in her life that she tried holding on to and love, that very moment she let it all go. What she felt at that very moment was more important to her than her sister, friend, or anything else that was in her corner for years.

"I'mmmm coming!" she moaned as Tyrone lay on top of her, reaching his climax at the same time.

Kemmiko then opened up and allowed her love juices to soak his penis as he shot off in her at the same time. Tyrone collapsed on top of her body whereby she immediately grabbed him tight and squeezed him.

"I love you," she stated from the bottom of her heart.

"I love you too," he replied as they held each other.

After two minutes of gloating in their new profound happiness, Kemmiko's phone rang. She looked over at her caller ID and recognized the number as being from Convict Jones. She blew out a short breath and did not answer the call.

Tyrone knowing that it was Convict Jones said, "I thought you told that nigga it was over with."

He was staring at her hard.

"I did," she replied in a fearful tone of voice.

"Well, he don't need to be calling here anymore," Tyrone ordered her.

"Well, he don't have nobody out here for him but me," she stated because she still had an ounce of love for his well-being, which would slowly but surely come to an end.

"I don't give a fuck. You either with me or you with him. I am here with you. That nigga ain't been with you in twenty years, and he damn sure don't take care you and your bills. I am here and he's not. What are you going to do?" he asked, forcing her to make a decision.

Kemmiko thought about everything he said, and she knew that he spoke the truth. She did not think about the bond she was destroying. She was a feeling doer. She makes all her decisions off of how she feels instead of what was logical to the mind.

Kemmiko looked in Tyrone's eyes, and said, "I'm with you."

Her phone rang again. She reached over, grabbed the phone, and answered it saying, "Hello."

"Excuse me, I am calling for Dyson. He gave me this number in case anything happened to him. Well right now their trying to kill him and, you need to contact somebody. I'm out," the male voice which belonged to Rodney Pitts stated.

"Look I'm telling him and you don't call here no more or I will call down to the prison tell them you got a cellphone. Fuck that prison shit," she replied, causing Rodney to hang up and look at Pig Sty and Black Nuk, shaking his head.

When Kemmiko hung the phone up, she looked at Tyrone and a smile spread across his face. He walked over to her, hugged her, and she fell into his arms.

"I love you," he stated.

"I love you Dys-I mean Tyrone."

"Yes, I'm calling in reference to one of my clients at this institution. His name is Dyson Michael Jones, prison number two-one-five-seven-five-seven," Debra stated when the Warden came on the line.

"Ma'am, at present I am in a very important meeting, but I will put you through to my Major and he will be able to assist you in any matter concerning your client," the Warden stated.

"Thank you," she replied as she was placed on hold.

Forty seconds later another male voice came on the line.

"Major John Riley speaking."

"Yes, this is Attorney and Counselor at Law, Debra Butler. I have a client at your institution, and I would like to speak to him immediately. It is very important that I speak with him now!"

She emphasized the now to allow Major Riley to know it was urgent and she meant business.

"I don't believe that will be a problem. Can you please tell me the inmate's name?" Major Riley replied, not thinking anything about this call might be for Convict Jones.

"Dyson Michael Jones and his prison number is two-one-five-seven-five-seven," she stated, looking at the paper that Tammy was holding for her while she drove and talked on the phone at the same time.

Silence filled the phone for a few seconds.

"Hello, are you there?" Debra stated.

Major Riley replied, "Yes ma'am, we do have an inmate Jones here, but at the present time this institution is on lockdown so it would be impossible for you to speak with him right now," Major Riley stated, thinking that he had to move fast if he was going to kill Convict Jones.

"Well, when will I be able to speak with my client?" she asked, knowing that Major Riley was lying.

"I really can't tell you that. That is confidential security information."

Debra knew then that Major Riley was bullshitting her. The Warden did not say anything about an institutional lockdown, plus the prison official she was talking to was giving off a vibe that made her uncomfortable. Plus, out of all the times she had been visiting institutions in South Carolina, she has never, not one time, not been able to speak with her client by phone or visit. This was even if an institution was on lockdown.

"Can you please inform me so that I can understand, why you don't know when I can speak with my client since you are the Major, and the Major is over security of the institution, and you're saying that the institution is locked down because of a security issue. Please explain that to me," she spat back, becoming frustrated and it was coming out in her voice.

"Ma'am that's confidential," he stated, short talking to her.

"Thank you very much, sir," Debra replied, not having time for the games. "But make sure my client stays in the best of health, make sure I hear from him in one hour, if not I promise you Major that I will have enough SLED agents down there in that county they'll classify it as a concentration camp within the next thirty minutes. The Chief of SLED owes me a favor. You would think that institution was a place for road cops," she said, sucking her teeth and showing her sassiness.

"Thank you Ms. Butler and have a good day," Major Riley stated calmly, knowing that he had to move fast then slamming the phone down.

Immediately after Major Riley got off the phone, he summoned Sergeant Jackson to his office. Sergeant Jackson walked into Major Riley's office two minutes later.

"You called for me?"

"Yes Sergeant. I need you to go get that shit eating Jones right now," Major Riley shouted, not liking that Convict Jones had people looking in on him, which was something he failed to calculate into the equation.

"That inmate is in the shit hole," Sergeant Jackson replied, walking over towards Major Riley's desk.

"Good then," Major Riley thought to himself and stated to Sergeant Jackson, "go get Shawn and Terry and tell them to report to the shit hole, and to bring their release papers."

Major Riley spoke in hidden message, being the release papers were actually knives.

"Yes sir," Sergeant Jackson replied, walking out of Major Riley's office and going to carry out his duties.

CHAPTER 51

Stephanie sat waiting for Debra to call her back with good news. She had been waiting there for the last two hours, and had not heard anything from Debra or Convict Jones. She got up from her living room couch, walked into her kitchen, and fixed herself a glass of orange juice. She then walked back into her living room, whereby the twins and her son walked in.

"What you doing home?" she asked, knowing that he was supposed to be at work.

"It's my day off. I just went in for a couple of hours because they needed my help," Decius replied.

Decius looked at his mother and knew that something was upsetting her. He also knew that it was his father, whom he did not know.

Decius walked over to his mother, wrapped his arms around her, and said, "It's us. It's me, you, and the twins. Don't worry about him 'cause he ain't been worried about us in twenty years."

He was holding a grudge, which he himself didn't know he had for his father.

Stephanie looked at her son and smiled.

"Y'all hungry?" she asked her children.

The twins began clapping and said at the same time, "Pizza!"

They were laughing, running, and hugging their mother's leg.

"So you think that it was a smart move, huh?" Major Riley stated, coming into the shit hole.

"Sir," Convict Jones replied, allowing Major Riley to know that he respected him, but only because he had the upper hand on him. "I told the officers I had important information for you that would resolve this problem or matter."

He was being very careful with the words he spoke to the mad man.

Convict Jones did not know that Major Riley had been contacted by Debra, nor did he have knowledge that Debra was representing him in this matter.

"Well Jones, guess what? I don't care who your lawyer is," Major Riley made this statement because he knew who Debra Butler was due to Reginald Harris' lawsuit case. "In fact, I think today is your last day causing trouble in society or my institution."

Madness filled his eyes as hate flooded his heart.

"Sir, can I please explain something to you?" Convict Jones asked with fear in his voice.

Convict Jones did not want to die like this. He would try to plead his way up out of the situation, even if the truth had to come out to this law enforcement officer who was playing the game like a gangster. The little that Convict Jones knew and whatever he had to say, Major Riley already knew the truth because he created it and to keep it concealed he would silence who he had too including his son, Rico.

"You can explain anything you want, but it still will not change anything about the conclusion of this matter," Major Riley replied, allowing Convict Jones to know that there was nothing he could do but to go through whatever he had planned for him.

"Just give me five minutes," Convict Jones pleaded, buying for time and looking for a way out of the situation he was in.

"Speak all you want. It's not going to change a damn thing, nigga!" Major Riley yelled, turning red in the face.

"Major, I say this to bring understanding," Convict Jones began moving around the cell at the same time. "I never knew Mechelle which was your wife. I have never seen the woman in my life. I also found out that O-Dog was her son as well. I remember that night. The guy that killed you wife and my friends was killed in Florida some years back," Convict Jones was stating what Major Riley already knew.

Major Riley shook his head because he knew that Convict Jones did not know everything, but because he was involved in the entire ordeal he also had to die. Convict Jones looked for any signs of a change of heart in Major Riley and saw none. Major Riley's eyes were void of any warmth for Convict Jones. His eyes were just as cold as his heart. Major

Riley then looked at Convict Jones like he was silly because Major Riley knew that the killer of his wife was not dead, because the killer was Rico, his son, who he hired to kill her for the two point five million dollar insurance policy.

"Major, your enemy is my enemy," he stated, looking Major Riley in the eyes. "Don't you think I want the same type of revenge for my friends that were also killed that night? The guy got away with my money, killed my friends, and got me this prison time, and I didn't do anything to deserve it just like I don't deserve this. Sir, I had no control over that night whatsoever, and if I could bring back your wife and homies I would without a doubt."

As Convict Jones spoke, Major Riley was thinking about what Reginald Harris told him prior to him delivering the final fatal blow to his head.

"Sir, if you think I am lying ask O-Dog what happened. He'll tell you the truth," Convict Jones pleaded.

"Terry has already told me the truth," Major Riley stated with a smirk on his face because in reality O-Dog didn't know the truth, and Major Riley wanted to keep it that way.

Terry Johnson a.k.a. O-Dog had been given information all his life by Major Riley, some truth and some lies. These lies mixed with truth were also given to police, just as Major Riley planned. When O-Dog was a little boy, he informed the police that Convict Jones killed his mother, only because the police had him handcuffed, he had blood all over him with a matching Pelle Pelle sweat suit. O-Dog had never really seen the killers face, and even if he had, he wouldn't have remembered due to the shocking trauma of the event in front of a ten year old boy witnessing the death of the person who gave him life. Convict Jones watched Major Riley pace back and forth in the holding cell. Convict Jones was waiting for him to strike at any moment, but he was hoping and praying that Major Riley came to some form of understanding. The holding cell door opened and Shawn and O-Dog came through it. Immediately fear filled Convict Jones. He was out numbered, out gunned, and out of time. Convict Jones looked up into O-Dog's eyes. The same intense burning was in his eyes. Had Convict Jones only knew how much O-Dog hated him, he would have hired an army for protection or had him killed.

O-Dog was serving his prison sentence for a murder he committed. When O-Dog was eighteen years old, he had stolen a car and came to Greenville, South Carolina looking for the killer of his mother whom he thought was Convict Jones. After a few days in Greenville and not finding Convict Jones, he was sitting in a *Burger King* parking lot eating his food when he saw a vehicle pull up. He watched as he ate his food and saw a man that closely resembled Convict Jones. The man got out of his car with his little son and went into the Burger King. O-Dog immediately placed his food on his seat, reached under the seat, and grabbed his .38 special handgun. As the man exited the Burger King, O-Dog ran up on him and shot him six times thinking that it was Convict Jones. O-Dog then turned around, ran back to his car, jumped in, and pulled off. The entire time O-Dog committed this assault the man's ten year old son stood watching. The cycle continues.

"I thought I killed you a long time ago nigga, but you keep coming back alive," O-Dog growled with fire in his eyes, pulling out a knife.

"What the fuck are you talking about?" Convict Jones replied, now moving around in the holding cell.

Convict Jones already knew that he was going to fight until they killed him, and if he died he planned on taking somebody with him if possible.

"You won't get away this time, bitch," O-Dog yelled, running towards Convict Jones and swinging the knife.

Convict Jones ducked the knife and landed a two piece to his jaw.

Convict Jones was moving off pure instinct to survive and live.

"Get that piece of shit!" Major Riley shouted as Shawn then went into attack.

The entire time Sergeant Jackson was sliding out the door to go get the welcome committee to assist Shawn and O-Dog but it did not rattle Convict Jones. At the same time O-Dog got back to his feet and rushed Convict Jones, tackling him. The two fell in a puddle of piss. Convict Jones was fighting for his life as Shawn came to assist O-Dog. Shawn stabbed Convict Jones twice with his blade, once in the rib area and once in the shoulder. Convict Jones slung O-Dog off of him and rolled to his feet. As soon as he was standing, a blow came out of nowhere sending Convict Jones right back to the ground.

Convict Jones was in a dazed state, but heard Major Riley say, "Kill that motherfucker!"

Shawn and O-Dog began kicking and stabbing him.

Blood was everywhere as Convict Jones lay on the floor going in and out of conscience. Convict Jones felt the blades penetrating his flesh. The more blood he lost, the weaker he was getting. Convict Jones lay on the floor looking up at the people who would be responsible for his death. He thought about Kemmiko, Stephanie, Decius, his father, several prisoners, and mostly Rafee. Convict Jones then repeated something he kept hearing the Muslims say.

"La illa ha illa la."

He watched Major Riley's boot come crashing down on his face and head, and that's when he lost consciousness.

CHAPTER 52

A twenty-one gun salute was given to Agent Williams. He had a closed casket funeral by request of his wife and the bureau. The only thing that was in Agent Williams' casket was his badge that Agent Johnson found in the rubble. The federal agents who cleaned up the rubble around the building from the explosion only found two of Agent Williams' fingers and his leg. Agent Johnson sat up front with the family, providing a shoulder to lean on and support. Mrs. Williams cried on Agent Johnson's shoulder, wondering what she was going to do now, being that Agent Williams was the one who brought home the money, coupled by the fact that she loved Agent Williams with all her being. When the funeral services were over, Agent Johnson went to his vehicle, got in, and just sat there thinking.

"Where is that son of a bitch?" he questioned himself because he had lost track of Rico.

As the American flag was being lowered and given to Agent Williams' wife in Agent Williams' honor, Agent Johnson started his unmarked car and pulled off thinking that he had missed something at the crime scene where the explosion occurred. Although it was ruled that the explosion had destroyed any and all evidence that may have existed, Agent Johnson just couldn't believe it. He would not allow his partners' death be in vain, but some things were just out of his hand. He pulled up to the abandoned building forty minutes later. He parked his vehicle on a side street and walked back over the building. As Agent Johnson stood watching, he noticed three identical pitbulls scuffling through the garbage for food. Agent Johnson then began running every detail of the case in the back of his mind. That's when he remembered what Agent Williams said the night after they left the cocktail lounge and it hit home.

"I know that Casper was in that car. I saw him."

As Agent Johnson looked up he saw a man in a trench coat by the garbage with the pitbulls limping away. Agent Johnson looked back down at his notes and the picture of the guy they pulled out of the car that night. Agent Johnson then spoke to himself out loud.

"Hmmmm Major Joe Riley, we need to have a talk."

Agent Johnson went back to his car, got in, started the car, and pulled off getting back into traffic.

Convict Jones was in and out of consciences, at least that is what he was thinking. He wondered why he kept hearing the Adhan being called. Over-and-over again he heard the Adhan being called, but he didn't see any Muslim rushing to prayer. All Convict Jones saw was a prayer rug that Muslims use to pray on. There was water all around the rug.

Convict Jones was far from a dream interpreter, but he knew there was something behind it. Convict Jones also knew he had to be dreaming, but what he was seeing seemed so real.

Convict Jones then remembered the last thing that was going on in his life. He remembered that he was being stabbed, kicked, and beat. As the thoughts went through his mind, he became very emotional and scared because he knew that he was dead. He could not make up for time he lost to spend with his son, Decius. He could not apologize to Kemmiko face-to-face for leaving her out there in the cold world. He couldn't apologize to Stephanie for doing the same, but with the exception he left her to raise a child on her own. There were many things Convict Jones wanted to do before he died, that he felt he would never get the chance to since Allah had called for him.

As Convict Jones thought about these things, the Adhan was being called again. As the Adhan was being called in Arabic, he could actually understand it in English. He then heard Arabic words being spoken. He did not see anybody speaking them, but he heard them loud and clear and understood them in English.

"Say: I seek refuge in the Lord of the dawn from the evil of all that he has created, and from the evil of the darkness of night, when it falls and from the evil of those (charmers) who blow into knots and from evil of the envier when he envies," Convict Jones, without knowing what he was saying, spoke back in English but sounded like Arabic.

"Oh Allah, I have been very cruel to myself, by ignoring my duty to you, and there is no one who can forgive me because you are the only forgiver and have mercy on me. Verily you are the forgiver and merciful."

Convict Jones' vision then slowly became blurry until it dimmed off into blackness.

Kemmiko sat on her bed crying when Tyrone walked in. He looked at her and didn't know what was going on.

"What's wrong baby?" he asked but she refused to say anything as the tears just rolled down her cheeks.

Little did Tyrone know was that Kemmiko had received a phone call from the South Carolina Department of Correction informing her of Convict Jones condition after the assault upon him. Convict Jones was listed as his closest relative contact in case of an emergency. She couldn't help but to remember the conversation her and Convict Jones had on visit about adding her as his closest relative contact in the case of an emergency. Here she was contacted first by friends of Convict Jones informing her of a dangerous situation he was in and come to find out his life had been threatened with physical force to take it. She swallowed the knot in her throat as she thought about the conversation.

"Kemmiko," Convict Jones stated, *grabbing her hands over the prison table. "Now if I put your name down here as the closest contact that means you're with me to the end, right?" he asked, looking her in the eyes while holding her hands in his.*

"You know I am with you, baby." She returned the stare and continued, "Just forgive me, and

forget about the past. We have found each other again and I am not going anywhere. I love you," she informed Convict Jones, trying to convince him that she was real, through-and-through.

"I will forgive you but I will not forget, because if I forget you'll do that same shit again," Convict Jones squeezed her hands, allowing her to know that he was serious.

"I'm with you, baby. Can't nothing come between us, especially no man," she stated.

Somewhere during the years, Convict Jones forgave and forgot, just as she forgot about the conversation they had. Today that conversation came back to haunt her as she cried.

Kemmiko looked up at Tyrone, and said, "It's nothing, baby. I was just thinking about my mother," she said, knowing that Tyrone knew her mother had passed away.

"It's going to be okay, baby. I'm with you always," he said, grabbing her hand and holding her in his arms, thinking about all the years he had been chasing her and finally got her.

CHAPTER 53

Convict Jones woke with a splitting head and body aches. His mouth was as dry as cotton balls, and he could not swallow.

He whispered low, "Water, water."

Stephanie jumped from the chair she was sitting in and ran to get a doctor or nurse.

Convict Jones' vision began to clear and the first thing he saw was some beautiful light brown hazel eyes.

"Hi, sleepy head," Stephanie stated, smiling from ear-to-ear.

Convict Jones tried to reach out towards her, but a sharp pain prevented him from doing so. Convict Jones' eyes began looking around the hospital room, looking for a certain person but Kemmiko was not there. His heart ached with hurt. A tear fell down his eye as Stephanie reached over and wiped it away with her thumb. The tear did not represent the fact that Kemmiko had left him without caring for his well-being, the tear represented the fact that he could now move on with his life away from Kemmiko.

She had always told him, "Go ahead with your life. I'm no good for you."

That was the truest thing she ever said to him.

Stephanie then said, "Hold it, big boy. Get your rest. Doctor's orders."

She rubbed his arms gently.

Convict Jones had been in a semi-coma for the last six months as a result of twenty-eight stab wounds, more than enough kicks, and blows to the head by other unknown objects. He also had three broken ribs, an arm out of joint, and a broken foot. Had it not been for a new prison guard being trained at that institution, named Peter Ashmore, who was not a part of Major Riley's crew two things would have more than likely happened. One, Convict Jones would have been murdered just like Reginald Harris. Two, Major Riley and his team would have gotten away with the murder of Convict Jones. Officer Ashmore was walking by the shit hole when he saw his Major standing and shouting orders for two prisoners to beat and assault another prisoner. Ashmore then became astonished when he witnessed his Major join in with the other two prisoners to assault the other prisoner, who was defenseless on the floor lying in feces and urine. The report given to SLED from Ashmore was that he saw Major Riley holding Convict Jones up while two other prisoners stabbed him with pointed steel objects. Ashmore, after seeing that, said he immediately ran to the Warden's office. Little did Ashmore know was that at that time, the Warden was in a meeting with some head officials from the South Carolina Department of Corrections head office in Columbia, South Carolina.

He started screaming, "They're gonna kill him."

He was hysterical.

The prison officials in the Warden's office jumped from their chairs in shock, wondering what this officer, who they did not know was talking about. The panic in his face and voice was all they needed to look into whatever he was screaming about. In the meeting was also a SLED and FBI Agent. They were there to clean up any other spills from the prior drug ring ran by Sergeant White. All the officials in the office exited the Warden's office and followed Ashmore back to shit hole. When all the officials got to the holding cell, the first thing they saw was Major Joe Riley jumping in the air and coming down with his foot, stomping Convict Jones' head into the urinated floor, which was the last blow that Convict Jones saw before his vision went blank.

The entire prison was shutdown, while the head officials got things under control. SLED agents and federal agents also contributed to helping get the matter under control. While Major Riley was being handcuffed and escorted out of prison, Agent Johnson showed up to question Major Riley about Rico and the night at the cocktail lounge.

"What's going on?" Agent Johnson asked, seeing his colleagues were already on the premises of the institution.

"We are trying to get to the bottom of the situation now," Another agent replied, who had worked in the same field as Agent Johnson.

Agent Johnson then looked up and saw Major Riley being escorted to a SLED unmarked vehicle.

He rushed over the two SLED agents, and asked, "What did he do?"

He showed the two SLED agents his federal badge.

The SLED gave Agent Johnson a brief update on the matter, which wasn't that much information and placed Major Riley in the backseat of their vehicle.

"Do you mind if I question him? He is also involved with another case I'm investigating."

"No problem. We're taking him to your federal facility anyway by order of your superior," one of the agents replied.

"Good. See y'all at headquarters," Agent Johnson replied, looking around at all the law enforcement agents working like bees.

Agent Johnson got back into his vehicle and rushed to meet back up with the agents who were escorting Major Riley to the federal building holding facility. One hour and forty minutes later, Major Riley sat in front of Agent Johnson and spilled his guts. He gave up information on Sergeant White and several other prison officials such as the welcome committee. He did not say one word about Sergeant Jackson because deep down in his heart he knew that Sergeant Jackson was his friend, and Sergeant Jackson cared for him. He also provided information about Rico in order to lessen the penalty that he would receive for his criminal behavior. All through the four hour interrogation and snitching, not once did he bring up Terry Johnson a.k.a. O-Dog, Shawn, or Dirty Dee's name. He looked at them boys like his sons. He loved them and figured that they had already wasted most of their life in prison. He felt that he could not be the one to further fuck up their lives.

CHAPTER 54

"Dearly beloved, we have come together in the sight of God and in the presence of these witnesses to unite this man, Tyrone Holloway and this woman, Kemmiko Davis in holy matrimony, which is a worthy institution proclaimed by God from the beginning of time. This ceremony signifies the great union which is between Christ and his church. Christ beautified this ceremony with his presence during the wedding at Cana of Galilee where he performed the first miracle and Saint Paul commended marriage as a sacred institution which all persons should embrace, and therefore is not to be entered into lightly, but to be taken seriously, realizing that this ceremony is ordained of God."

The preacher preached as Kemmiko's sister and brother stood around watching as the preacher continued,

"Into this holy estate these two persons come now to be joined as one. Therefore, if anyone can show a just reason why they should not be united as husband and wife, let them speak now, or forever remained silent," the preacher stated in which one of Kemmiko's family members should have taken exception to the marriage because it was believed by many that Convict Jones and Kemmiko were actually married but none spoke up.

After a minute of silence the preacher said, "I now pronounce you two husband and wife. You may kiss the bride."

They kissed as her family clapped and wished her well. The entire time she was being married, Convict Jones was lying in the hospital fighting to live.

Three months later after Convict Jones came out of his coma, one early morning around four thirty when the prison cell doors popped, Shawn and O-Dog's crew members were found hanging from the top tier when the unit returned from breakfast. It was later said that Shawn and another young prisoner who was fresh meat in the South Carolina Department of Corrections had robbed a head member of the Aryan Nation. The member of the Aryan Nation was an old man who hated the ground that black men walked on, which was one of the reasons why Shawn and the young prisoner picked him out to rob. However, the old white man was powerful. Other blacks did not help Shawn because due to all the dirt he did to them when he was rolling with O-Dog. Shawn did not have the protection around him like he used to when Major Riley was there and the Aryan Nation brotherhood knew this. Shawn was dealt with properly for violating a common rule.

Dirty Dee finally stopped bullshitting around and gave his life over to Christ, thinking that he was serving the one and true creator. He now sings in the prison choir, and is looking to make parole in the next six months. O-Dog was transferred to another prison. Word shot through the system that he was still doing the same old bullshit that he was doing at Evans. Some say that O-Dog had been released from prison, and some say that he is serving the rest of his time in supermax, but one thing is for sure, no one has seen him or heard from him since. Major Riley, after posting his bond, went home and got intoxicated to unbelief. He then took his .38 special and blew his own brains out, leaving a letter behind that read:

When it's time to die, no one can stop the wrath of death. I've had my life long enough. Because of my actions, I have now become a disgrace to my family, friends, co-workers, and most importantly, my sons. I am a failure. I'm turning up the bottle of E&J, taking a long, hard gulp. However, I do not regret anything I have done to several prisoners. They make me sick with the exception of my sons. I really hate that prisoner, Convict Jones. He thinks that he can just do anything and get away with it.

Major Riley had been living the life of a lie so long that he actually started to believe his lies. He actually believed that Convict Jones had something to do with the murder of Mechelle, when he, himself, knew the truth. Major Riley's letter continued to read:

It's all a part of the games we play. The games are over now and the cat only peeped his head out of the bag. To my sons, and you know who you are. I made sure that you all would be taken care of. There is enough money for you to live semi-comfortable. It all depends on what you do with money. Upon your release, someone will come to you with your share of the money.

He was speaking of Sergeant Jackson.

I love you all with all my heart. If you ever find out the truth concerning this entire ordeal about your mother, brother, and me, Terry, just know whatever happened I did it for you, son. I could not allow you all to go through life struggling for the things you needed and wanted. I now can no longer live this life I have been living. I cannot continue to fail my family, friends, and the people I love, which is few. So until we meet again at that lovely place in the sky, my sons carry the legacy on. I love you.

The letter ended with Major Riley's signature.

Blood and brain mater was spread all over the letter and the desk he wrote the letter on. Also found in the basement of his house was a little tin box, hidden behind a water heater. Inside the box were several photos of his first born son, Chris Taylor, a.k.a. Rico Cross a.k.a. Nightmare, which the agents referred to as Casper. After a proper and intensive investigation was complete by the Federal Bureau of Investigations evidence pointed out that Major Riley had Rico kill Mechelle for a two point five million dollar insurance policy.

The plan was simple. The killing was supposed to look like it was drug related. That part played out perfectly, but there were unseen matters that popped up that Major Riley had not planned for. Being Rico was in the drug game, Major Riley offered his son the hit so that he could make some real money. Major Riley also figured that by having his son pulling the hit, he didn't have to pay money to outside contractors to kill her. He could keep all the money in the family being that was the reason he had Mechelle killed, to make sure his son would be alright after he left this Earth. Had Agent Johnson not seen the photo in the tin box found at Major Riley's house, he would have not been able to compare those photos with the photo him and Agent Williams used to track Casper. Because of those photos and a birth certificate with the name Chris Taylor on it, Agent Johnson also found out that Chris Taylor and Casper were the same person and that he had not been murdered in Florida. Agent Johnson couldn't believe what the evidence was pointing to as he read the paperwork report. Major Riley had his very first-born murder his wife for insurance money.

Agent Johnson then thought to himself, *I wonder if the stepson knows.* No one knew where or that O-Dog was the stepson.

CHAPTER 55

After several months of being out of the semi-coma, Convict Jones was also given parole. That happened five days after Kemmiko and Tyrone got married. Debra had pulled a lot of strings to get Convict Jones parole. However, the parole was revoked a month and a half later because Kemmiko and Tyrone called the parole board and informed them that they were scared that Convict Jones might come after them. Convict Jones couldn't believe that he loved a rattlesnake for all those years.

Tears fell from his eyes as he thought to himself, *How could she do me like that?* Thinking about Kemmiko he thought, *You can never turn a whore into a housewife.* A lesson he intended to keep with him for the rest of his life.

William Ham also appeared before the parole board and was about to be released until Mrs. Turner's granddaughter and Smith's old girlfriend showed up at the hearing and protested against his release. Last Convict Jones heard was that William Ham was at *Crenshaw Correctional Institution* working in the multipurpose building as a gym worker. Smith was released from prison one year later. He tracked down Pam and beat her till she was blue. Several jocks stopped the beating by holding him on his ass. Smith is now serving a fifteen year sentence under the eighty-five percent law in the State of Texas for assault and battery with intent to kill. Rodney Pitts was transferred from Evans to a level one camp. He later made parole. Six months after making parole, Rodney was killed by several police officers. Convict Jones had seen the shooting of Rodney first hand on TV, while lying in the hospital bed. As Convict Jones watched the news, he saw Rodney holding court in the streets. Convict Jones' heart dropped to his belly when he saw the first two bullets from police guns rip into Rodney's chest.

Convict Jones remembered Rodney always telling him, *I am not coming back to prison, not alive anyway.*

Convict Jones waved his hand for Stephanie to change the channel or turn off the TV.

Black Nuk was not heard from again. Word was that Black Nuk, when he was released, went out West with a girl he met on the chat line. Family members of his said that he was out there gangbanging. Some say that he was up North putting it down on young boys coming into the drug game. Pig Sty is still serving his life sentence. Last heard was that Pig Sty had caught another body, and began raping white boys. As for Luther Moses, a.k.a. Mo, it was last heard that him and Dirty Dee attended church together every Saturday and Sunday and have become best friends.

It was now two years later and Convict Jones had been shipped from Evans to another institution named *Ridgeland Correctional Institution*. In the next couple of months, he would be released after serving all the time in prison for a crime that was out of his control. As Convict Jones stood in a crowd of prisoners, his name was called.

"Inmate Dyson Jones," a female prison guard yelled his name for mail call.

"Yeah, right here."

He was thinking it was from Stephanie being she was the only one writing him besides the court and Debra.

The mail was handed back to Convict Jones. Convict Jones looked at the piece of paper and realized it was a money order. Convict Jones tore it open, thinking that Stephanie had sent him some money which he was against except when he really needed it. When he opened the money order, it read one thousand dollars and the sender's name was David Bell. Convict Jones could do nothing but smile from ear-to-ear.

"Inmate Dyson Jones," the female yelled his name again and handed back a letter.

"Yeah," he replied again, grabbing the letter.

Convict Jones opened the letter and began reading it.

Dyson: Hope all is well with you. I have been released and I am in Detroit. My address is at the bottom of the page as well as my phone number. I sent you a money order too. When you are released come see me in your draws if you must. I got you.

The letter ended.

Convict Jones smiled, stating to himself, "David is alright."

He walked to his cell for the remainder of the night.

Allah who ack bar / Allah who ack bar / Allah who ack bar / Allah who ack bar / Ash sha du anna la illaha illa la / Ash sha due anna la illah illa la / Ash sha due anna muhummada ra sual Allah / Ash sha du anna muhummada ra sual Allah / High yalel salat / High yala salat / High yala falate / High yalel falate / Allah who ack bar / Allah who ack bar / La illa ha illa Allah.

The Adhan was being called.

Convict Jones got off his bed while the Adhan was being called and went over to his sink and placed his hands under the water and washed them. He then put some of the water in his mouth and washed his mouth out three times. Next, he sniffed some of the water three times. He then washed his arm three times, as well as his head and ears. Finally, he washed his feet three times, going in between the toes. What Convict Jones was doing, was purifying himself before going to stand before his Lord. When Convict Jones finished making Wudu, he thought about when he took his Shahada. He was laying the prison infirmary when Rafee came with three other Muslims to perform the Shahada. Rafee had been coming to see Convict Jones when he was at the medical facility at Evans. Rafee would read the Qu'ran to Convict Jones and teach him several Surahs and Hadiffs. Convict Jones had actually studied before taking his Shahada. He studied the Bible as well as the Qu'ran before taking his Shahada. The day he took his Shahada, he pointed his finger outward and repeated after Rafee.

"Ash-hadu. An-la-ilaha, Illa-lahu wahdahu-la, Shareekalahu-wa ash-hadu, Anna-muhammad-abdudhu wa-rasuluhu," Rafee stated.

Convict Jones repeated after him what it means in English, "I bear witness that there is no other deity worthy of worship, except Allah, who has no partners and Muhammad is his slave, servant, and messenger."

Upon the completion of taking his Shahada, Rafee and the other three Muslims yelled in union, "Allah who akbar."

They yelled that three times as the Muslims all reached down and hugged Convict Jones.

Convict Jones' attention was brought back to the present when a Muslim brother named Hakeem came to his door, and said, "They lining up in ranks for Maghrib."

Convict Jones came out his cell and followed the Muslim brothers to the prayer room.

Once in the prayer room, Convict Jones who they now called Shakur, walked up to the front of all of eleven Muslims, and said, "Uh comma."

Another Muslim brother named Abdual began calling the uh comma.

Convict Jones then informed the eleven Muslims to consolidate the line and to state their intention for making prayer. After the Muslims were lined up in a straight line, Convict Jones standing in front of them began quoting the Fatee hah and continued on with Surah Ikhlas and Surah Nas. After seven to ten minutes the prayer was over and the Muslims disassembled and went back to what they were doing. Convict Jones left the prayer room and went to the wall phone and made a phone call.

CHAPTER 56

Two years had passed since Convict Jones was released from the South Carolina Department of Corrections. Debra after putting in paperwork, applying pressure on the state but the reminder of state prison officials wanted her client dead. The state came to a nice settlement to keep the incident out of court and mostly out of newspapers. Convict Jones accepted a settlement for eight hundred and fifty thousand dollars in state court and another one point five million for the violation of Convict Jones constitutional rights. Debra refused to take any of the money, but Convict Jones forced her to take her share, if not more. Debra and Convict Jones now have lunch every Thursday at the same time and place that Mike Jones and her would have lunch at the café on Main Street in downtown Greenville.

Debra would always tell Convict Jones, "You look and sound just like your father."

She was smiling at him and looking him directly in the eyes as Convict Jones returned the smile with a mouth full of food.

The ex-con, Mr. Dyson Michael Jones, sat in a honey and candy apple red 500 Benz with twenty two inch rims on the tires. Gold chrome sparkled off the metallic paint job, which had silver and gold crystals in the paint. The system in the vehicle was loud as it played 50 Cent's old school classic, *I'll Teach You How To Stunt*.

Mr. Jones sat parked in the parking lot of an *ABC Store* waiting on his main man Herbert Wakefield a.k.a. Waco. Waco came out of the ABC Store with a fifth of Crown Royal and got in the vehicle. Soon as he closed the door, Mr. Jones pulled off.

"Damn nigga! Let me get in first."

Both of them began laughing because that was the norm for them.

"Yeah, you right."

He made a right turn and headed towards Laurens Road where *Fuck the World Studio* was located.

For the last six months, *Fuck the World Records* was up and running and doing numbers. Waco was scouting for new artist instead of his normal routine of laying nigga's down or out. Waco then pulled a CD from his backpack and inserted it into the CD player.

"Check this cat out. I got this from my peeps down in Savannah, Georgia."

He turned the volume up on the CD player.

"Who is it?" Mr. Jones asked as the music began coming through the speakers.

"That cat everybody been talking about. Say he's the new mad fool," Waco stated, laughing and knowing that statement would fuck with his man.

"Yeah right. Hum!" Mr. Jones replied then continued. "I don't hear nothing."

As the music played the rapper they had been talking about began spitting in a wicked flow and talking about prison life.

Mr. Jones began bobbing his head, and said, "That boy hot right there."

He was pumping his fist as he made a left turn.

"Oh sit, you heard that?   Rewind that shit." Waco shouted with excitement.

"What this cat's name?" Mr. Jones asked.'

"He goes by the name of Top Dawg."   Waco answered fucking with the CD player.

"We got to sign this nigga to "Fuck the World Records" before somebody else snatches him up." Mr. Jones informed Waco.

"Already done baby, that's what I'm here for." Waco replied.

"No, you here because I love you.   We here because NTP is everywhere. "   Mr. Jones stated laughing, but meaning every word he said.

"True, true."   Waco replied feeling the same way.   "In fact, I got the rapper and his manager waiting at the studio for us right now."   Smiling.

"Say word."   Mr. Jones asked making a right turn on to 291 bypass.

"Word to the motherfucker."   Waco replied, bobbing his head to the music.

Mr. Jones and Waco whipped up into the parking lot of "Fuck the World Records".   Mr. Jones' cell phone began ringing.

"What's poppin' baby girl?"   He asked Stephanie, who was now his other half.

"What time will you be coming home?"   She asked, watching her two twins running around with football gear on.

"Give me two hours. I am handling some very important business right now. He replied parking the car in his parking space.

"Okay. Well on your way home, please stop by the BiLo and get me some Butter Pecan Ice Cream, a dill pickle, and an extra large pizza from Pizza Hut." She replied giggling.

"Damn!" Mr. Jones screamed laughing, as Waco looked at him like he was crazy.

"Well you know I am eating for two now, plus the twins got to eat."

"Steph, you know damn well them twins ain't going to get none of that pizza." Mr. Jones replied, laughing.

"You can't blame a girl for trying." As both of them laughed hard.

"Anything for you baby. I got you, Ishaallaah." Opening the vehicle door.

"I love you daddy, and don't get in any trouble." She stated hanging up the phone.

Jones sat in the vehicle for a minute thinking while Waco got out of the car. He couldn't help but to consider that since he had been released from prison, Stephanie, every time they would talk, she would always inform him not to get in any trouble. What Mr. Jones thought was a jinx, was actually concern for his well being. She would always remind him of his past life in prison, forcing him to relive the experience. Hell, Stephanie had now become Mr. Jones parole officer and warden, but she did it for good reasons.

CHAPTER 57

The sun shined down on Rico, who laid back on a beach chair in Cancun. As he sat on his beach chair watching the tide roll in and out, sipping on a fruity daiquiri. He noticed a tall heavy set black man with a limp coming walking his way. It had been years since Rico had left the states, and had no intention to return, unless he had to. He had left the states with over four million dollars, and since he had been in Cancun, he had doubled that amount. As a speed boat floated on the water with a skier on the back doing tricks, he lay back and stated to himself.

"Life is good now." As two beautiful Mexican women ran by him in two piece bathing suits, waving at him.

A smile spread across his face. To Rico, he was God over in Cancun. He got whatever he wanted, whenever he wanted it. Rico had damn near sexed every woman he could in Cancun, so sex was nothing to him anymore. He now wanted more out of life. He was ready to settle down with a wife and build a family. He sometimes thought about his father, Major Joe Major Riley, but as quickly as the thought arose in his head it was gone. Rico then got off his beach chair and was preparing to go back to his seven room house he had built from the ground up for thirty-five thousand dollars, due to cheap labor from Mexicans. As he took up his beach chair and grabbed his drink, he noticed the older black man with the limp fall to the sand. Rico dropped everything in his hand and ran over to help the man. Since Rico had gotten over to Cancun with everything he could ask for, he started becoming soft. He began caring for others, which in the life that he lived in the states was a no no. Rico began reading the Bible and the Qu'ran, which showed him that he must forgive others in order to be forgiving for his sins he committed. Taking all that in, Rico also began trusting people. He even paid Zakat/ charity for homeless people on the island, and monthly sent money over to Africa for the starving children. Rico's life had changed for the better. He even sent money for animals that did not have homes and had been beaten. The strangest thing that Rico ever did, being who he was, was cry tears watching the movie "Boys in the Hood" when Tray's friend got killed. Rico had changed. Being who Rico was now, and people on the island loved him for the things that he did do for them, he rushed over to the old black man and began helping him back to his feet.

"Are you alright sir?" He asked.

The man gripped Rico's arm getting up. Rico looked at his hand and noticed that the man only had three fingers. Rico then looked in the man's face. The man had a beard just like Rico. Rico looked in the man's eyes and thought to himself.

"Damn he looks familiar."

Rico didn't think that anyone would recognize him, being that he had gained over one hundred pounds, coupled with him having a beard. Rico studied the man's face a little bit and then it hit him.

"Oh shit!" As two slugs from a weapon attached with a silencer shoved the words back into his mouth.

Rico's body dropped right there in the sand.

"Got cha nigga." Agent Williams stated, limping off without anybody knowing what had just happened.

After Mr. Jones finished talking with Stephanie, he and Waco exited his vehicle. Walking towards the building that his studio was in, they were stopped by three women standing outside of the studio. Mr. Jones continued to walk in the building while Waco stayed outside talking with the three women.

"What's wrong with your friend?" One of the females asked Waco.

"Business baby, that's all." He replied.

When Mr. Jones got into the building, he saw the track master messing around on the boards mixing down a track.

"What's going on, Ishmael?" Smiling knowing everybody was doing what they were supposed to be doing.

Ishmael stuck his finger to his mouth, informing his boss to be quiet while he was doing the final mix down. Ismeal then pointed towards Mr. Jones' office indicating that some people were waiting for him in his office. Mr. Jones walked to his office and entered. The first person he saw was a fat guy who's name was Jimmy. The dude was so big that when he got up to shake Mr. Jones' hand, he left a dent in Mr. Jones' leather sofa. After shaking Jimmy's hand, which was wet, Mr. Jones asked.

"Where is your hot boy at?" Looking around his office because the rapper was not in the office.

"He's using the bathroom right now. He'll be out in a minute." Jimmy replied thinking about all the money he was about to make off of Dawg.

Jimmy then began bobbin his head to the track that was being laid down by Isheal. Two minutes later the rapper Top Dawg walking out of Mr. Jones' bathroom buttoning up his pants with his head down. Jimmy immediately stood to his feet, to make the introduction of the best rapper in the streets at that time. Mr. Jones looked at the rapper as Top Dawg raised his head.

"What the fuck!" Mr. Jones shouted shocked.

"What's wrong sir?" Jimmy asked seeing something was not right.

"So we meet again." Top Dawg, aka O-Dog, stated as Mr. Jones and O-Dog stared each other down.

CHAPTER 58

Agent Johnson sat on his front porch playing with his yellow Labrador retriever.

"Here boy, fetch," Agent Johnson instructed his dog.

While playing with his retriever, he noticed a Fed Ex truck pull up. He then watched the man in the Fed Ex truck get out and walk up his driveway with a box. Since Agent Agent Williams was thought to have been killed in the explosion, Agent Johnson had been working a desk at the agency, just to earn his paycheck. He would be retiring in the next two years, and he and his wife and children decided to move out west somewhere. He thought about Agent Williams often. Agent Williams was a true blue friend and partner. Williams had saved his life on several occasions, and he did the same for Williams. He just hated that he couldn't save his life back then. Since the trial had gone cold on Casper years back, Agent Johnson had felt like he had let Williams down, and that was one of the reasons that he was now working a desk, and seeking to retire early. Agent Johnson had given up chasing Casper two years prior, because everywhere he turned, was a road block or dead end. The Fed Ex worker came up to Agent Johnson and said.

"I have a package for Mr. Johnson. Can you sign here for the package?" Handing Agent Johnson the clipboard with a piece of paper on it.

After Johnson signed for the package, he called for his dog and they went into the house. Johnson took the package and placed it in his office on his desk in the basement. He decided that he would open it later, being he had a lot going on at the time. He planned to open it when he returned from his daughter's graduation.

Four shots erupted from Mr. Jones .45 Magnum. The four slugs ripped through O-Dog's chest, face and throat area. Jimmy, his manager, not knowing what was going on quickly moved out of the way, but was shocked as he watched his money cow go down the drain. Waco, who heard the gunfire, immediately stopped everything he was doing and came running to check on his partner, since the shots came from his office.

"What the fucks going on?" Waco busted through the door asking.

Mr. Jones stood there with the smoking forty-five in his hand. Mr. Jones, without a second thought, turned towards Jimmy, pointed his weapon and squeezed off three more rounds, killing Jimmy before he could plead for his life.

"Shit!" Mr. Jones stated knowing that he might have fucked up as he thought about everything he could lose.

Without hesitation or instruction, they immediately started cleaning the area up. He rolled the bodies up in the office shag rug. He then wiped down the entire office of any finger prints of Jimmy or O-Dog. Mr. Jones and Waco did not want any trace that Jimmy or O-Dog had even been in the studio. Although the track master knew they were there, he did not hear the gun shots, because he was in the sound proof booth when it went down. Ishmael did not even see the bodies being moved out of the office, because they were taken out the back way through Jones' office.

"Man, we were almost there, homie. We were about to take over the rap game, and what did you do and do? Kill our number one artist, shit!" Waco stated picking at Jones as they began lifting the rug and half carrying it and half dragging it down the back stair case.

"Where there is one hot nigga, there are always two." Laughing as they struggled moving the bodies. "In fact, I know this real young cat, about twenty years old. He has a handicap father he's been taking care of by himself. His father is paralyzed from the waist down. His father was shot in a Burger King parking lot some years back when he was only ten years old. He's going to need our help." Mr. Jones informed Waco.

"Is he good?" Waco asked dropping the rug and cursing. "Shit! This shit heavy as a motherfucker!"

"He is what the business is needing right now. Plus, I owe his father dearly." Mr. Jones stated thinking back to the truth.

The two bodies were removed from the studio and placed in the back of a van. They then moved the bodies that night, but first they wanted to make sure that they had several eye witnesses, who would testify truthfully, if need be, that they were in another spot, rather than the spot where the bodies would have last been seen alive. After dropping the bodies at least three counties over from Greenville, having the murder weapon melted down, and destroying any and all other evidence that may link back to them, the two went to a new strip club to establish their alibi.

"Damn this shit packed as a motherfucker." Waco stated walking by a crowd of women scantily clothed.

"What's happening nigga's?" A big heavy set red nigga spoke to Waco and Mr. Jones.

"Joey, my main man." Mr. Jones stated excitedly hugging Joey, just as Waco did.

"Hey Waco." Some girl walked by speaking to Waco.

A large crowd was all around the parking lot. The new strip club's name was Big Butts, and ran by associates of Mr. Jones. In fact, this was the opening party of the club. Mr. Jones, Waco and Joey walked into the club. When they walked through the entrance, the owner was standing at the door.

"What's hood, nigga?" The owner stated whose name was Joel.

"You know what it is. NTP for life nigga." Joey replied.

"True that." Mr. Jones and Waco stated at the same time, while Mr. Jones cell phone went off.

Mr. Jones looked at his cell phone and saw that it was Stephanie.

"Shit!" He yelled forgetting that he told her he would be home in two hours until the bullshit happened.

"What's wrong?" Waco asked.

"Nothing, just wifey." He replied as he looked at Joey, when Joey said.

"Dyson, look what the wind blew in." Directing Mr. Jones attention into the crowd.

What Mr. Jones saw was horrible. He couldn't believe his eyes. He felt a tug in his heart as he watched her slide down the strip pole. The bad thing about the entire ordeal is that the woman looked to be sixty something years old, in which she was nothing but fifty years of age. For a brief moment, the female and Mr. Jones made eye contact. It seemed as if the entire club became silent. Mr. Jones dropped his head and began shaking it, thinking about all the love he used to have for her. As bad as he wanted to reach out and grab her in his arms, he couldn't. Too much hurt was between the two. She destroyed whatever bond they had, she was no good for him. She was what she was. A whore, and she proved it even further by standing on the stage stripping for money. Mr. Jones came back to his senses when he watched a guy place a one dollar bill inside her pussy. He noticed while looking in her eyes that she was under the influence of something, but at the same time, she knew who Mr. Jones was, because the tear that fell from her eye confirmed that. Mr. Jones, followed by Waco and Joey, began walking towards the stage.

"Here we go." Waco stated knowing that Jones loved him some Kemmiko.

Joey began laughing. When they got in front of the stage, Jones reached inside of his pocket and pulled out a knot of hundred dollar bills and handed it down to Kemmiko and said.

"That's for holding me down as long as you could. That's ten grand there. Thank you." Turned around and walked away with Waco and Joey following.

After forty five minutes had passed and establishing their alibi defense, Mr. Jones and Waco left the strip club, and went home to their wives.

CHAPTER 59

Agent Johnson returned home with his family from his oldest daughter's graduation. The Johnson family had dined out already at the Outback Steakhouse, where Johnson surprised his daughter with a brand new blue BMW seven fifty. He received more kisses and hugs from his daughter than he had ever received in her entire life. After returning home, and tucking all the children in for bed, Johnson and his wife retired to their master bedroom. Ten minutes later his wife had dozed off to sleep. Unable to fall asleep, Johnson got up out of bed, put on his house coat and went back downstairs to his study, in the basement of his house. After browsing the internet, surfing for information and unable to come up with a lead on Casper, he turned the computer off. This was something that Johnson did every day. He felt that it somewhat justified the fact that he had failed his partner Williams in catching the bastard that killed him. Some days Johnson knew without a shadow of a doubt that Williams was turning over in his grave because of his failure to track down Casper. Johnson then looked at the package he placed on his desk earlier that day. He grabbed the package and stationed the night lamp on the package preparing to open it. Once the package was open, he began removing several of the contents form the box and placed them on the table.

"What is this stuff?" He asked himself as he continued to remove items from the box.

Inside the package were photos, and paperwork log ins and outs. Johnson picked up the photo, which were identical copies of Casper photos that he and Williams had when they began first investigating the case, which was the same photos that were supposedly destroyed in the explosion. The second photo he picked up was a recent photo of Casper relaxing on a tropical beach in Cancun. There were several photos with different dates on them of Casper in Cancun. You could tell that Rico was investigated for well over a year, due to the dates on the photos and document log in sheets. The third photo showed Casper lying on his back in the sand with a hole in the middle of his head and his eyes open. There was a person standing over him holding a gun with three fingers. Johnson looked further in the box and noticed that a note was also inside the box. He reached and grabbed it and began reading it.

"Case number: 93-GS_23-8435 is now closed. Casper the Ghost is no more." Causing Johnson to drop the note on his desk with his mouth wide open. He couldn't believe what he was reading. It couldn't be is what he said to himself.

"But I saw......" Johnson stated out loud, but never finished his statement because he was trying to put things together in his head. He picked up the piece of paper and continued reading it.

"Come see me sometime, signed off Big Willie." As a smile spread across Johnson's face as he stated out loud.

"You old sly dog." Thinking about his partner, Agent Williams.

Mr. Jones exited his vehicle quietly as possible by pushing the door up to the car slowly without making noise. He then tiptoed into the house without making noise. It was three o'clock on the dot, and he knew Stephanie would be mad when he got there because he was more than just late. However, knowing his woman, he made plans for his tardiness.

"Where in the hell have you been?" Walking over toward Mr. Jones fast as he moved further around the table. "I have been crying and worrying myself half to death. I didn't know if you were dead or alive." She screamed.

"Shhhhh! Before you wake the twins up, I'll explain. Damn!" Mr. Jones was trying to calm something down before it got out of control.

Mr. Jones knew that at any moment a flying object could come flying his way, so he played the situation with caution. Stephanie was standing there with her hands on her hips, tapping her feet awaiting an answer, in which Jones would never provide her with the truth.

"Don't calm down baby me. I want to know where you've been all night?" Staring him directly in the eyes. "And I don't want to hear you been at the Temple, because I called down there already."

Mr. Jones without warning took off running around the table because he knew her next move.

As he ran around the table, she chased him. The entire time he was laughing and smiling at her, while she was pissed off.

"What the fuck do you find so funny?" Now smiling because she could not resist Jones' smile.

Mr. Jones then reached in the breast pocket of his jacket and pulled out a jewelry box.

"Honey, I had to ride all the way to Atlanta to cop this special gift I had made for you." Looking her directly in the eyes, hoping and praying that it would work.

"Special gift, my ass." She replied, still moving around the table trying to catch him.

Mr. Jones then stopped moving and opened his arms and said.

"Come here, baby." As she began coming to his embrace. "Here, I love you." Handing over the box.

"Nigga, it better be good, or I'm busting your ass." She replied as they both began laughing.

She opened the box and a smile spread across her face so big that you thought the sun had came out at night. Mr. Jones could tell by the smile on her face that he wouldn't be in the dog house long. Once she looked at the piece in the box, she dropped it on the table and took off running and jumped into Mr. Jones' arms, kissing him all over his face.

"I love you." She repeated at least ten times while kissing him.

The gift that Jones had just given Stephanie set him back fifty thousand dollars. There were more blue and pink diamonds in the earrings with the matching bracelet, than the South Carolina Department of Corrections had inmates. The two then began kissing which ended up in the bedroom where they made love for the next hour and a half until they fell asleep in each other's arms.

CHAPTER 60

Mr. Jones was awakened by the phone ringing.

"Can you please get that phone, baby?" Being she was closest to the phone.

He rolled over and realized that Stephanie was not even in the bed with him. He figured that she was in the kitchen, because the house smelled like I-Hop. He reached over and picked up the phone.

"Yeah, tell it." He answered the phone.

"I see you don't let shit slide, do you?" Debra asked.

"What are you talking about?" He answered a question with a question.

At the time he asked Debra that question, Stephanie came walking in the room with a tray full of food. Debra and Stephanie then stated at the same time.

"Turn on the news." As Jones grabbed the remote and turned on the TV.

There was a wooded area on the TV that looked real familiar to Jones. He propped up his pillow, waiting for the magic word from the reported that he wanted to hear. As he listened the news reporter stated.

"An up and coming hip hop icon rapper Top Dog, real name Terry Johnson, and manager Jimmy Hicks were found brutally murdered in a wooded area right outside Rickhill County. Several gunshot wounds were shown around the neck and chest area. One slug was also placed directly in the center of the rappers forehead. The police are saying that this is a crime of passion. The rapper Top Dog was to drop his new CD "Feasting on the World" this coming September. The police also stated that they think the crime was drug related, and from listening to the rapper's music, it's not hard to believe. There were several guns and a kilo of crack cocaine found in Jimmy Hicks' vehicle, which was at the crime scene. The police states that there are no suspects yet, and are asking that anybody with information about this crime, to please come forward with that information. As the investigation continues, we will keep you posted as the news rolls in. I am Charlie Gert for News Center Four, back to you, Tim." The news reporter signed off.

The police had no clues, and that was all Jones wanted to hear, because there was no evidence left at the crime scene. Jones sat back and smiled with his ear to the phone.

"So, what were you saying Debra?" He asked while Stephanie wondered what he was smiling about.

Well baby boy, if you need me, I'm seven digits away." Debra stated.

"I'll see you Thursday at our spot." Jones informed her, watching Stephanie set the breakfast out over his lap on a tray.

As Jones hung the phone up, Stephanie laid her head on his chest, as she watched the news on TV, which was now showing a picture of O-Dog. Stephanie's mouth dropped wide open as she remembered seeing his picture years back concerning what Jones went through. She snuggled up closer to Jones, as the news reporter stated.

"Anybody with information about the slain rapper, Top Dog, aka Terry Johnson, please call 1-800-CRIME-STOPPERS." As Stephanie looked up at Jones and said.

"Baby, we made love all night." Allowing him to know that she was setting up his alibi defense.

"Thank you baby, but I honestly don't have nothing to do with that." Jones replied sincerely.

"Okay, well then, where is my Butter Pecan ice cream, dill pickle, and large pizza." Staring him down since he thought he had covered all his bases, rolling her eyes and sucking her teeth.

"I knew I forgot something." He replied laughing.

"Oh, I forgot, you got mail." Handing him a letter which came from an Institution in the South Carolina Department of Corrections.

Jones looked at the mail, and smiled when he saw the name. He ripped the mail open and began reading it.

Dear brother Shakur :
As-salamu alaikum and eid Mubarak!
I hope this letter reaches you in the best
state of health. May Allah give you patience, bless
your life, and make things easy for you. I would like
to thank you for your monthly donations to the
Umma here. May Allah bless you here on Earth and
the hereafter. I was speaking with some brothers
last week, and I received very disturbing news about
a brother who bumped his head with us. It seems as
if he had forgotten about Allah. Allah will bring you
through all things, if your intentions are pure, and
you're sincerely with this deen. Ask Allah and you
shall receive. This brother I am speaking of, is
brother Hashaun. He is much younger than you, but
he is from the same county you are from. If you
wouldn't mind, I need you to check in with him and
see how all is going with him. Lastly, we should
want for our brothers, what we want for ourselves.
I love you for the sake of Allah. As-salamu alaikum
and la ilaaha illa-allah.
Brother Rafee

Jones placed the letter on his night stand and
knew what he had to do later on that day for his
brother. He then reached over and grabbed
Stephanie and held her in his arms. He then looked
at the news, and watched a news reporter speaking
about the overcrowding of the South Carolina
Department of Corrections, and how bus loads of
prisoners were being transferred to Institutions, only
to have them turned around because the prison did
not have space to house them. As he listened to the
reporter speak, stating that the Governor planned to
pass a bill which would release only non-violent
inmates. Jones reached over and grabbed his

remote and took one more look at the picture on the news of the South Carolina Department of Corrections Flag and symbol, and turned off the TV. He got up and walked over to the corner of his bedroom and made two Rakat prayers for the convicts in prison.

There is not one man on earth that does good and sin not……

www.ingramcontent.com/pod-product-compliance
Lightning Source LLC
Chambersburg PA
CBHW060531180626
46817CB00002B/515